teach the free man

PETER NATHANIEL MALAE

teach the free man

stories

Swallow Press / Ohio University Press

Athens, Ohio

The author gratefully recognizes the magazines in which the following stories first appeared:

"Turning Point," *Cimarron Review* (Fall 2002)
"Before High Desert," *EM,* no. 2 (2002) (as "Before His Time")
"Smuggling a Kiss," *North Dakota Quarterly* 70, no. 3 (Summer 2003)
"Guts and Viscera in the Chicken Farm," *Red Wheelbarrow* 4 (2003)
"The Once-a-Week Performance," *Santa Clara Review* 89, no. 1 (Fall/Winter 2001/2002)
"What You Can Do after Shutdown," *South Dakota Review* 39, no. 4 (Winter 2001)
"Tags," *Witness* 20 (2006)
"Get It One Last Time," *ZYZZYVA* (Winter 2003)

Swallow Press / Ohio University Press, Athens, Ohio 45701
www.ohio.edu/oupress

© 2007 by Peter Nathaniel Malae

Printed in the United States of America

Swallow Press / Ohio University Press books are printed on acid-free paper ⊗ ™

15 14 13 12 11 10 09 08 07   5 4 3 2 1

Library of Congress Cataloging-in-Publication Data

Malae, Peter Nathaniel.
 Teach the free man : stories / Peter Nathaniel Malae.
   p. cm.
  ISBN-13: 978-0-8040-1098-6 (acid-free paper)
  ISBN-10: 0-8040-1098-6 (acid-free paper)
  ISBN-13: 978-0-8040-1099-3 (pbk. : acid-free paper)
  ISBN-10: 0-8040-1099-4 (pbk. : acid-free paper)
 1. Prisons—California—Fiction. I. Title.

PS3613.A423T43 2007
813'.6—dc22

                                        2006034871

This book is for my father,
Peter Falefatu Malae,
the most aptly named
man on the planet.

Jesus to Simon Peter: "You are the rock
upon which I build this church."
Fale: "house"; fatu: "heart";
Falefatu: "househeart" or
"heart as big as a house."

In the deserts of the heart
Let the healing fountain start.
In the prison of his days
Teach the free man how to praise.

—W. H. Auden

contents

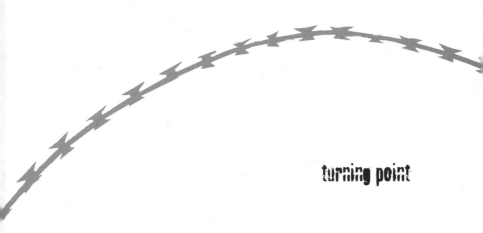

turning point

A BURLY SECURITY GUARD WAS PATTING DOWN THE entrants. He wore a thick, black cotton-lined parka jacket to keep his tattooed arms warm. On the chest pocket was a stitched "TP" encircled by a stitched arrow. It looked like a formula to recycle waste and was the Turning Point emblem. The security guard, himself a recent graduate, said, "Nothin' on you, right?"

"Nah," said Haimona.

The security guard nodded. "All right, homie. It's Healing Room 3 up the stairs. Right past HR 1 and 2."

Haimona walked past him officially confirmed and patted down. He was two days out of the penitentiary. He went up the patched-up stairs into an enclosed hallway. In line along the wall were framed quotations by Mahatma Gandhi and a self-help guru, Marianne Williamson. Haimona stopped at the third frame, bordered in lavender and reading between two groves of artificial roses, "Show us not the aim without the way."

Everyone in room HR 3 was a man. Haimona looked around without looking, a skill he'd picked up in prison. About half were Hispanic and the other half black; the way he could tell was that blacks sat with blacks and Hispanics sat with Hispanics, just like in the penitentiary. Each man had a spiral notebook in his lap or at his feet. A few were sleeved-down with jailhouse tattoos. One of the Hispanics had a "14" tattooed to his cheek and he winked at Haimona when he came in. "Another *ese*," he said.

Haimona said nothing. He would correct him later on when the time came. Anyway, it wasn't exactly a greeting, saying he was Mexican. The Hispanic was looking hard out the window, sagging yet inflated in his chair. Haimona was used to this kind of stuff among men, the feeling out and silent assessing.

A dozen chairs outlined the perimeter of the room, which was small and intimate. On one wall hung a framed circular diagram split into six wedges, and on the adjacent wall was the same wedged diagram in Spanish. There was still one available chair next to Haimona, under which the rug was thinner, almost torn.

The security guard stepped into the doorway and then ducked back out and a smiling woman walked in. She wore a body-tight ankle-length dress.

"Thanks, Lopez," the woman said to the guard.

Lopez said, "No prob, Boss-Ma." Like a barroom bouncer, he had a stool just outside the door.

The dress seemed out of place to Haimona. He'd never been to a formal dinner where formal dress was required, but he figured that if he had, he would have seen gowns like this, or maybe gowns aspiring to this. It was navy blue and finely cut and there were subtle frills along the bottom which matched the subtle frills along the V of her bosom. She was ravishing, she was bustling with the confidence of true wisdom, she was spearheading healing. Most of the men sat up when she came in, and one of the blacks said, "Ooooh! She ready to heal tonight!"

The woman laughed and said, "Good evening to you, too, Jazelle."

The men shifted in their seats. Haimona did not move, did not even sit up. He had seen her without seeing. There was something in her confident gait he immediately despised. He was instinctively certain that she considered the out-of-placeness of her high-class outfit to be an act of generosity: It was sharing candy with underprivileged kids.

"We're running a little bit late," said the woman, the smile somehow widening. She creased the hem of her dress and dragged both palms from the top of her buttocks down underneath her legs as she sat. She deeply inhaled once and raised her eyes to the room. A binder covered her lap. "Does anyone want to begin?" she asked.

"I'll start," said Jazelle.

Many of the men put their heads down so as not to look at the speaker.

"My name's Jazelle and I'm feeling content right now. It's been a long week for me. Work's been tough and my boss ain't right. But things are getting better."

The woman smiled. "And how did your homework go, Jazelle?"

"It was tough but I did it, you know what I'm sayin'? It was tough findin' all them people and even tougher tellin' 'em I was sorry."

The woman nodded. "And how did you feel about it afterwards, Jazelle?"

"I felt all right."

"And your wife? Did you apologize to her, too?"

"I did."

"And?"

"It made a landslide."

The woman sat up and put a pencil to her lips. The lips were wealthy and brown like the bosom, and artificially full like it too. She was intrigued by the healing potential of the situation and it showed. "You mean a landslide of emotion, Jazelle?"

"No, man." Jazelle dusted some lint from his slacks and shook his head. "I mean a landslide on me: She went crazy with it. Tol' me an apology over last week's fuckup ain't enough. Said I need to apologize about the week before that and the week before that and when I was done doing that, she said then we'd start talking about months."

The woman glowed, tapping her lips with the pencil.

"I been with this woman for eight and a half years."

The woman nodded. "Now what did we say about that term, Jazelle?"

Haimona looked around unknowingly. *I didn't hear no term*, he thought.

"I meant," Jazelle said, "my wife."

"But how do we *feel* about that term, Jazelle?"

Jazelle said, "It's a outdated term. It's male privilege."

The woman nodded slowly, raising her voice so that the group at large could hear: "That's right. For a man to say 'woman' implies possession. It devalues her role in your life. Now who wants that anyway, guys?"

Some men shook their heads.

"Wounds need closure, guys. When these deep-seated things fester, what happens to communication?"

Some of the men mumbled in varied volume, "Amputation."

In an instant, Haimona's institutionalized mind, in which everything always gets worse, jumped from amputation to emasculation to, finally, and perhaps mercifully, execution. He had to rapidly blink the thought away. He suspected felonious fakery: ex-cons doing their time right by nodding away the hour, keeping their mouths shut and avoiding the wrath of the system. Getting in, getting out, going home.

"Well, thank you, Jazelle," said the woman. "And who's next?"

There was a tangible pause while no one moved. The woman regally sat up, inhaling and smiling at the same time. "Well, I'll go next, I guess. Helloooo. I'm Athena . . . and I'm feeling . . . confused. Things with Jeff are still the same. He's refusing to go to our weekly healing meetings and it's frustrating for me. I care for him very deeply. He has a lot of issues but he's a wonderful lover. I want our loveship to survive the perils of most loveships, but I'm afraid. We should stop the problems before they occur, right, guys?"

The men in her line of vision half-nodded; those in her periphery did not move. "That's why it's essential for us to start therapy now, to take care of these things early. Jeff doesn't think a couple should attend therapy until something is wrong. I guess he thinks it's like a jinx. Oh, well, I can't control him and I can only control myself. And I can only hope for the best."

The same men in her immediate vision nodded again and Athena inhaled at the same time, smiling. "Okay," she said. "Who's next?"

The Hispanic with the "14" tattooed to his face raised his hand slowly. Haimona saw that his hand was also tagged with "14s" and it went no higher than his chin, then came down to his lap just as slowly as it had come up, like a waving mannequin in a department store window, its batteries dying.

"Okay, Pablo. We'd love to hear how you're feeling."

"*Soy* Pablo," he said, his voice like the heavy hand in his lap. Some time passed and he said, "And I'm feeling content."

More time passed. Athena checked her watch and played with it for a while and then inhaled and said, "And how did your homework go, Pablo?"

"Okay."

"Did you apologize to the people you've hurt in your lifetime?"

He looked up at her and said, "Sure."

"And how did it feel?"

Pablo smiled and nodded. Time kept at it. "It felt good."

"And has it improved things with anyone in your life, Pablo?"

"Sure."

"Okay, Pablo. Like who? Your wife, maybe?"

Pablo smiled. "Oh, *simón*. Hell, yeah. She loves the big loveship now."

A few of the men lightly snickered. Athena said, "Well, good, Pablo. And I'm glad you've made the distinction between relationships and loveships. You can have relationships with anyone, but loveships are another thing. Loveships need work and loveships need constant cleaning."

There was more light snickering. "But it's also important for us to address these things with our enemies, not just loved ones. I told Jeff that no matter what happens between us, even if we harbor irredeemable ill will, we'll always be able to communicate."

Haimona was listening to every word she said with the outward appearance of indifference. After listening to her speak for five minutes, he had summarized specific aspects of her life: She was a divorced, wealthy, anal-compulsive, Buddhist daughter of upper-class hippies. He knew she was divorced by the speed with which Jeff had gone from the loveship to a potential enemy; he knew she was wealthy by the facial and frontal implants and, in confirmation, the gown; he knew she was anal-compulsive by the way she sat; he knew she was Buddhist from the nonjudgmental, tip-toey way she was talking; and the parents, he just presumed.

"Lao-Tzu stresses the importance of balancing our contrition with those we see and those we don't see, those we take from and those we give to. Life is not just about taking care of ourselves, though that's where it begins. It all starts with us taking care of ourselves."

Seemingly relating to the thought, some of the men nodded. Jazelle said, "That's right. Gotta take care of yourself."

Athena smiled at the group response. She said, "Who's next?"

In the ensuing half-hour, the men introduced themselves in a kind of subdued cooperation. Though there was a steadiness in their dialogue with Athena, the monotony in their voices seemed either Prozac-induced or spaced into the programmed repetition of a test administrator at the Department of Motor Vehicles. A few times Athena asked the speaker to raise his voice, and invariably he did, though sometimes with a noticeable delay. Some of the men went into more detail than others, and a select few had disastrous results with their homework: one had lost his temper apologizing to a cousin who refused to apologize back; another had apologized to the wrong person. Athena reassigned the former the very same homework of apologizing again for losing his temper in the original apology and told the latter that it never hurt anyone to give or to hear an apology, even if it was to or from the wrong person. It was finally, circularly, good karma.

Then, with nearly all the introductions completed, a young Hispanic with a Raiders beanie and the same "14" ink-running the span of his forearm asked how you apologized to the dead. The beanie was suspiciously low over his brow. Athena quickly scanned her file and, smiling, dismissed herself from the room.

When her office door clicked shut, Pablo whispered, "*Qué pasó*, Javi?"

Javier had his head bowed, deep in remorse. Like every other man in the room, Haimona was watching, eyes between the floor and the ceiling and out the window.

"Hey, homie. Javier. Hey."

Remorse was on his face.

"*Necesita* shut the fuck up," said Pablo. "Don't say another word, *ese. No digas nada.*"

Javier put his head back down.

Pablo slapped Javier's arm and grunted, "Hey, homie. That bitch'll snitch you off, fool. She's calling your parole officer *right now.* She'll send you back. Come back with a fucking tape recorder. Don't get soft, *ese. Me entiendes,* homie?"

"Yeah."

"This ain't *El Día de los Muertos.* This ain't about yesterday, homie. This about staying out that hole. 'What's gone and past help is past grief,' homie. Kill it, *ese.*"

Javier mumbled halfheartedly, "All right, homes."

"Kill it."

Haimona didn't speak Spanish, but he understood what had just occurred. He had the same parole officer as Javier, as did Jazelle and Pablo and everyone else in the room. His homeboys had told him just before he got out the penitentiary, "That mutherfucker ain't no joke. He sent me back here for sneezing. He's always doing dirty on a homeboy." And so she was checking on Javier, his files, whether or not his case number had been murder. Haimona chuckled and thought, *She gave him an opening. If he got pinched for mur-*

der, he wouldn't be in this goddamned classroom right now. He'd be in the ground or up with twenty-five to life. She should have rolled the tape if she wanted him. She should've never left the room.

The office door clicked open, and seconds later Athena came back into the room smiling. None of the men looked up and least of all Haimona. She sat in the same wrinkle-free fashion she had sat earlier, hand to the ass, almost a slap, down the length of the hamstring in smooth, descending motion.

Smiling, "Well, okay. Sorry for the delay everybody. Javier?"

"Yes?"

"Did you want to share how you feel about it?"

He rubbed the corner of his eye. "All right."

Smiling. "These things are tough, Javier. Take your time."

Some of the men were shaking their heads no, with more water coming up in Javier's eyes, and the collective huff of a jam-packed holding tank. Javier said, "I loved them both."

Haimona shook his head, Athena nodding empathetically.

"And I never got to see them before I got out. Mama died. Then Papa died. Then I got out the pen. Never said sorry to either one of them for getting locked up."

Athena said, standing, not smiling, "Oh my God, Javier."

"Well, what should I do?"

Now smiling, "Go to the cemetery, make amends, bring flowers. My parents taught me that family peace comes before world peace. I'll be back shortly, class."

When he heard the hurried slam of her office door, Pablo said, "You scared me, *ese*," and Jazelle crossed race lines: "You crazy, nigga."

Haimona merely sat, sagging in his chair, bitter and very close to anger. At least in the penitentiary a man had a little silence to ruminate. To let the anger build and do bad with it, or let the guilt build and try to get out. No good came from the penitentiary, but sometimes you got out.

And to what? Haimona thought. *A classroom of sobbers and a lying bitch.*

Athena returned after a minute more and came rushing in. She sat in her customary wrinkle-free way and fingered the face of her watch. "We've got to hurry. I have to set aside fifteen minutes for the film, guys. Who's next?"

No one said anything. Everyone but Haimona had introduced himself and everyone but Athena was feeling "content." Athena had been "confused" for the second time in three meetings.

Athena smiled and said, "Is that it?"

In a confined moment of hope, Haimona thought he might be spared from speaking as a first-timer at Turning Point. But better sense deemed otherwise: The strained confessions of men who'd been to the same places he'd been, maybe worse, tiptoed the same lurid yards and the same four-by-eights, maybe longer, worn the same torn-up state-issued threads and slept in the same hanky-thin sheets, maybe less, eaten the same slop wearing the same stoic, institutionalized scowl meant that, law-ordered, he wouldn't get off. And when Athena asked him the proper pronunciation of his name, he knew he was done for.

She said, "Mah. Sue. E. Sue. E. Is that right? Sounds maybe Kenyan? Or is it South African? I once was in a loveship with a young Kenyan poet: But he was a projector. He shot all his problems with life off on me. I'll never date a Kenyan again. Or a poet. Jeff says he wasn't my type, anyway. Well, what kind of name is that? Ma . . . su . . . i . . . su . . . i?"

"Mine."

"What's your ethnicity?"

"Samoan."

"That's why you're so big," she said. "Well, welcome, Haimona. Did I say it right?"

Though she hadn't, Haimona opted for silence. He raised his head at Pablo. Haimona was indeed brown, but he wasn't an *ese*, and he wanted a silent confirmation from Pablo, who'd drawn a race line when Haimona first walked in. In the passing moment, Pablo raised his head back, the same gesture. No bond between them, no sweat or debt, Pablo looked off to another staring point just as hard as Haimona.

"Soooo," Athena said.

She was organizing papers, sliding papers out and silent-counting, licking her fingers, sliding more papers out, handing specific papers to Haimona, who, like her, was head-down. On one handout there was a pie with six wedges that seemed remotely familiar. He glimpsed at the two frames on the wall and saw why: Abuse, Coercion and Threats, Intimidation, Emotional Abuse, Blaming, Male Privilege. He turned the paper over and saw the therapeutically sound alternatives: Partnership, Negotiation and Fairness, Non-threatening Behavior, Respect, Accountability, and Shared Responsibility.

Athena turned, smiling, still organizing some remaining papers, and said, "What you're gonna need is a notebook for the class. You'll want to bring it with you every week. You'll have a homework assignment, usually having to do with the class discussion and healing." Haimona didn't move from the sag. "And . . . " she said, looking down again, missing something, finding something, thinking it over, fingering again.

Haimona handed her a paper. "I need this signed."

Athena smiled at the class and held it, awaiting words from the group. None of the men said anything. "Pablo?" she said. "Do you want to explain to Haimona our policy on signing attendance sheets?"

Pablo did not look over at Haimona. Neither did any other Mexican. Blacks and Samoans kicked it together in the pen and so some of the blacks took a peek. Pablo stared at Athena and said, "She'll sign it at the end of class."

Haimona scrunched the paper back in his pocket.

"So," said Athena, "how are you feeling?"

Haimona said nothing.

"On the second sheet of paper, you've got a list of emotions. So," Athena said invitingly, "how do you feel?"

Haimona looked down at the paper and saw happy festive serene comfortable peaceful joyous ecstatic enthusiastic inspired glad pleased grateful cheerful perplexed dismayed frightened apprehensive horrified cautious grumpy secure afflicted aching ardent zealous stretched hollow feisty immobilized pathetic desirous daring offended courageous somber gloomy fidgety content

"Content."

"And what do you expect to learn from the class, Haimona?"

"What?"

Athena said, "What do you expect to get out of the class?"

"A completion certificate."

Suddenly Athena sat up in the chair, and the smile withered away. The stares of the men crossed at points but never met. Lopez the security guard shifted in his stool by the door.

"Does anybody hear what I hear?" Athena asked.

The men looked away as if they had neither heard what Athena had heard nor heard her ask about what she'd heard.

"Pablo?"

Pablo looked up slowly, not at Haimona.

"Would you say that Haimona is being a little bit rigid?"

Pablo acted like he had been selected to clean the urinal. He looked over at Haimona, down at the notebook in his lap. Like any other man, he didn't want unnecessary problems and so he tempered his answer accordingly. He shook his head. "A little bit."

"And what does rigidity lead to, guys?"

"Doomed friendships and loveships."

Haimona said to Pablo, "You don't know shit about me, homie, and neither does she."

Some of the Mexicans sat up, including Javier. Lopez spun slowly in the stool and faced the class. Haimona's stare was steady, chest out.

Pablo said, "Take it easy, homes."

"Mind your own then, homie. Keep it real."

"Now, guys—"

"Who you think you're talking to, *ese?*"

"Guys—"

"I don't give a fuck who I'm talking to."

"Guys, if you're getting a little hot under the collar, just take a time-out. Just tell yourself you need to step back and take a break from it all. That's what we learn in here, right?"

Pablo said, "I'll take a time-out."

"Yes, Pablo," said Athena. "That's very good. Just be back before the hour to sign in."

Pablo stood just as slowly as he had done anything else. He brushed the lint from his slacks, rolled the sleeves of his jacket, and billboarded the tats on his forearm. The labyrinth of green ink nearly preceded his exit from the room. When he hit the door, his eyes were on Haimona, who returned the same stare. He passed Lopez in the hallway and commenced down the steps.

Lopez came in the door.

"Oh, it's all right, Lopez," said Athena. "Everything's fine. Pablo's just been here a little longer than Haimona. He understands the benefits of self-control. He has the tools to take a time-out when he needs to and Haimona doesn't. Yet." She looked over at the first-timer. "Well, Haimona. Tell me again what you want out of the class."

"A certificate of completion."

Athena nodded, the smile coming up, and began to read the file: "Yes. Well, you've a history of violence now, don't you? You came from a violent background, an abusive family. Your father beat you at a young age, almost killed your mother."

Haimona looked down at his "Feelings" sheet. He felt like he'd been zapped below the belt with a cattle prod. He didn't want her talking about things she wasn't entitled to talk about, and family was one of them. But he didn't know what she knew. There were files and files of accurate and inaccurate biographical tidbits on him, and she probably had every one of them in her lap. And any tidbit she didn't have, she could get. He didn't know what she knew, but he didn't want any other man to hear one detail unqualified. In a confessional age, there were still men who were still silent and went against the times.

Athena told Haimona what she knew. "You've been arrested for assault and battery, assault with bodily injury, assault with a deadly weapon, your fists; you nearly killed your girlfriend and the man she was with, for which you served out a . . . six-year term. You've been out now for two days and already you're creating problems for yourself. If, by saying you want a certificate of completion, you mean you want to get to the bottom of these problems, you would be right on. If, by saying you want a certificate of completion, you mean that you will approach this classroom with an open mind to healing, you would be right on. If, by saying you want a certificate of completion, you mean to not waste the class's time with meaningless rigidity, rigidity which will serve you in the same faulty fashion it has served you before, you would be right on."

Athena had the full-on smile again, a vague, gaping whiteness in Haimona's peripheral vision. All along it had been a bold and bright insult, growing in stature in a lengthy half-hour. It was deviously sensible: she had backing all the way around in silence. He'd go back to the pen for sure if he walked out on her for good. The other men would silently applaud with smiles, admire his rebellion, and maybe tell some stories to their homeboys, and he could retell the stories to kill time while locked up. But it would mean nothing. They didn't care about him; he was just another story. He wanted out of the system, and this was the first step. This was the turning point and she knew it. They knew it, too, because they were doing it, step by weekly step. Confining themselves in freedom as they confined themselves in the penitentiary. And the worst if he walked away: he'd be back here again some day, once he got out. The elephantine State of California never forgets.

And if he opted for the route of violence that got him locked up to begin with, something worse would occur: that prehistoric phenomenon of men protecting the other sex, an urge which must be the benevolent side of violence, a phenomenon no more alive in life than in the penitentiary itself, where Haimona had watched in wonder young women preachers, guest singers, and correctional officers prance through the block in giggles and hair spray, more certain of their safety than he himself, banking on prehistoric protection, that last core value of every man when stripped down like a convict—that he could protect his woman, he could still do that; all of this would come crashing down upon him with the fisted, booted, forearmed force of twelve stripped men, enraged at his violation of the code in their face. Enraged that he couldn't internalize the urge as they did, that he couldn't cut it for even a week.

He lifted his head to the room and Jazelle met his gaze with the conspiratorial surreptitiousness of a crime partner. Jazelle was the friendliest of the pack, two weeks from finishing the class. He half-nodded and pinched his eyebrows together. The gesture said, *Don't bring us all down, nigga.*

The smile was almost in front of him. "Now would that be correct, Haimona?"

"Sure," he said.

"Good. I'm so pleased. Well, welcome, Haimona. We're all very excited to have you with us." The smile was in his face and then gone. "Now, we've not much time left. Let's begin the video. It's the follow-up of last week's presentation on male privilege."

Athena smiled Lopez out of the doorway, pranced out under its arches, and reemerged with a television on a shelf with rollers. The shelf fit perfectly into the space of the doorway, like a puzzle piece. Lopez was directly behind the television, his back to the class, his shoulders twitching now and then. He looked back once at Haimona and then sat down on the stool.

Athena pressed play and, even as he registered the action on the screen, Haimona began the process of preparation. Turning Point was a year long. After tonight, there were fifty-one weeks left. At twenty-five bucks a pop. When it's over, a thousand bucks to the state—Don't think about that. Gotta say hello and your name and then an inside-feeling and gotta lose the rigid face. Think about that, do it. Keep a feel on the woman, her mood, her tone, her ideas, her smile, and hover about like a bumblebee. Keep your stinger to yourself. Be there every week, sign in, sign out, perfect attendance, or it's back in the joint.

And Pablo. Will return before the hour for the same reason. And he'll be back the next week, too, back with a scowl.

Maybe to get you. Maybe he'll get on the horn next week and call up some homeboys or maybe he'll show up next week with a piece. Maybe he'll slash the tires on your ride, smash the windows, maybe he'll follow you home. But whatever happens next week, a time-out doesn't mean take a break from it and cool off in the corner and come back and forget about a slight and shake hands and hug and start over. Especially in a roomful of parolees.

Gotta patch it up somehow. Gotta remind Pablo who the enemy is, who's on what side, who's on the same side, who's got choice in the matter, who doesn't. Gotta show him it's one big setup to lose. Gotta work toward male neutrality, like two lions passing on the range. Gotta do it front of the class, still strong, but smart-strong, and if the woman's there watching, fuck it: Gotta do it. Keep your back to the wall and head-up, just like in the joint. *But if it comes down to it and you can't get out of the fix, fuck it: Do what you gotta do to survive.*

The presentation ended and Athena stood and pranced over and bent down in front of the set. No one admired her ass but Jazelle. Still facing the screen, she asked the class: "Did you see how they resolved their problem through open, frank discussion? No one raised their voices, no one made threatening gestures. That's one good thing about Jeff. He hasn't threatened me yet; he just goes off by himself when he's mad. But if we all keep the idea in mind that our partner has a problem to be resolved just like us, we're one step closer to healing."

The buzz of the machine rewinding accentuated the silence in the room. No one but Jazelle moved about in the seat. Athena three-stepped back to her seat and removed a felt marker from the flap of her binder. The marker was purple-pink and fat like a cigar. When she uncapped it and began writing on the board, Haimona could smell the ink.

He looked around the room. Javier was watching him, brooding. Haimona nodded and Javier looked down.

"Sooooo," said Athena. "What did you notice about the way the couple conversed?"

Jazelle said, "He asked her questions."

"Okaaay." Athena was still writing. She was redrawing the wheel on the wall. "Can you say more about it, Jazelle?"

"He didn't tell her what to do once."

Athena stopped writing and turned to face the class. "That's right," she said. "There was mutual respect between them. Jeff says that's the one thing he loves about our loveship: He knows I give him respect. Did you see it, guys?"

Most of the men nodded and Jazelle said, "Yeah."

Athena was waiting for Haimona. He was looking down in his lap, and when he felt the silence he looked up. Javier had found something else to focus on. "How about you, Haimona? What did you notice?"

"Well, no one tried to be the boss. No one tried controlling anyone."

The smile came back. "That's right. Both parties were on equal ground in every facet of their conversation. That's what we all want, really, equality in our relationships, friendships, loveships, the workplace: Everything we're involved in, we long for equality. Haimona, you've pointed out an essential problem people have in resolving problems. Look at the Anger Wheel, guys."

Athena pointed at the board and circled a wedge. It was the same wedge on the wall and on the paper in Haimona's lap. Inside the wedge the words *POWER* and *CONTROL* were underlined twice in wavy lines. She circled the same wedge in the other wheel. It read, *EQUALITY.* She drew an arrow from the first wedge to the second wedge, not smiling yet, frowning.

"This is our life goal, guys," said Athena. "Treating everyone we meet with equality. By eliminating our own insecure desires for power and control, we optimize our chances of healing. And plus, guys, it's good karma. Good chi. No one wants to be told what to do, not your friends or your kids, not your wives. What happens, guys, to problems dealt with equally?"

Jazelle said louder than the others, "Absolution."

The smile came up and Athena capped her pen. "Absolutely absolution. Okay, guys. I'm gonna let you out a little early so I can talk to Pablo when he returns. Your homework for next week is—let's think of something good—"

"You're gonna gimme homework on my last week?"

"Do you think you're different than everyone else, Jazelle?"

"Hell, yeah. I got two weeks left. I must be different than everyone else."

"Okaaay. Then it's fair for you to have different homework than everyone else, right? Your homework is to tell the class next week what you've learned in the past year. The class'll be yours for the first ten minutes." Jazelle winced. It made the smile come back. Jazelle matched it, as if he needed to cover for the remaining unsmiling men of the group. "Good, Jazelle. Everyone else, write out a re-creation of your crime, whatever it was, how you would deal with it now, what would happen."

Jazelle said, "That's easy. What happen is you won't be here."

Athena laughed and the men stood and got in line and Athena signed their attendance sheets one by one. There was some muffled discussion in the rear of the line, lessening towards the middle of it and altogether gone by the time the parolee reached the front of the line. Some men offered harmless, obsequious flatteries to Athena, and she took each one gracefully, equally harmless.

Javier cut in line in front of Haimona. The Raiders beanie pushed his ears out like flaps. He said, "You got a long time left here, homie. Wanna take it easy."

"This life is a long time."

Javier was at the front of the line. "Sometimes it is, sometimes it ain't."

"Hello, Javier," said Athena. He turned slowly away from Haimona. "Thanks for sharing with us tonight."

"You're welcome," he said.

Haimona reached the front of the line. Javier went out the door. It was just Haimona and Athena in Healing Room 3. She said, "I'm very happy that you're with us, Haimona. If you have any difficulty making the payments, just tell me. We can arrange an alternative payment plan. Okay?"

His mind was on all the things opposite of healing. He said routinely, "Okay," and then gave her the sheet.

"There you go," said Athena. "See you next week."

"Thank you."

Haimona came into the hallway and took three steps to the bathroom. The door cut the hallway into two equal sections. He would check the head, HR 1, and HR 2. He gripped the doorknob and opened it. He bent down and peered underneath the first stall. No feet. He pushed the stall door open: No one propped up on the porcelain. He did the same with the second stall: The bathroom was empty. No breathing, no noise, no one but himself in the head. Just the hum of the overhead waterline and the trails of a song beneath the door. The song sounded like distant, repetitious orchestral music. It almost sounded like the waterline.

Haimona stared into the mirror, an institutionalized menace on his face, and told himself to relax. This wasn't the joint, he didn't have to hold his breath or tiptoe. He wasn't walking the yard, bottling himself into scowls, signs, and vernacular. Keeping with the manic, universal concern for safety. This was where the Jeffs and Athenas of the world dallied about halfheartedly, where noncommital union was okay and you could walk away from the past. This was the "outs," this was freedom. Forced freedom maybe, the state still holding the strings of autonomy, still calling the shots, but it was the best he'd get for awhile.

He smiled and said to himself in the mirror: "Take it easy, man. Just like that *ese* said."

He came out the door and almost collided with Lopez. Lopez was breathing hard, like he'd been exercising. He put an index finger to his lips. The deep, mysterious chant which Haimona had heard in the bathroom was filling the hallway. Lopez wiped the sweat from his brow with a sleeve and motioned at the office of Athena. "It's the boss-Ma," he said. "She's meditating."

"Oh."

"Don't worry, man. Just head on out."

"Should I wait until she—"

"Nah, nah. Go now, man. She don't like people hanging around."

Lopez began softly whistling a tune. Then he stood in the doorway of HR 3. "Go ahead, homie."

Haimona shrugged and started down the hallway. He vowed to walk past her office without acknowledging her presence. He passed the other two rooms of healing and the eerie chanting grew louder, no longer distant, possessive of hallway ear space. Haimona defied the vow and, still walking, glanced into Athena's office. Her back was pressed evenly to the wall, her ass flat on the rug, legs crossed beneath the dress, eyes closed, head up, ommm-ing. Her tone was as controlled as the chant filling her office, but there was an undercurrent of narcissistic ecstasy in the pitch. She seemed to be separate from life itself. As if both the healing and the horrors of every man who ever set foot in her office were of the very distant past. Haimona was happy her eyes were closed. He didn't have anything at all to share with her about his first meeting at Turning Point. It made him feel better when he passed undetected.

He came down the steps of the Turning Point offices feeling alive. When he'd walked from the prison gates two days back, he'd felt something of the same family of bliss. Yet the feeling then was a little closer to relief, like the cool water after an exhaustive ten-mile run. Tonight he felt a release of invigoration.

The cold snuck up on him and he made a bowl with his hands and blew into the palms, a smoke cloud forming around his face. He had been sweating in the hallway and only knew it now from his steaming cheeks blurring things a bit. Yet the cold shadow of night was almost comforting. He softly chuckled: the steady, rhythmic chanting was still coming from the office.

He had not reached the bottom step when he felt a tremor in the wood frame. He knew what it was and who it was before he even thought of turning, and almost simultaneously a blow to his ear confirmed what he knew. He was thinking he shouldn't even turn at all, since it was better to be knocked into oblivion and land in the hospital than return to the penitentiary for fighting, but already he was falling down the steps to the concrete below.

A quick shuffle step and drag step and the endorphin-adrenaline–awakened anxiety prevented a total loss of balance, and almost immediately again he was struck in the ribs from a different angle, thinking, *That wasn't a fist. It wasn't wasn't.* The needle-point pain made him turn toward it and swivel his hips on his pivot foot, and he aimed for the Raiders logo and struck Javier upside the temple. Javier's steel knuckles shot off into the bushes from the blow and he was collapsing to the ground like an accordion condensing and Haimona turned and swiveled again and swung and grazed Pablo's cheek. He was moving in reflexive immediacy, decisions in quarter-seconds. Everything snapped in black-and-white pictures, yet behind it all were the molten images of the meditating woman coursing through his mind. He was growling like an animal, thinking, *Bitch You did Bitch bitch you did this.*

Steady on his feet, circling Pablo, he was blazing cognizance. Pablo lunged like a fencer and Haimona stepped to the side and clutched him by the shoulders and drove him to his back. Pablo hit the pavement at the same time Haimona hit the cushion of his body and bounced up to his knees. Pablo was straining in timed, bodily surges, like bodily hiccoughs, bodily convulsions. Haimona's left hand balled into a fist and struck the face again and again while the other stretched for the "14" on his neck, and somewhere between that very moment and his knuckled fist blooming and draping the open, already choking hand, Haimona thought, *Fuck it Too late done Dead.*

It was forced freedom gone down the drain, and it was blood geysering from Pablo's nose and mouth and his eyes rolling up. A louder tremor than before came, and Haimona knew it was the inside of his untamed head, a train wreck, and then—not. It was too loud to be his head, like overhead thunder, a herd of bison, the deep, resinous cough of a choking wood frame. He was squeezing Pablo's neck harder and was struck again in the same spot of the rib cage and shoved aside to the bushes. As he was already rolling to his feet, he was thinking, *Here come the Here they.*

"Get the hell out of here, man!"

Haimona didn't step back or forward, huffing, spitting, shivering, blinking.

Lopez said, "Get the fuck out of here! Before that bitch wakes up and calls the cops!" Then, to Pablo: "*¡Ándale, ese! ¡Arriba!*"

Haimona's feet were backing him up one by one, but he did not turn. Lopez wiped at Pablo's nose with the jacket of his sleeve and then took the jacket off altogether. His arms were covered with green and red and a half-dozen tattooed "14s." There was a forceful soothing in his voice, the steady, paternal intonation of experience: "Come on, *ese.* Get up, homie. Come on. Straighten up, *ese.* Gotta clean you up and sign in."

Javier was out cold in the bushes, and Haimona's institutionalized mind was registering everything. The moment Lopez was completely draped by Pablo, he would attack again. Yet when he heard Lopez grunt, "Get up the steps, *ese,* get up there," it was like a license to leave the scene.

A rush of blood came to Haimona's legs. The unsteady staircase leading to the Turning Point offices was still trembling. They were already up it and gone, had never been there, efficient ex-cons just like him. He turned and stretched out in a hurried but composed stride. His ears were ringing, his eyes and ribs stung, the swollen knuckles a pulsating heartbeat. He was cupping the blood flowing from his ear, wincing at the thought of next week.

He did not think it mattered much beyond the inconsequential bounds of pain. Just live in it, just die in it. Everyone he knew felt pain, and there was a hell of a lot more on the horizon: This healing stuff would always be in business.

reliable vet dad, reliable con son

DAD TELLS ME ABOUT THE TIME HE WALKED OUT OF his lieutenant's rank tent and avoided military charges of assault with a deadly weapon and kidnapping. The man he'd beaten has not yet died and the evidence is his name on the thirty-five-year reunion list for the Special Ops Pathfinders team to be held in the Mexican café La Paloma in the San Diego County city of Oceanside. Including my father, there will be five men attending.

I say, "You should go, Dad," and he says at once, "I'll shoot that bastard in the head."

I have twenty-two years of life under my belt, including two-and-a-half years in the penitentiary, and all twenty-two with my war-seared father. Nothing in this life can surprise me, not even murderous thirty-five-year grudges. Though still on the virginal side of an official coup de grace, I myself will kill a man if necessary (it's the only thing I'd known for certain prowling under the orange corrugated iron of the

San Quentin chow hall pillars for the baptismal time and seeing two hundred mutherfuckers knowing the very same thing). Doing time has taught me to keep my head down and my back to the wall in a way that imparts to any given threat that I will kill a man if necessary. If I get out of the rotting gates of San Quentin State Penitentiary without a single external scar, it's because I will kill a man if necessary.

But Dad was looking at real time in March 1967, a sentence that carried at least ten years. The general rule about time is that a military charge carries double a civilian charge. So some homeboy pinched for possession of weed on the streets of East San Jose, and serving, let's say, a year in the Santa Clara County Jail, would probably get prison time from the brass if caught in the lush greenery of Vietnam.

"I guess you had a lot of that," Dad says, both forearms pressed into the surface of our shared visiting table, S.Q.V.R. 24. "You had certain leg units who smoked so much that their eyes were sealed shut. But not our team. Everyone had been in country for two tours each. You had to qualify with guts and blood to get on this team. We trained in Malaysia with the local Gurkhas and the British SAS. And you didn't do that shit because you were needed. That's how you survived. Relied on one another. Dopers went to leg units and dopers went home in bodybags."

I read my first book of fiction about Vietnam here in Quentin. I didn't like the book because I knew at once the author belonged to a doper unit and in the one scene of one story where the main guy flies his girlfriend from the states over to Vietnam because he's lonely, I knew my father would not only consider the tale inconceivable ("If you could do that," I could see Dad saying, "all of 'Nam would be infested with American hussies") but, more importantly, damned cowardly ("You ducked bullets and ate c-rats and watched your black lab die with a hole through its chest and you're gonna bring your woman to the bush? What kind of coward does something like that?"). Then when the girlfriend has the textbook training and internal fortitude and jungle radar to walk point on reconnaissance missions for the Green Berets, I knew Dad would consider the book a literary insult to his team. ("See, this what happens in doper units. The dope distorts their reality. Why you reading this shit? Fuck the bullshit writer.") So I sold the book for a smoke to a peckerwood heroin addict named Scooter who claimed he'd gotten high for the first time in Vietnam.

Even well before that day, I was familiar with the military terms that pop up in Dad's vocabulary any time he deems a situation serious or worthy enough. I had known before my first fistfight what *REMF* stood for. And what a *leg* unit was. And what *STRAC* meant, and *BRASS*, and even *KISS*. All that good stuff. You can remember it this way: So your basic *R*ear-*E*chelon *M*uther *F*ucker was often in a nonparatrooper *leg* unit of less combat engagement because they weren't *S*trategically *T*ough *R*eady *A*nd *C*ompetent, never learning or abiding by the fundamental laws of wartime protocol, like *B*reathe *R*elax *A*im and *S*(*S*)queeze when firing your weapon and *K*eeping *I*t *S*imple *S*tupid in matters of field strategy and the management of personal philosophy.

In the privacy of my own cell, working the heavy bag of my upright burrito-rolled mattress, I'll flatter myself: "I been through it, soldier. I ain't no leg REMF, boy. Got more lead in my body than bones." And as near as last night even, I knew that Pop's imaginary words were right on: Fuck the bullshit writer.

WHAT HAPPENED to Dad was he got caught in a ravine between the 861 Hills. He was the team leader and heavy gunner, and so he had an M60 automatic machine gun, over twelve hundred rounds of ammunition, and an upper-lip tobacco-chewing shot-up hick from Tennessee, duly named Tennessee. Tennessee had one bullet in his elbow and the other in his forearm because the series of stripped napalmed bamboo stumps they were hiding behind was big enough for Dad and everything of Tennessee except the wrist and the elbow which protruded as he was feeding the M60 its ammo.

"Assistant gunner bad luck," Dad says. "Bad angle."

Dad was down there for a day, "peppering the tree line," putting out fire in sparse, timed spurts so as to preserve ammunition while still, as a must, maintaining a perimeter. Anyway, Dad put down a dozen of the enemy and ended up throwing Tennessee over his shoulder, who, by that time, had also gotten clipped in the foot, and humped him up the hill and down the other side to a chopper which arrived the standard—for they, the pilots, were legs, too—two hours late.

I already know what you're thinking: There's something fraudulent about a framed story, especially from the glowing eyes of the given hero's son. Hearsay never stands in a court of law, so why should it stand in a story? And who can rely on anything about Vietnam from someone who just hit twenty-two and has admitted heretofore to the dubious autobiographical descriptor of convict? It's almost disrespectful, especially when people are dying in the tale and the person involved is your own father: fifty-eight thousand dead and your goddamned progenitor is at risk of being one of them.

No matter how it's relayed, if you're honest inside, you should damned well feel a sense of guilt, all right? It's blasphemy. But if I merely write that Dad was nominated for a Medal of Honor and ended up with a Silver Star for Valor and then leave it at that, the point of the story will be missed entirely, and Thomas McMalley, private first class of 173rd Airborne Pathfinders Special Ops Team, beaten to disfigurement and thrown into a monsoon rain–filled eight-foot-deep ammunition ditch on 17 March 1967, might have the nerve to take the moral high ground on Dad in the safe and sound ditch of Oceanside, California, 2002.

FUCK THOMAS MCMALLEY.

Each team had a runner, and the job always fell to the newest team member. The runner would report back to Saigon any activity he'd seen in a given period, usually two or three months. Thomas McMalley was the runner. He had over half a tour under his belt, but no one in the unit had seen his goods, and therefore no one in the unit respected him, especially Tennessee. He hadn't earned his bones with the team, and that was what mainly mattered. And then, too, he'd been transferred to their unit fast, real fast, and without explanation. The general feeling was that they were playing bodyguard for some brass baby misfit, some senator's son who wanted to play hero and walk the line, a jinx for whom they'd all pay the price in the place where it counted. They didn't know anything about him, really, and that's scary.

That's how it is here in Quentin, same principle. I came into this mutherfucker not knowing anyone. If I wanted to get hyperbolic and sentimental, I could pen that I didn't even know myself, that it was, ultimately, the beginning of an incarcerated journey of self-discovery. Like Dostoevsky before the gallows in Siberia or Rubin "Hurricane" Carter growing his 'fro out in the hole. But I won't pen that now, can't really. I wouldn't give the California Department of Corrections that much credit, and, anyway, what kind of bullshit is that? There are lifers in the East Block of San Quentin who are, decade by decade, discovering the hell out of themselves, and then, damn, not wanting to jinx myself either, my mission is getting out this mutherfucker with my skin unslashed.

Some kid named Darwin didn't. He came into East Block the third night of my sentence and went out the next morning on a blood-soaked gurney. No one knew who the hell he was when he first came in, ducking-like, looking no one in the eye, not even a first-termer nobody like me. He passed my cell like a priest: head down and breath held, cast-iron gray blanket folded across his forearms. I was on my stomach on my bunk looking out the crisscrossed iron grate the cops put in so you won't get firebombed and silently mouthed to myself, "Leg."

The catcalls started up over the wire an hour after his arrival, white catcalls since he was white. "Who is that there just came in, Red Dog?" "Don't know, Scooter! Ask Harley!" "Harley!" "Yeah?" "Who was that?" "Don't know!" "Hey! Well, find out, dog!" "Hey!" "Hey!" "You!" "Fourth-tier white boy just came in, hey!"

Darwin never answered the "Hey!" and that was about all the information anyone needed. When you come into East Block at two in the morning and there ain't a busload of convicts with you, then you're either a snitch, a chester (*ch*ild mol*ester*), or a crooked cop who got caught, or you just got punked somewhere in another block and it was time for you to move out. You asked for protection from the cops, a transfer to another block, and that's chum for the sharks.

Darwin slit his wrist that night, and they didn't find him until five in the morning, when the black in the cell directly below shouted out a few minutes before chow, "Mu'fuckin' blood drippin' down fourth tier! Start up a trickle, end up a river! Got me a crimson waterfall! Some nigga bleedin' hisself up 'bove!"

Then the "Man down!" calls started up, and after everything finally died out and the blue-skinned, supine-forever youngster that everyone still didn't know went rolling down fourth tier, I said to myself, "Darwin said you couldn't cut it. Wouldn't survive. Good-bye, leg."

ANYWAY, Dad says it was Tennessee who first said he didn't trust Thomas McMalley. Tennessee had been with Dad for two tours' worth of two dozen firefights and a guns-drawn race riot in the rear at a PX in Saigon. American on American, so to speak. Dad had negotiated with the blacks to put down their weapons, and they had only listened because Dad is Hawaiian not white and he promised to get Tennessee to stop using the word "nigger" in their presence. That night Dad's team left the PX and all the blacks of the racially mixed 101st Airborne Division behind on a mission. It was moved forward a week by some cherry leg West Point second lieutenant who was pissed because he had no authoritative say whatsoever in the scrap, and Tennessee kept on with his nigger-saying ways.

But Tennessee could track a gook through bush triple-canopy thick, had the nose of a (Dad laughs here) black Labrador retriever, the ears and fierceness of a German shepherd, and (never telling Tennessee, of course, Dad laughing) the light-footedness of a native. He was tiny like a native and red and lean like a carrot and had a Confederate flag on his shoulder which always showed because he'd roll that sleeve of his T-shirt, leave the other sleeve down. And what Dad'd never tell anyone but me in 2002 is that he trusted Tennessee precisely because he *was* a racist hick.

I know exactly what Dad means: I'd seen it in Criminal under the pillars of the East Block chow hall my first week in Quentin. Criminal drove (and still drives) our Polynesian car, the smallest racial crew in East Block. There were nine (now eight) of us total, five Samoans including Criminal, three Tongans (now two), and one Hawaiian, me. The loudest Tongan, streetnamed Rambo, had words in his cell with a northern Mexican streetnamed Flaco from East San Jose, my home kick. Before eleven that night, Criminal dangled a sheet-torn fishing line with his signature arrow-cut milk carton (a tribute to his Indian hero, Crazyhorse) in front of my cell. I quit beating my mattress for a minute and reeled in the line and detached the kite and tugged on the line to indicate reception, and read the kite on the steel toilet in the rear of the cell:

Get ready to get down when the cells pop, Hawaii. Welcome to Quentin, homeboy.

I thought immediately, *That's right. KISS it up, Criminal. Keep it simple.*

At five the next morning, I put a shield of folded cardboard over my chest and my stomach and tied everything at the sides with an interwoven shoelace. I pulled my T-shirt down to double secure it and buttoned the state-issued jean jacket to the neck. I stabbed the panoply with the chiseled point of a toothbrush and then put my face in the steel mirror and gritted my teeth and pinched my eyebrows down. When the cell popped for chow, I came out with a palm wrapped around a sharpened pencil in the pocket of my jacket and the laces of my boots double-knotted at the tongue, STRAC as hell.

I grew up with Vietnamese and Mexicans in an East San Jose suburb, understood *El Día de los Muertos* before ever trick-or-treating on Halloween, could cook chorizo as well as any Oaxacan crew at the local taqueria. All my homeboys growing up were Mexican. (The Vietnamese homeboys abandoned me the day I came out the neighbor's house smelling like tripe and La Victoria salsa: I ain't mad; gotta be down with your own.) And my first lay was a Mexican girl named Dora Muñoz who cried the day I left her for another Mexican girl, my second lay, her cousin, Esmerelda Muñoz. Anyway, Dora was Flaco's sister and that mutherfucker remembered me. Or found out about me from Dora. It doesn't matter. We (Criminal's Polynesian East Block car) were gonna get down not because I'd fucked Dora or left Dora for her and his cousin but because he questioned my ethnicity (mutherfucker) to Rambo, said I was a Mexican snitch hiding out with Polynesians since he'd once heard me speak some cheap street Spanish to an old *paisa* man on fifth tier who needed help filling out his paperwork for canteen, or that why would a Hawaiian screw a Mexican girl, anyway?

I found out all this afterwards, didn't know any of it that morning. Truth be told, I wanted to hide my history with the enemy in the way a wife keeps from the husband her cast of former lovers. We call Mexicans in the pen "Mexi-*komos*," because "*komo*" in Samoan means "fuck," so that "Mexi-" and "*komo*" combined will translate into "Mexi-fuck." Criminal bypasses the Hispanic prefix altogether, so that when he says to me, "Hawaii, those *komos* over there are spotting up," I know exactly who he's talking about.

Anyway, we all met at the dead yellow pillars of the first tier, the nine of us, ready to get down. Northern Mexicans are at least sixty deep, the largest racial segment not only in East Block but in all of San Quentin. So there were ten strategically positioned groups of six northern Mexicans deadeyeing us as we spotted up in our own semicircle, a Polynesian half-moon, every man facing out.

I was to the immediate right of Criminal, to the left of Rambo, both of my hands in the jacket, one around the pencil, the other balled into a fist. I had a sincere belief that everyone at that moment must've had their hands in their pockets, STRAC as hell, though the belief, in retrospect, was probably some kind of sly psychological assuaging of the guilt I felt for my own hands, which were, I remember, so full of nervous violence that I nearly broke the goddamned pencil. I wanted to perform: I was amped, STRAC, and ready to go. But I decided fast that I could probably kill a man with my bare hands just as easily as I could with a sharpened no. 2 Ticonderoga, maybe easier if I went for the Adam's apple, so I pulled both hands out and BRASSed: breathed, relaxed, and got ready to squeeze.

It was damned quiet, unprecedentedly quiet. Quentin's like a cathedral, nineteenth-century high-walled and everything going up and down in echo, even silence. All the races were split and quiet, blacks and whites on the periphery watching, us and the northern Mexicans in the center at the pillars, also quiet. The cops abided the silence, too, maybe, somehow, directed the silence, only the metered click of the gunner's boots on the cast-iron walkway above breaking the quiet. His steps sounded like an eerily perfect metronome, the kind that Pound (my favorite leg poet) used to time his poems when he was locked up for insanity.

The shot-caller for the northern Mexicans was a bowling ball named Bam Bam. He had arms like two big cuts of tri-tip, his chest a whole other regional entity, and when he walked it wasn't just his legs that moved, everything moved. He was short and wide and held the East Block record for consecutive pull-ups with thirty-eight. Big fucking deal, right? Who but a coward REMF leg worries about muscles or pull-ups or being badly outnumbered in battle? He probably couldn't raise the fork to his lips without colliding with some goddamned hindrance of muscle.

I thought, *I'll bomb on this leg REMF first. Put five punches in his face. Go for the king.*

Criminal was at least a foot taller than Bam Bam and, with his afro, a foot and a half taller. He looked down on Bam Bam like a cop.

Bam Bam said, "We got a little problem with your home-boy Rambo."

"Then you got a problem, dog," Criminal said, "with *all* of us."

Right there my breath went halfway down my throat and caught and I gritted my teeth and shot the air back out. Bam Bam looked at me suspiciously, trying to detect some schematic diversion in the exhalation of air, but I just looked at him with a murderous menace, STRAC as hell.

Bam Bam looked back at Criminal and said, "I'm comin' at you with respect, *ese.*"

Criminal said, "I got no problem with your people."

"How about your homeboy?" Bam Bam nodded at Rambo and I felt Rambo move.

Without looking at anyone but Bam Bam, Criminal said, "Nah. No problem, dog."

Bam Bam said, "So is this thing squashed or what, *ese?*"

"I'm asking you the same thing, dog."

A concession in the pen is like a sign on your back saying, *Stab me.* Criminal and Bam Bam said simultaneously, "Squashed," and that was it.

There was nothing noteworthy about the pseudoevent except two things: First, we—Criminal's East Block Polynesian car of nine (now eight) men—all pointed up together on the basest and truest of terms, and then, second, there was one who didn't: Rambo, all six-foot three, 280-pound crip-from-Long Beach of him, tagged down with more claims of homicidal menace than Charles Manson himself over in Vacaville, all of the murderous machine of him stood in the rear at the pillar making a hole in our phalanx four feet wide. Rambo had been nowhere near me the whole time. When we went under the pillars to chow, I looked at him like the leg that he was.

"Rambo," I said. "Got a book for you to check out, REMF mutherfuckin' Rambo."

SO WHAT Dad must have meant about Tennessee was this: Death is simple. The way you get yourself home, everyone learns, is by getting your team home. And the way you get the team home is through a down-to-the-bone loyalty, an esprit de corps tantamount to some backwoods hick believing in the worn-out ways even and especially in the face of emerging evidence to the contrary and the nullification of his very soul. Nothing but Death is simpler than that. No one beats Death, but you can sidestep it, stiff-arm it right on the point of the chin.

Because Dad knew even then that the self alone and an ideology alone ain't enough. You need someone to lean on. I remember my first time through the rust-iron frame of East Block. I stripped to my skins, got deloused and watered down, and then, just like Darwin, shot up to my cell shivering in boxers with powder-blue issues and a blanket draped across my forearms. I was nineteen years old, dizzy as fuck and looped as hell, and during our first visit Dad had said, "If you need an ideology, son, think of me. If your self ain't enough, son, think of me. Don't let this place drive you nuts. Survive in this place, son, thinking of me."

For two-and-a-half years, Dad has visited me twice a week, the maximum number of visits for a convict. He drives an hour and a half down from East San Jose, hour and a half back, straight trooper is Dad. Except for the eight months I just spent in the hole (as it turned out, Rambo's ducking in the rear had to be addressed, and so I volunteered to initiate the beating almost two years later: Rambo, bastard-coward-crip, must be rotting in a lock-downed protective custody cell wherever the hell protective custody bitches hide out),

Dad's always the first to walk into the San Quentin Visiting Room at eight a.m. sharp, frowning under the frame of the door like he owns the place, death-conscious as hell.

It's always tough talking to Dad alone. Mom has refused to visit (another story in itself) and it's okay by me: no son wants his mother to be searched and disrespected by cops, hustled in and out by the small of the back, lectured and then left at the door for not observing the eight-page dress code to the last button. What kind of selfish mutherfucker would want that for his own mother?

Still, her absence makes the conversation between father and son unfiltered. We're both right there, Dad and I, tethered to the gist of this survival thing like two mute maniacs chained to their own cursed silence. After the first four visits, we ran out of things to say. A long time passed on the crunch of Doritos and worn-out war stories. The same redundant reliable thing until Dad walked in with the invitation list for the Pathfinders Special Ops Reunion in Oceanside, California, and Thomas McMalley's name was on it.

SO TENNESSEE didn't trust Thomas McMalley, even before he'd been shot up in the ravine feeding my father's M60. He'd told Dad about his misgivings and Dad'd said, "You're probably right." Dad made Thomas McMalley walk point in his first three reconnaissance missions with the team. He passed all right, but not enough to satisfy Tennessee. A week later, Dad and Tennessee got caught in the ravine between Hill 861A and Hill 861.

THE FOURTH and fifth member of the Pathfinders Special Ops team are exonerated of any act of cowardice due to a lack of evidence and the Purple Hearts they both earned for catching multiple slivers of shrapnel in (a physical and geometrical miracle, really) nearly the exact same spots beneath the liver and in the ass and hamstring of the same leg, and, principally, to their unconditional post–Thomas McMalley beating support of my father, which suggested, possibly (I write, but Dad didn't say), that their story of being pinned down by enemy fire was true.

Dad says that Doc and Red disappeared from their flank in a single ground-pulse of explosion and that, while he harbored a private concern for Doc and Red missing and ordered McMalley to immediately search their circumferential radius at fifteen meters, he still had to operate on the tangible evidence that the remaining three, Thomas McMalley, Tennessee, and himself, were still alive and together and not divvied up into body parts in a tree. He'd have to assume Doc's role of medic, patch anyone up that went down, recognize that Red's customary flank cover fire wouldn't be there.

Dad whips right through Doc and Red's disappearance and I don't ask why. The only thing I can write about any undercurrent of suspicion is that it rests solely in my own damned felonious failing, all right? Quentin's a fucked-up place, what can I say? It makes a man crazy with suspicion. But can you imagine the deconstruction of Dad's innards and Dad's soul and all of his expectations in people and himself if a blood brother like Doc or Red sold him out and voluntarily vanished into the bush up the hill? How could he close his eyes at night, make a statement of certainty on anything? On what inner hallowed ground would he stand? What could he say about people except we're alive in one moment, dead the next, everything in between the two moments a straight-up variable?

THE RAVINE was at the base of two conjoined hills, Hill 861A and Hill 861. They had come down the face side of Hill

861A, by far the barer of the two. There was the waist-high cover of cut and napalmed bamboo and some elephant grass. At thirty meters from the ravine, they made contact with the enemy, a single, soot-faced, middle-aged gook who fired from the hip at once, spun on his heel, almost fell, recovered, bounded twice like a deer up the base of Hill 861, and, just before catching a bullet beneath the lung from Tennessee's M16, let out a string of nasal utterances fast as a machine gun. He was the point for a company of NVA at least fifty men deep.

Ten seconds later, Hill 861 exploded with fire. There were infinitely more nasal utterances and Dad's team caught ground fire without any discernible pattern. It worried Dad because groups in large numbers are invariably imprecise with their fire. It's power in numbers, overwhelm the enemy.

In the perpetual fire and leaf-rustling chaos, Tennessee yelled, "Kanaka! Set up behind the bamboo! See it?"

Dad nodded on his stomach and, after the one-two-three slaps of his right hand on the dirt, alligator-crawled with his weapon out front, his chin in the dirt, his pack riding the hump of his shoulders high in the line of fire. With Red and Tennessee's sharpshooting spot cover, Dad made it dirt-mouthed to the destination of bamboo in the deepest spot of the ravine and set up his 60 on the short-range V-shaped bipod and went to work.

Dad was worried about the tree line. If a sniper set up, he'd potshot the team to hell. Dad'd have to make it seem like they were larger than a five-man team. He'd have to toss some grenades, work the angles with his 60. He knew he'd have to pepper the tree line as Tennessee worked the ground, especially, he discovered in one fast look over his shoulder— "Poom!"— since Doc and Red were gone.

But Thomas McMalley was still there and stayed there for the next eight hours. He had run out of ammo in the first twenty minutes of the firefight, watched from a clump of knee-high bamboo Dad and Tennessee cut down at least a dozen of the enemy, probably more.

"Cowered just like a damned leg," Dad says.

Thomas McMalley had had a thirty-round clip in his M16 and five thirty-round clips in his pack. Anything more than that was too heavy. It didn't matter. Dad had over twelve hundred rounds for his smoking sixty, and the gooks froze their fire for an hour and a half, which allowed Thomas McMalley to escape up Hill 861A and alert someone of the need for relief and cover since the NVA were regrouping and bringing more men.

DAD WOULD NEVER say it here in the East Block visiting room of San Quentin, but I know that he loves Tennessee. I can tell in the way he talks about him. He knows the doubt that could come up in the crazy head of a modern man, so correct and politically sound, so safe. Dad's sagacious nods are little confirmations not of the veracity of the story—that he kept it to himself for three decades is proof enough for any challenge—but the point of the story itself. There's gotta be a point.

Because if he was to trust Thomas McMalley to get up the hill and summon support from the nearby First Cavalry and some medics for Tennessee's elbow and forearm, which, by now, were getting meatier and bloodier by the hour, what the hell did he have to fear with a blood brother at his side and a smokin' 60 putting lead into Hill 861 like a dynamite excavation? Oh, for sure, deep down there somewhere in the middle of his stomach was a pocket of outright con-centrated fear, pushing out against all those intangibles lost in the blood and breath of the body, and yet, deep in the malaria-ridden jungles of Vietnam (and top secret parts of

Laos and Cambodia) and even as far back as the days Dad'd walked the streets of 1953 Honolulu as a sixth sibling of fourteen brothers and sisters scavenging for food like jackals—even then those intangibles were refining themselves into outright concentrated courage and loyalty. And that's why Dad loved Tennessee: he'd courageously and loyally stuck.

A lot of time passed down in the ravine—at least, Dad says, eight hours—and Dad knew he had to make a move before the gooks returned en masse. He told Tennessee, "Ten. We gotta make a move. They're gathering up, coming back."

"My fuckin' foot's shot up, Kanaka."

"I know, I know. Makin' a move now."

"Go ahead, Kanaka. Go ahead."

"Nah. *We're* goin' now. I'll put up some fire and then toss you on a shoulder. Get some grenades ready. Toss 'em if you can."

"Yeah."

They made it up the first quarter of the hill without any enemy fire, zigzagging through the labyrinth of knee- and waist-high bamboo, Dad hunched by the weight of Tennessee and almost a day in the ravine on his stomach. His leg cramped but he kept running. That's how you fight through a cramp: keep running. Hill 861 blew up with fire when he and Tennessee came into the open patch of Hill 861A, and what Dad says about that half-minute is this: "You keep running."

He kept running, and they made it to the top and back down the other side, where a crew of medics of a First Cav leg unit were smoking Marlboros and whistling Smokey Robinson to a synchronized finger-snap, and just under four months passed before they saw Thomas McMalley again at the Special Forces Camp seven clicks south in Lang Vei.

YOU SEE, the funny part of this tale is Tennessee not dying. If Tennessee dies in the ravine of the conjoining 861 Hills, then Dad probably gets his Medal of Honor, Thomas McMalley definitely gets what he wanted, and poor old Tennessee either gets shot back to Nashville with a form letter from President Johnson stapled to the terry cloth of his body bag or ravaged for his wallet by the first NVA on the scene. But Tennessee lived with a right-legged limp and a twitching trigger hand and a grown-to-its-fullest grudge, and it fucked everything up for Thomas McMalley.

He was the runner, remember? And, like Dad says, Thomas McMalley kept right on running as ordered, straight on into Saigon to report what eventually became known as the Day-Long Battle in the Cup. In the Lang Vei Special Forces Camp four months later, he'd told Dad, Doc, Red, and Tennessee that he'd "indeed" gotten on the horn at the base of Hill 861A and the reinforcements had "indeed" arrived but how could he help it if the reinforcements were REMF legs who "indeed" couldn't be STRAC with the buttons of a pinball machine? That was fine by Dad because he'd heard a different version of the same thing from Doc and Red four months earlier and seen the honesty in their eyes and remembered each and every dig they'd been in together and known that the possibility of lying was not, after all, a possibility, and they each popped another can of Schlitz with their P-38s and toasted Thomas McMalley, who, in his prodigal return, had to be one of them, and then Tennessee, grudge-bound gimp, asked McMalley for his medal.

McMalley said, "What, indeed?"

Tennessee said, "Where's my medal?"

"Take it easy, Ten," Dad said. "Take it easy."

"I didn't play babysitter with this REMF for nothing. I didn't get laid up in bed three months for him. I got enough lead in me to make a thousand pencils and I want at least some silver in exchange. Now where's my fuckin' medal, REMF?"

Dad said, "Hey, Ten. Fuck the medal. What's wrong with you?" and Tennessee said, "Fuck," and limped around the corner of the kennel of the tracker dogs.

Dad, Red, Doc, and McMalley kept drinking. Red asked if the whores in Saigon were clean and could be trusted, and McMalley shouted, "No VD, indeed!" and as McMalley explained in precise detail the best spots to frequent, Tennessee limped back round the corner of the dog kennel with his Walther PPK pistol drawn and pointed at McMalley and a brand-new rucksack over the other shoulder. His sleeve was rolled and the big flag on his shoulder was blazing red.

"Fuck," Dad said. "Put that shit down, you fuckin' hick."

Tennessee threw the sack at McMalley's feet and said, "Open your ruck up, McMalley."

McMalley hesitated in the cloud of dust rising. Dad looked at Tennessee and back at McMalley, and Doc beat Dad to the punch with a single directive: "Open it up, man."

Dad said, "Come on. Get it open."

McMalley unbuttoned the main part of the ruck and put both hands in. The sack split open from the inside out like a blooming rose, the buttons popping like distant semiautomatic machine gun fire, pop, pop, pop. There was the promising shine of canned goods—Vienna sausage, Spam, and Beanie Weenies, the olive green and pale gray of cartridges and knife sheaths, and, somehow, three department-store-folded, clean white tees. One shirt bulged at the bottom like the belly of a pregnant mother. Tennessee reached down and unraveled the shirt like a flag, and three rolled shirts fell out from the bulging shirt's center. They'd hidden like a secret a sealed manila envelope, and Tennessee grabbed it with his bad hand before McMalley could reach down and get it with both of his own good hands.

Inside the envelope were two carbon copies of an official military document. Dad was being recommended for a Medal of Honor for "action exemplifying courage in the American infantry man . . . and keeping the enemy at bay for eighteen hours until suitable reinforcements could reach a point of support . . ." and that was it, the first document. The second document described everything that went down per the assistant machine gunner, Tennessee's angle, except that Tennessee hadn't been shot; that, in fact, Tennessee was never even there because his name, Lee Robert Warren IV, had been spelled out in print on the document as Thomas McMalley, recipient of the Silver Star.

Dad pistol-whipped McMalley in the temple and Red reached down and yanked his arm behind his back, breaking the elbow like a wishbone. The snapping sound of it rang out in the eerie silence of the compound. Doc spit in McMalley's face and then slapped it and thrust his hand on his waist and stripped his pistol from the holster. They dragged him by his arm and his leg and his boot to the eight-foot-deep ammunition pit, Tennessee limping on his bad foot and skipping on his good foot five feet behind, and loosened his boots and threw them at his head and pushed him like a package into the miniature man-made abyss. That was ten minutes after four o'clock, 1610 military time.

For a little over an hour, they pissed and spit on McMalley and threw empty and half-full beer cans at his head, but that's not why he was unlucky. He would "indeed" be purged of the mess by the violent rain of the Vietnamese monsoon season. The buckets of rain sloshed through the trees and canopy at 5:36, 1736 military time, and only the septic southern molestations fired from the rim of the pit—"You think

I'd die from a bullet in the elbow, boy! This rebel got mo'
guts in his pinkie than your whole goddamned stomach!"—
kept McMalley from going under.

DAD WOKE the next morning to a blinding light. The light
was like the ball of white sun at the end of the near-death
tunnel. A pistol was at his head and two M16 barrels were at
his eyeballs. It would be at least three bullets each through
his cranium. His hand slid to his trousers. His gun was gone,
and he heard from a few feet behind the light and the guns:
"We gotchu, Kanaka."

"Shut up, private," said one of the nearest guns.

"Fuck you, REMF pig," said Tennessee. "Don't worry,
Kanaka. We gotchu. You're covered."

"Out of the bed now, sergeant."

"Get that light out my face."

Dad put a palm gently on an M16 barrel and, raising himself to a sitting position, gently extended his arm. The other
MP put his own barrel closer to Dad's face, prompting Doc,
Red, and Tennessee to move in a step closer to the three MPs.
Their own M16s were locked and loaded. The MP with the
pistol and the light and the MP baseball hat said, "Put your
shirt on. You're coming with us."

Tennessee said, "We gotchu, Kanaka."

Dad slid into his shirt and stood and assumed point of the
procession: Three MPs in erect and formal step gun-drawn
on the back of his head; shirtless and barefoot Doc, Red, and
Tennessee in skivvies and a jungle crouch gun-drawn on an
MP each.

WHEN I GOT SHOT to the hole eight months back for
lumping Rambo with the sharpened end of a steel dustpan,
not one of Criminal's East Block Polynesian car snitched on

me. So they had no witnesses. Each one of the homeboys went into Lieutenant Spinos's Dallas Cowboy office (he's got football cards of Troy Aikman, Emmitt Smith, and Michael Irvin framed on the plane of his desk, a tiny little trinity) with pure dirt on me and all seven came out just as dirty. No one leaked. That's how a car of eight men walk the East Block yard of Quentin. No one leaks. Lieutenant Spinos was pissed. Because they had no witnesses. Couldn't get me on anything. They searched my cell for contraband, put me in the hole for a trumped-up charge of insurrective behavior (I didn't stand on the wall like they'd ordered), and I was back in the block in eight quick months getting called for a visit from Dad.

THE LIEUTENANT'S TENT was rank. It stunk like a mud pit. Papers were scattered across the floor, and there was a lump of laundry in the corner. The lieutenant had stubble across his face as if he'd been fighting in the front, and his hair was knotted and twisted on his head. Dad was disgusted. He didn't salute and it didn't piss the lieutenant off. He yawned and said, "You're facing a lifetime worth of charges. Assault with a deadly weapon and kidnapping. Could add some others. You'll be in hell before you know it."

"I'm in the 'Nam."

"You'll never see light again, sergeant."

"He's a piece of shit. 'S lucky we let him live."

"That's the only reason you're walking out of this tent, sergeant. Look at me. Starting right now, we're forgetting everything that's happened in the last twenty-four hours."

"Nothing to say," Dad said, and lifted the flap of the tent to leave.

"Including meeting me."

"Nothing to say."

"Oh, hey," said the lieutenant, yawning. "Here. No Medal of Honor for you, sergeant." He handed Dad four citations and the accompanying medals and said, "Get out. And take your monkeys with you."

So everything was settled. The brass's ass was covered, Dad had his punishment of a Silver Star, Tennessee exchanged his lead for a Bronze, Doc and Red had a Purple Heart each, and the swollen and bloodied Thomas McMalley filled a seat on the first Starlifter Troop Transport back to the states.

IF YOU THINK the only reason the lieutenant let Dad walk was McMalley not dying, then you probably won't understand why not one of these cops can touch me or my father. The only thing keeping Dad from breaking me out this mutherfucker is a Southeast Asian mission of settling a debt with Thomas McMalley in Oceanside, California. The cooks and waitresses of the authentic Mexi-*komo* cuisine La Paloma are going to be in for a big surprise. Better duck down *en la cocina*, better keep their Mexi-*komo* asses out the fire.

Dad says, "Don't listen to these stories, son. I just wanted you to see why I said it. Why it came out like that. It was a fucked-up time and, even now, I got shit stored up in my head. Forgot about my head until today. It's no good. These stories don't mean anything."

I can't contradict Dad, even when he's wrong. Owe him that respect, the noncommittal, yet supportive disparity of silence. I look off at the cops with the mixture of placidity and menace unique to the man in the pen. There's a cop here named Rodriguez that I'd placidly and menacingly kill if I could. He's got eyes that never stop moving and a mouth to match.

Back in the block, that mutherfucker goes through a convict's house like a hurricane, ripping Britney Spears and Jennifer Lopez from the walls, tossing and kicking everything off the tier like a schizophrenic in need of his meds: When you see papers and posters swaying down in little U's and mattresses plunging past your cell, you know that Prozac poster boy Rodriguez is somewhere up above doing his thing. That schizo jumps on the PA system and shouts, "Here I come, boys! Who's the lucky tier gettin' stripped out their drawers? Get ready to touch your toes, boys! Flush that dope down the toilet! Pass that porn to your homeboy! Dismount at once from each other's asses! Here I come, boys! Here I come!" Then sure enough, the catcalls start up and the fishing lines vanish and the whole damn block is oscillating from a hundred toilets flushing simultaneously.

Dad says, "Do you need money on your books for food, son? Canned goods, soda pop?"

I say, "No, Pops. I'm fine. I'll survive."

"I'll put money on your books tomorrow."

"Okay," I say.

Rodriguez rises from the desk to take his rounds. He stops at the first table and noses his big Mexi-*komo* head into the conversation, moves onto the next table when the conversation gets too boring. I mumble, "Why don't he just pull up a fuckin' chair?"

"What?" says Dad.

"That pig Rodriguez," I say. "He's a piece of shit. Like McMalley." Dad looks sad and I say, "That piece of shit. I'll kill that coward Irishman myself. Right after I get out this mutherfucker. I'll hunt his ass down, treacherous bastard."

"Son," Dad says, "listen to me. I know how it is in here. But try to think of me and all our visits when you're down. Our mission is getting out of here fast as we can. In one piece. You got a year and a half left. Don't want you picking up other charges. Gotta stay outta that hole. Don't get looped. Gotta take care of yourself."

"Yeah," I say. I look around for any Mexi-*komos* from East Block. The visiting room is a haven of jumping beans, no one but Dad and I speaking English. It's twenty to two in this mutherfucker, *veinte* REMF Mexi-*komos* to two down-ass Hawaiians, me and Dad. "That's right. Gotta take care of yourself. Fuck these leg cowards. Fuck that pig Rodriguez and—"

"Son," Dad says. Though my eyes are on the Mexi-*komo* schizo pig making his rounds, I listen as attentively as possible to Dad. "Are you listening to me? Son, you need to step back and listen to what I'm saying. I'm worried about you. Try to keep your head up."

I look Dad in the eyes. "But you kept your head *down* in the bush."

Dad shrugs and his lips are crooked and pressed together like two puzzle pieces. It means he doesn't want to talk about it. But I'll pick up the ball for Dad, will pay homage to his story just as I should.

"Don't worry, Dad," I say. "I ain't gettin' picked off by these leg mutherfuckers. I'll be right in the front line doing my thing. They'll never break me."

Dad takes a deep breath like the kind you take at the doctor. "Are you all right, Dad?" I ask.

He lifts his eyebrows in confirmation. He looks tired, goddamnit, too tired. This STRAC trooper shows up the day I get out the hole for a visit, the very day I get out. We don't need to talk about the hole, Dad and I, we both been through it. Even mention of a single moment of suffering is meaningless surplus. The mission now is survive and be STRAC and get Dad some sleep before his big trip.

"Dad, you should split and get some rest."

He sits up, inhales, and says, "I'm all right, son. Listen. You gotta take care of yourself."

"Don't worry, Dad. Don't worry."

"Remember our mission. Getting you out as soon as we can."

"That's right." I duck down to hide the little gleam in my eye from any mutherfucker unworthy to see it: That makes for everyone in the damned visiting room save Dad. "Are you flying or driving to the reunion, Dad?"

"Neither," he says, shaking his head. "I ain't going."

"What?"

"I ain't going," Dad says. "I owe that to Tennessee and I owe it to you. I ain't debasing the story any further."

"Well," I say, nodding, "That's all right. Tennessee will take care of that bastard."

"No," Dad says, "he *won't*. They *won't* and I *won't*. Mc-Malley's alive: good for him. That's the *point*, son: good for him. I'm coming to see you instead, listen to your story for awhile. I'll go home tonight and come back tomorrow."

So there *are* things in this life that can surprise me: I guess nothing in the world fazes Dad, not even a living Thomas McMalley. But he doesn't have anything to worry about: everything he taught me about death is grooved into a circuit in my head forever. No one's better prepared for this place but me, and I got that bastard Thomas McMalley to thank. You gotta learn what not to do in this lifetime, too.

We don't say anything for awhile, and I think Dad might be hungry. He's been sitting here for two hours talking about Tennessee, Doc, Red, and that piece-of-shit Irishman, and he hasn't eaten a thing. I say, "Dad. Are you hungry? Go ahead and get a sandwich if you want."

"You want a sandwich? Better eat now while you can, son. How about some chips?"

The question's a formality. Whether I say yes or no, Dad's coming back with a sandwich and chips for me. That's the way we do it. He knows what it means to live off canned sardines and top ramen, how essential food becomes in survival situations. When you've got a twenty-minute line and a limited supply, you stock up at the vending machines. Gotta take care of yourself.

"Okay," I say.

Dad gets up and walks placidly and menacingly off and I think if he were locked down in this mutherfucker, he'd be running Quentin in a matter of weeks or however long it'd take for something to pop off where courage and loyalty came into play. He stands in line like a San Quentin pillar, steady and time-scarred, quiet and looming, holding all the shitheads up on his shoulders. He has his Pathfinders Special Ops T-shirt tucked into the khaki trousers, STRAC as hell is Dad.

A Mexi-*komo* family is in line before him. Two young kids as high as Dad's hip jab and parry on one another, the old lady with Eskimo eyes and a rosary resting on the shelf of her stomach scolds them in Spanish. Their father, a *paisa* with a black-and-tan cowboy hat, a gold tooth, and a pair of faded, soiled Wrangler jeans, could care less. They look like they've just left the lettuce fields to attend Mass. The woman nods and says something to Dad and Dad nods back, pats one of the kids on the head. The kid freezes exactly as he should with my father.

I can't watch Dad for too long. Two cops roll into the visiting room on either side of Criminal. He's got his 'fro all blown out like Don King and his issues all tucked in and ironed down just like you'd think he would, shot-caller for the East Block Polynesian car. My issues are never as clean and ironed out as his. With Criminal's arrival, that makes three of us here, six back in the block. As you know, we're the smallest unit in both places, but, as you know, we live off Polynesian esprit de corps and a down-to-the-death reliability.

Criminal walks directly over to me, shedding the cops off his elbows, and says, "'S been too long, Hawaii."

"Wassup, Crim." He's got no family in Cali or Samoa and I ask him about it. "Where's your people?"

"You *are* my people," he says, just like I'd known. "Came to watch your ass, get your back, dog."

"I'm mellow, homie," I say, looking over at the vending machine where Dad is still patting little Mexi-*komo* heads. "Kickin' it with Dad being mellow, homie. Hearing about hills and heroes."

Crim says, "Listen, Hawaii: I don't wantchu thinkin' you're alone, dog. You know we all still love you. Even Rambo."

I look at Crim and he's nodding.

"That's right," he says, "I explained everything to him, homie. He had eight months to heal up. And, anyways, he don't want no trouble with no one: He's short to the gate, got four months left. So don't worry about that shit, 's squashed."

I don't know what to say.

"Just get your mind right, dog. We want you back on that yard, homie. Need you back. We're eight men deep. A ninth mutherfucker means ten feet of space in the yard. You know that. We need you back, dog."

Criminal lifts his head and I grit my teeth and dutifully nod.

"Just gotta make sure it's all good. I know what it's like to come out that hole mad as fuck. That place is no good."

"Nah, nah, nah," I say. "I took it all out on my mattress, homie. Worked that mutherfucker over every night. Jabs, straights, hooks, headbutts. I chewed on that mutherfucker like a dog. Time flew, ain't no thing."

"We were worried about your head, Hawaii, if you lost—"

"Nah, I'm mellow, Crim. Respectin' Dad and his story and that's it."

Criminal looks over at Dad and says to me, "All right, all right. What about all that 'stracked' shit you yellin' at Rambo last time? All that 'legs' and shit 'fore you cracked him? You ain't gonna lose it on us?"

"Fuck no, Crim. I'm down like a mutherfucker, you understand me?"

Criminal smiles our perfectly symmetrical Polynesian smile and he says, "Yeah, yeah, yeah, Hawaii, crazy mutherfucker. Just want make sure it's all cool. You're still on this side of sanity."

"You know whose side I'm on, homie."

"I know, I know. We know who to rely on. No one doubts your loyalty, dog."

If you're gonna do time in Quentin, you gotta be prepared for filth, ambushes, and rudeness. Filth from the cranksters and junkies and queers, ambushes from Mexi-*komos* and in the letters from your girl, and rudeness from cops. That Mexi-*komo* schizo pig Rodriguez is so damned short that he doesn't have to lean very far over to put his rude-ass elbows on table S.Q.V.R. 24, right where Dad was sitting. Rodriguez has demons and tombstones running the ink-canvas of one arm, "CELLBLOCK" in three-dimensional Old English on the other, a foundation of letterhead for the gun-tower on his biceps. Big bad gangbanger is Rodriguez.

He says, index finger tracing the grooved graffiti on the table, "That's about it, Criminal. Take you back to the block."

"Thanks, Rodriguez," says Crim. "'Preciate the time."

Rodriguez looks up at me and then over at the vending machines. He wants me to say, "Thank you for letting us talk," but I don't say a word.

"Your father's a big man," he says, little Mexi-*komo* hand on Crim's elbow.

He doesn't leave so I say, "That's right."

"Ever done time?" he asks.

"What?" I say.

"Come on," Crim says, "Take it easy, Rodriguez."

"Your father. He's got that look. He did time, didn't he?"

Crim puts a hand on my forearm and I say, "Fuck you, pig."

"Your visit's done, boy. Going back to the hole. Get on the goddamned wall."

"I ain't goin' nowhere, leg pig."

"Nowhere'd be 'bout right."

He goes for his stick and I twist the hips and put a fist in his face. His knees yield no sound whatsoever striking concrete and, just as I'd imagined a hundred times a visit, Officer Rodriguez is a one-hitter quitter. All fluff, no stuff, just mouth. He dropped like a sack of potatoes. I hear like a grunt, "Fuck it," and watch Crim play soccer for a second and boot Rodriguez across the chin for the goal. He goes to his back like a bitch doing yoga, his uselessly tagged-down leg arms flailing above his block-ass Mexi-*komo* head, and everything in the East Block Visiting Room freezes and goes quiet except the jingling of the chains and a table being knocked from its feet by a herd of rushing pigs.

You think that moment scared me?

I saw Dad's time-worn hand at the vending machines snake to an empty pocket, twitching for the grip of a gun.

before high desert

IN CELL 3CARSON16 AT SAN QUENTIN STATE
penitentiary, Ya-Ya packed his property as ordered. He was
nineteen years old, a week and a half from twenty, and three
months into his eight-year sentence for attempted murder.
Above the sheet he'd been sleeping on for the past three
months were a bar of soap, two razors, and a picture of his
girl. He kissed the photo once, a practice traditionalized during the same three months, and then brought the frazzled
corners of the sheet together. After he tied everything up, he
focused on breathing through his nostrils, and then paced in
the four-by-eight-foot cell.

He looked down at the mass of man asleep on his bunk.
The lower bunk was officially his, but as he crept along the
narrow five-step track, Ya-Ya realized that he would never
get a chance to sleep on it.

"Reg," whispered Ya-Ya. "Yo, Reg."

He reached down and gently shook Regulator's mattress. "Reg," he said.

Regulator did not move. He had just done a ten spot up at Soledad State Penitentiary and could sleep through anything. The last time he had shown any real human emotion was at the trial three months back when they had struck him out with twenty-five to life for petty theft. He had spun on the state-appointed attorney and spat in his face. "You public pretenders. Buncha dump-truck mu'fuckas."

After the incident, there were additional charges of assault and contempt, but Regulator had not heard any of it. The judge had asked the newly appointed public defender if her client was medicated. "No, Your Honor," she'd said, looking down at the back of Regulator's tree-trunk neck. "He just likes to sleep, I guess."

"Reg," said Ya-Ya.

"Wassup?"

"I'm out, homie."

"Where?"

"High Desert. Level IV."

Regulator rolled over. "Sweet Jesus."

"I'll drop you a kite, Reg."

"Do that. Keep ya mouth shut, boy. Those ears open." Regulator yawned, but his hands stayed where they were. "Not ya ass," he said. "Ya ears."

"All right, Reg."

Ya-Ya put his hand out, but Regulator was already nodding off, and his hands stayed where they were. At times, it seemed to Ya-Ya that his cellie and the bottom bunk were virtually one and the same. The first time he had entered the cell three months back, Regulator was in the identical position then that he was in now. It wasn't so much a matter of things coming back to full circle, or a cycle of some sort. A lot of things just never changed. Regulator rolled to his side and tucked the sheet under his chin, and then the snoring came. That hadn't changed either. Ya-Ya had said that first night, "You're on my bunk, homie," then he'd heard, "What'd you say?" and then nothing else. He had tossed his property on the top bunk, unrolled the mattress, and as near as he could figure, that was the last sound decision he'd made since arriving in prison.

He scratched at his head and felt the lump. The catcalls were dying down now, and there were spaces of silence through the block. Ya-Ya preferred the shouting to the unpredictability of silent quarters. His cornrows disguised the lump now, but at first even the thick ridges of hair could not hide what had happened. And anyway, the disguise was pointless: Everyone in the block knew about Ya-Ya, and what they knew would travel with him to High Desert.

His first week in San Quentin had been time-counting. To counter the inner effect of the endless hours, Ya-Ya had outwardly strutted through them. He slapped hands and jived and whooped it up in the block, on the yard. He pretended to know everyone. He threw up gang signs and made claims. His chest was always inflated and pushed out, and if his back was to the wall, he leaned.

On the third day, his neighbor called out from his cell, "'Ey, kid! I heard you a killa!"

Ya-Ya asked, "Wha's your name?"

Casper laughed. "No, I'm askin' you, killa. I said, I heard you a killa."

Ya-Ya said, "You heard right, homie."

An immediate chaos of catcalls:

"Oh, you a killa, is you?"

"Well, it's Manson hisself, boys!"

"Good ol' Charlie showed up at Quentin!"

"Yeah!"

"Charlie sure talk like a nigga now, don't he?"

Even the whites in the block laughed for awhile, and when the chanting ended deep into the night, Ya-Ya hadn't moved from the bars.

Still, the time passed tangibly slow in Ya-Ya's heart, and so the strutting remained. By the end of his first week, any man interested knew the precise details of his crime, and the indifferent were told the tale regardless. For mainly that reason, by the end of his second week at San Quentin, they thumped his head. As he had never seen the assailants, Ya-Ya was not quite sure who "they" were. The only distinction he could make was that more boots than fists struck his body, and that deduction was premised upon two facts: When you're lying facedown in the gravel, it's impossible in the short span of an attack for the fist to get underneath your stomach like the foot can; and then, secondly, a fist is not plated in steel.

When it happened, he was watching a steamer in the bay through the barbed fence. It had appeared every day for two weeks, and Ya-Ya made a habitual point to watch its voyage until the end of yard. He liked to keep little structural habits in his program, an idea romanticized by all the prison flicks he'd seen as a boy. The boat was so close that he could see the passengers watching him, their elbows resting on the rails. At least he had assumed they were watching him. He earnestly scanned the deck for any sign of connection, a crinkled brow, a curious squint, binoculars. But the faces on the steamer were always expressionless, and then when the fog came were gone.

The crash of the first blow was kind. His equilibrium turned upside down, and Ya-Ya's knees collapsed beneath him. They struck the gravel hard and there was nowhere to go but forward. The speed of the assault effectively veiled the pain, but somehow he could consciously tally the blows to his ribs. He had been struck twelve times, ten by the steel of the boot, the first and last blows to his head by the fist. In the fog of the yard, he had one silly thought rising to his knees: *Seagulls sure get up in the air slow. No wonder those Asians got a easy time catching 'em for lunch.*

In the cell that night, Regulator woke from his slumber and sat him down. He rubbed the sleep from his eyes, and got out one last yawn. Then a little life came to his face. Regulator had the deepest voice in the block, a kind of Barry White ghetto basso. Back at Soledad, he used to scare the dope fiends by announcing in an official tone that a sweep of the block would commence in ten minutes. They'd fumble and tussle about and the catcalls came in their cryptic codes and there were multiple flushings of the toilets. Then Regulator would yell out, "That's why ya gotta get off that dope! I told you! You mu'fuckas be swimmin' in the toilet in no time! Lookin' for dolphins if I told you to!" He'd laugh and there'd be curses, his homies throwing water out their cells and onto the tier.

Ya-Ya's lip was swollen. A streak of strawberries crossed the line of his palm. His head was bowed and there was water in his eyes. Regulator said, "Ya fool ass mouth gon' get you in trouble, cuz. That's why they put hands on you. They don' care who the fuck you are, cuz. You nobody. They don' care whatchu did or who you ran wit' on the streets—westside players, all that bullshit. That's old shit. E'body come from the streets. Whatchu think's worse, homie: 14th and Jackson, or third tier Carson?"

"I feel ya, Reg."

"You better feel me, cuz. That time you lookin' at ain't no joke. When they ship you outta here, that's your real time. Reception ain't shit. They gon' send you to a straight war zone, boy. Shit be poppin' off right befo' yo' eyes. Fuck that thumpin' shit. Mu'fuckin' throats openin' up, homie. You play the fool and you gon' play dead man, feel me?"

Ya-Ya nodded.

"I'm telling you this, homie: Mu'fuckas don't like some youngster showin' up sayin' what's what. New kid on the block, dead punk on the block. Happens every time. *This* the bigger picture, cuz, and you better recognize."

In the next two and a half months, nothing truly significant happened to Ya-Ya. He'd heard a few times in passing "Killa," and once when he pointed out at chow that his dinner tray was missing the entree, the response had been "Get the fuck outta my line then." He didn't watch steamers on the yard any more, and sometimes stayed in his cell to read Sidney Sheldon novels. He had heard rumors from his homeboys that the lumping had been set up by his own race, but it seemed as if addressing the incident would only increase the chance of another, and so Ya-Ya said nothing.

He was actually relieved when the block was locked down for a week. A southern Mexican had been stabbed in the shower by a northern Mexican, but Ya-Ya cared little. The days went by fast in the cell and it was Sidney Sheldon, Ya-Ya, and Regulator doing his time asleep on the bottom bunk. There was little talk over the intercom, and the catcalls were limited to the jaycats who were running for president once they got out. Not a single Mexican in Carson block yelled out over the wire, and this was just fine. When the lieutenant finally approved yard for every race except Hispanics, the old worry returned to his throat, and Ya-Ya swallowed.

"Prison gon' reduce you, boy," Regulator had said one night between naps. He yawned and Ya-Ya nodded.

"'S about reduction, homie," he'd said on another night, and again, Ya-Ya nodded.

He awoke out of his sleep, startling Ya-Ya on his thirty-sixth day in prison, and said, "Listen, cuz. They gon' reduce you."

And on his forty-third: "Get my line," and Ya-Ya did. The string of sheet dangled out the cell, and Ya-Ya reeled it in like a fisherman. A smoke cloud formed up from the wick tied to the end of the sheet and Ya-Ya said, "You need to get yourself a lighter, Reg. Big shot like you."

An index finger went to Regulator's mouth. "Shhhhhh," he said. He lit the cigarette and put the snipe to his lips. Through the grill of his teeth, he blew some smoke, all the time eyeing Ya-Ya. "That's right, boy. Shhhhhhhhh."

Regulator sat up in his bunk and cleared his throat. He roared, "Hassan!"

"Yeah!"

"Hassan!"

"Yeah! Right here!"

"Touchdown!"

"Okay!"

"Thanks for the shine, cuz!"

"All right, Reg!"

The cell was filling with smoke and Ya-Ya jumped up on his bunk. Hardly any time passed before he heard, "Now."

Ya-Ya leaned over on his side and looked down at his cellie. Regulator was lying prone on the bunk, somehow smoking and speaking perfectly without the use of his hands. They were both wrapped smugly behind his head. His face was without emotion but Ya-Ya thought he saw the beginnings of a smile, something.

Regulator repeated, "Now."

"Now *what*, Reg?"

Regulator shook his head in disbelief, still without moving the hands. "Now, what'd you *just* learn?"

"I ain't followin' you, Reg!"

Regulator took a drag, blew it out his nostrils. "What's the most you seen me speak?"

"Well, just now over the wire, Reg. You don't say but ten words a day!"

"That's right." The ash was growing dangerously long, but to Regulator it only meant there was less cigarette to smoke. "So whatchu figure they got *me* reduced to then?"

Ya-Ya focused on the wall two feet in front of him.

"Ya-Ya," he said. It was the first time he had used the name. "I'm the meanest, most killingest mu'fucka you ever met. But I tell you this, homie. They done reduce me. When I gon' thank a man, I thank him for real."

Ya-Ya took some time to think about the words, but he needed more. He was on the verge of speaking when the snoring started up. It resonated through the cell. Ya-Ya shook his head and then laid back on the bunk, curling up and falling asleep within minutes.

That was over a month ago, and tonight was his ninety-first in prison. Recalling the words of wisdom, Ya-Ya committed himself to making a change. He was on his way to High Desert to do the remainder of his time, and everything started right now. He knew that Regulator was right about something, but even as a nineteen-year-old first termer, he could identify the flaws in what had been said. How confined and reduced, after all, were the shot-callers down on first tier with their late-night cassette-playing radios, personal runners through the block, stocks of canned goods? They never looked over their shoulders, or at least were never caught doing it. One night he'd even heard the white shot-caller tell a rookie cop to "keep it down and show some respect." The cop had ended the speech over the PA almost immediately, "Good night, then, gentlemen."

The rattling of keys disturbed the silence. Ya-Ya grabbed his property from the bunk and hefted the bundle over a shoulder. He leaned with the other against the wall and waited for his cell to pop.

The cop keyed his lock and said, "P31772."

"Yeah."

He came out the cell, looking back at Regulator on the bottom bunk. The sheet was moving up and down like the rhythm of a heartbeat. The cop said, "Wait here."

Ya-Ya put his chest on the railing, looking down to first tier. There were paper airplanes and torn T-shirts and confiscated fish lines scattered along the floor. The majority of it was swept into a corner, and Ya-Ya watched one of the lines going in and out of the pile, pulling in objects. On the end of this line was an empty milk carton. Its hollow had been squared off, and an issue of *National Geographic* tied to its bottom for weight. It swallowed up anything in its way, and Ya-Ya followed its journey across the floor, collecting redeemable items from the pile, toilet paper, sugar packets, toothbrushes. His eyes were set, his mind transfixed.

"Ya Ya."

Ya-Ya spun, knowing in midspin, who'd said it. He recovered instantaneously. "Wassup, homie."

Casper's sea-blue eyes sparkled in the floodlights. The grease of his jheri curls matched the shine, and the big, toothy smile seemed impossible, misplaced. You could count the freckles on his face: Big Dipper here, North Star there, no more than twenty. Casper was whiter than most of the whites he loathed, and had earned his nickname long before arriving in prison. Casper said, "The High D awaits, Ya-Ya."

"Ain't no thing."

"Uh huh. Them gang signs you throwin' up ain't nothin', mean nothin.'"

"I'll handle mine."

"Oh."

Ya-Ya turned back to the rails, watched the fish line being tossed out, maneuvered about, jerked in for the catch. "I'll handle my business."

Casper chuckled. "Oh, we seen that."

Someone down below yelled, "Shut the fuck up! Let a man sleep!"

The cop was approaching with five other men on their way to High Desert. They all had their property tied in a sheet and were quiet. There were two peckerwoods, two northern Mexicans, and a black. Casper took a step toward Ya-Ya and whispered, "We done see how you do business, killa." Then he grabbed his property and slapped hands with the black.

"Wassup, homie!" he cried.

From below: "Shut the fuck up!"

"Let's go," said the cop.

Ya-Ya followed, and some of the homies started jiving. The cop said, "Shut the fuck up." As they descended the staircase in perfect step, finally there was silence.

The gunner's walkway and all the barbed wire were passing before Ya-Ya. Empty milk cartons and underwear were entangled in the sharpened spirals, and every now and then a magazine. The hot water pipes ran along the wall to the shower, and there were black and yellow lines pointing in the same direction. The cold water ran the opposite way, fingering past the five tiers of fifty cells, up along the roof and then back down. One thin vertical line of stained glass bisected the block wall, giving no light. He'd seen it all on the way to chow and yard and canteen a hundred times; a hundred more out his cell sprawled along his bunk on his stomach late into the night, the eyes squinting and straining, trying to find focus through the dark mesh of crisscross and wire. Facedown on the mattress, he'd seen it in his dreams, vivid enough to draw an accurate picture from memory. He'd sent the art to his girl with a few lines of bravado and inflated hubris, waiting for her reply. She had written back, "Oh my God, babe! I can't believe you live like that . . . " and, stupidly, he was happy, proud. But now he took it in as nostalgia.

Things gon' change, thought Ya-Ya.

As the jingling keys neared first tier, the fish lines vanished. They came down the steps and the pile of trash and garbage in the corner seemed untouched, maybe even bigger. A group of men already waited along the wall, all from the three other blocks—Alpine, Badger, and Donner—and they were mixed in race, though mostly black. Some sat on their property and some stood and looked up for any of their homeboys.

With the six from Carson Block, there was one over the thirty five-man capacity of the transportation bus. Fortunately, the problem had been solved by Sergeant Wayne the moment he tallied the numbers: the two smallest men would be squeezed into the protective custody cage in the front of the bus, and the delivery would be made as planned.

Casper and his homeboy slapped hands with another homeboy from Alpine Block. The cop walked off to the control panel and nodded at Sergeant Wayne, who was reviewing the departure list one last time, head down. Everyone sidled up and divided into race, and at the end of the line Ya-Ya squatted and put his back to the wall.

Just above Ya-Ya's head, Casper said to his homeboy, "I gon' get at that phone." He nodded at the three collect phones on the wall.

"I wouldn't, homie. John Wayne in a bad one tonight."

Casper said, "That white boy in a bad one every night. I oughtta know. Carson get John Wayne four times a week.

Carson know John Wayne. How many times y'all get 'im over in Alpine, Country?"

Country said, "Well, what? You can't count the days o' the week, nigga?"

The other homeboy from Carson laughed.

"Oh, I can count," said Casper. His neck was turning red, and he licked his lips. Ya-Ya repositioned on the wall down below, and Casper looked down. "Oh," said Casper. "Say, Country. This my homeboy Yo-Yo."

Ya-Ya looked up and nodded at Country.

"He whatcha call too hard for this place. Gotta take 'im to the desert with the snakes and coyotes."

Ya-Ya thought of Regulator in the cell, and said nothing. He took the jiving in stride, like he and Casper really were homeboys. He tightened his lips and lifted his eyebrows. Only those from Carson Block knew the old Ya-Ya, and so the new Ya-Ya stood.

The other homeboy from Carson looked back at John Wayne. "Well, go ahead then, homie. But you know John Wayne gon' getcha. One way or another, he gon' getcha."

"Yeah. Go on, all-star. Start your time in the desert from the hole."

Casper stepped over to the phone. He said, "Give me a look then."

His homeboys stepped from the wall and positioned themselves shoulder to shoulder. It blocked Casper from the cops' view. They tried to appear natural, but it was no use. Every one of the thirty-six men was on the wall except them. Just as Casper lifted the receiver, the cop said, "Hey. Get on the wall."

They didn't move. Casper hung the phone up. The cop marched over, yelling as he walked, "Get the fuck on the wall!"

They all three did as they were told, but with no urgency. The cop asked a rhetorical question: "You mutherfuckers wanna show up in the D in chains?" He looked over at the phones, unaware of the real violation that had just occurred. His eyes came back and he answered the question: "That's what I thought. 'Cause you're gonna end up at the D either way. Stay on the fuckin' wall."

The cop returned to John Wayne at the control panel and someone said down the way, "You gon' get us all laid up, nigga."

Casper said out the side of his mouth, "We don't need any more cops in this mu'fucka."

"That's right," the other said. Casper did not turn his head to see the speaker. "What we need is more convicts who can do their time right."

No one said anything else, not even Casper. Ya-Ya felt the threat of silence building along the wall. He directly faced the cells on first tier, listening. He heard breathing and some of the homies repositioning. Somehow he was conscious of being too close to Casper and his two homeboys, but for the moment he remained with his back to the concrete, his property between his legs. He had the feeling that if he moved in any way, even simply rising to his feet, the focus of the tension would shift from Casper's shoulders to his own, and he did not want that. His was a mission of obscurity until the time came for a change, making the homies forget the old Ya-Ya of Carson Block. He wasn't sure when he would get his chance, but with the accrued wisdom of three months in San Quentin, he knew that it could come any time, and in the vigor of youth that had not yet been rubbed out, he hoped that it would come soon. He consciously told himself that when they finally walked through yard to the bus, it would be best to distinctly separate from Casper.

Three hours later, John Wayne placed his cup of coffee in its holder and came over to the wall. His hair stood in the same orderly fashion that it always had, evenly cut pricks of blackness at squared attention on his head. The homies were spread along the wall in various positions. Some of them were asleep, but Ya-Ya was wide awake, and promptly stood when John Wayne began the issuing of directives.

"We will commence," he said, "across the yard to R and R. Any approved property you may have will be packaged and sent to High Desert. You can claim your property within the first week of arrival through whatever necessary channels you are provided. If it is lost, do not 602 San Quentin for your property. Appeal High Desert. You are no longer ours once you get off that bus. We will commence to R and R in a single file line in complete silence. Let's go, gentlemen. And act like gentlemen."

The homies formed up a respectable line and made their way out of the block, John Wayne at point, the cop at the rear. Up above, the gunner came to life and rose to his feet, watching the powder-blue caterpillar slink through the double doors. Immediately, their breath became little clouds in the cold and they blew into the palms of their free hand. Everything was blue or black and the cold seemed to encapsulate even those root functions of breath, blink, take another step.

They were at the fence of the yard now, the boats on the bay just beyond it, the precise spot of Ya-Ya's group thumping two-and-a-half months back. It could have been any number of men. It could have been his own homeboys. Maybe the word had spread to the other blocks by now, but probably not. The six others from Carson knew for sure, Casper and his homeboy, the two northern Mexicans, and the two peckerwoods. Ya-Ya walked the fastest and made distance, trying to pass the point of shame. Then he heard the impossible from behind, a mocking whisper.

"Havin' flashbacks, boy? Or maybe you can't remember, all punch-drunk."

Ya-Ya kept walking.

"You sure movin' fast, killa. Gonna make a break?"

Suddenly the line stopped and it was colder standing. The homies shifted from one foot to the other and the scowls froze on their faces. John Wayne had stopped the line. He advanced to a point in the yard where everyone could see him and put both gloved hands to his mouth. He blew once and the same little cloud came up. "We have some major problems here, gentlemen. Major."

The homies stopped shifting.

"I am known as a fair man. I don't ask for much from you."

The teeth of some of the homies began to rattle.

John Wayne looked beyond the line of men. In the mist of the bay, the red fluorescent warning lights flashed just beyond the lookout tower. Its own white light scanned the surface of the water and made pink when crossing the warning lights. John Wayne blew the little cloud over his hands again. "We have people in this line that presume to use the telephone without permission." He did not look in Ya-Ya's direction, nor Casper's. He raised himself to his tippytoes and scanned the details of the bay. "We have people in this line that presume to speak contrary to the direct order of silence."

One homie looked over at Casper. Casper did not see the menace in his eyes, but Ya-Ya did. And despite the cold, a warmth grew inside his chest. The menace brought a kind of shameless comfort to Ya-Ya, bordering on giddiness. For the first time since arriving at San Quentin, he knew exactly what to do. Ya-Ya shifted his feet and blew into his hands like all the other homies on their way to High Desert.

John Wayne looked up at the gunner in the tower and mysteriously nodded. "It's my opinion that due to the insurrective behavior demonstrated by this group, a strip search is not only necessary, but essential."

Ya-Ya heard a grunt and rapid breathing, and he wasn't sure if it came from himself or somewhere down the line.

"We will begin at the rear of the line, and then commence forward."

Ya-Ya felt anger. John Wayne stood directly before him, blowing clouds, awaiting the group disrobing which would start at the end of the line. Ya-Ya's eyes fell to the ground and then he blew out his own smoke cloud: "Can't do it, John Wayne."

Another said immediately, looking over at Ya-Ya. "Yeah, that's right."

And then another: "I ain't even taking off this scowl."

"I ain't catchin' pneumonia so you can look up my ass."

One pointed at the tattoos on his arms. "Whatcha you want me to take off next? These tags?"

"This ain't gladiator days."

"I got my rights!"

There were a lot of untraceable "Yeah! Yeah!"'s and vulgar denunciations in Spanish and a variety of grunts and hisses. Many breath clouds came up at once and a movement in the line, and then the blue lights along the fence flashed. John Wayne stepped back and the other cop ordered them down on the yard. All except Ya-Ya fell to their stomachs. You could hear the cuffs and chains through the block and then the slam of the double doors and the squad of cops flowing out and the first thump of a warning shot from the gunner. The miniature beanbag struck its target and Ya-Ya gasped and dropped to a knee, clutching his chest. He hurt more in the shoulder region from a twisting ripping hand, and, for a brief flash of a moment, his eyes and John Wayne's came together. Nothing registered or clicked but the gunner reloading for live ammo up above. Things were spinning out of control, and John Wayne's elbow crashing like a bullet into his cheek straightened everything out. He was spun to his stomach and the world rolled over again and the gravel pushed up toward him until he mouthed, nosed, and eyeballed it. And the jingling was coming all along and was right there. And then the clicking torque of cuffs and chains on his wrists, ankles, and amazingly, somehow, wrapped underneath and around the hips like a belt. They dragged him like a package down the line and then off to the cages in Carson, and, just like that, there were twenty-five cops in the yard.

Miniature speeches and diatribes ensued. The cops were mad. John Wayne breathed heavily between sentences: "You sonsabitches . . . You wanna make it hard? . . .You and that jackass are just prolonging this process . . . The High D awaits all of you, one way or the other."

The strip search started on the other end of the line, one by one, away from Casper and Country and their homeboy from Carson Block. They were all on their stomachs and the breath clouds were coming up from the ground where it was warmer. Country pointed his head in the direction of the cages inside Carson Block. He mouthed a question, curiosity frozen on his face:

Who's that nigga?

Casper silently mouthed back: *I told you. Ya-Ya.*

Who?

Casper looked back at the cops occupied and hunched over, talking amongst themselves, giving orders. "Calls him self Ya-Ya," he whispered in a boast. "That nigga's crazy."

the arms of brian flintcraft

I. The First Hour

Seventeen years, two months, and two days passed before he looked back at a family in a car through a smashed windshield, nothing in the empty street except glass. The night was cold but he did not feel it. They were still alive but petrified, and when the shivering old man said, "Just do it son put your arms down you're just a kid they're not gonna hurt you," he laid the gun on the hood of the car, and immediately heard stomping steps and the pleasant jingle of handcuffs. He fell facedown from a blow to the back of his head, massaged into the bed of shattered glass by a six-palmed creature, and now he could feel the cold.

Three weeks and a day later, he arrived at the California Men's Colony with a seven-to-life sentence for armed robbery. No longer than ten minutes passed when his first visitor arrived. He had a little bird tattooed to his neck, and on his arms were matching thunderbolts. The wrinkles on his pale, ashen face were not wrinkles. The labyrinth of grooves shifted when he spoke. He said, "How you doin', brother?"

Young Brian Flintcraft nodded respectfully.

"What'd you catch, brother?"

Young Brian didn't understand the question. He knew, however, that he did not like being called brother. He had one out in the world somewhere, and this wasn't him.

"Well, it can't be more than six or seven. Did you shoot the gun?"

Now he understood. "Yeah. Once."

"Seven then. But you're young. It'll go fast, brother." The term embedded itself in Brian's mind. "Listen, youngster. I'm Del. If you need anything, come and talk to me. I'm right up the way. Three down. Don't hesitate. We gotta stick together. Every white boy in this place knows me. Soap, razors, whatever you need I got. And you gonna need something, brother."

The irritation inside could not yet be anger. Young Brian began to speak.

"No, no, no. Don't say a word." Del tapped on his forehead thrice. "I got it, youngster. But we'll see how long it lasts. I's the same way when I first got locked up, brother. Didn't ask anyone for anything."

Del looked once up the tier and then started. He walked with confidence and noticeably close to the cells. He was the only one on the tier. Young Brian Flintcraft watched as far as he could and vowed never to ask for anything from his newly met brother.

He was surprised by the cleanliness of the cell. The walls were white and unchipped with hardly any graffiti across their surface. Even the sink in the corner was whitened with paint, and the two parallel shelves above it. The top bunk was folded up against the wall, the iron hinges unreliably locked into position. Young Brian Flintcraft lightly shook it and a book fell out, landing diagonally across his bunk. It had been squeezed between the wall and the smooth steel of the top bunk. The pages were ruffled and weathered like a paper bag used over and over again. There were creases across the cover from reading and perhaps other unforeseeable things, but most strange to Young Brian was the combination of words beneath the wrinkles of age. He pondered the title's meaning for a bit, but came up with very little. He was seventeen years old. He did, however, recognize the functional utility of any book that size: *A Farewell to Arms* would make up for the pillow he was not provided upon arrival in this whitened-down, lead-laden cell.

All was quiet for a few minutes, and then Young Brian Flintcraft heard several conversations on the tier. The words were all mixed in together, but he found that if he focused, a single conversation would become isolated, like the sound of a radio station caught between frequencies. Everything echoed through the block, and he forced himself to concentrate above the static of both new and former retorts.

For some untraceable reason, his mind latched onto a discussion two cells down. It was in the opposite direction Del had come from, and the opposite direction he went in leaving. Brian noted that Del had not even looked in the other direction where this conversation was coming from: it was almost as if half of the tier did not exist. That was strange to young Brian, but perhaps normal in the schematic makeup of this place. Go out the same door you came in. He closed his eyes to focus and discovered, coincidentally enough, that his arrival was the topic at hand.

It was not coincidence. When young Brian came to the bars, he saw that Del was not the only one out of his cell. One of the conversants two cells down was leaning against the bars, his back to young Brian Flintcraft and the other fifteen caged white men behind him.

Above the static, young Brian heard him say, "Nah. 'S a white boy."

"For real? Well, where's he at?"

"He two down, home. Right next to Ya-Ya."

"Damn, he's the last on the line, in't he?"

"You know dem cops. Throw him into the mix right from the start. Gotta test a man."

"Well, now I know. Won't have to check in on that mu'-fucka when I walk down the tier."

"You still want dem smokes, home?"

"Yeah, homie. I been stressin' for the past two days."

"Wassup?"

"'S my girl's birthday."

"Oh, shit."

"Yeah."

"I'll get dem smokes fast, home. I don't wantchu thinkin' 'bout Sancho for too long. There's nothin' you can do, home. Sancho gon' be there whether you like it or not. Gotta roll with it and keep Sancho outcha head, whoever that nigga is."

"Just get my smokes, homie. Whatever happens, Sancho gonna do his thing with her, right? I just hope he's still around when I get out. Then I can do my thing."

"Be right back in here with us, home."

"I'm just jivin'. If Sancho wanna hit it, more power to that backstabbin' nigga. But I gotta smoke. "

The inmate on the tier said, "I hate Sancho," and then walked in the opposite direction Del had come from. He stopped and slapped hands a few times along the way, and then strutted through the double doors of the block. Young Brian had never heard a more mysterious conversation in his life.

II. The First Day

The chow hall was divided into two sections. There were three gray columns bisecting the layout of two dozen square steel tables, and everywhere the buzz of flies. He stood in line knowing no one except the fraternal Del, who seemed to know everyone. Everyone who was white. He was several men up from young Brian, leading a discussion with three other pale white inmates who had the same birds on their necks and the same two thunderbolts on various places on their arms.

The line was patched by race: clumps of black, pale white, and other degrees of brown. When the men took their seats for chow, all the color perfectly organized itself into two halves: whites on the entrance side, blacks on the exit, three gray column barriers in between.

He carried his tray to the white side and began to eat. The menudo had spilled into all three sections so that little triangles of tripe combined with the peas and fruit salad. His last meal had been on the bus that morning, and so he ate. Young Brian Flintcraft chewed ravenously, if at all.

He felt the surrounding blackness just beyond the three gray columns, like someone's shadow all around him. He could clearly hear their conversations, but could not decipher the codes. As he ate, he concentrated on the diminishing menudo on the tray, but in the fore of his mind was the periphery of black threat. No one had said anything to him about the split, neither black nor white, maybe because any mention of it would be insultingly redundant. The separation itself was the threat, pure threat, and it didn't require anything but vision to understand. In the span of seventeen years, young Brian had never felt anything as powerful as this shapeless, unstated concern. He pushed the unfamiliar blackness from his mind, but the residue of breathlessness lingered like a cough caught in his stomach.

Another white sat down next to him, but he did not eat. He had been jiving with Del earlier in the line. The eyes were steady as he stared at young Brian Flintcraft and said, "Whatcha got for me, youngster?"

Even at seventeen, young Brian's hands were big, but this man's hands were bigger. They were white five-legged crabs on the table top. Del and his crew were watching from an adjacent table, but their sporks remained on the path between mouth and tray, mouth and tray, mouth. Young Brian Flintcraft looked back at their table. Del put his head down, as did the other three men, and the sporks in motion were the same. Young Brian's lip curled up, and he began again to eat.

"I said, 'Whatcha got, youngster?'"

Brian shook his head with meaning. The response went no further back than childhood, which, at seventeen, wasn't that far back. Any time his father had spoken to him, it was always safest to say "no," and that was that. When one of the crab-hands reached out for his arm, Young Brian swung first with the fist, and then followed with the other forearm. It was the ultimate expression of "no."

Crab-hand fell to the ground, and before he was struck again an officer arrived. He grabbed young Brian Flintcraft from behind. Brian turned and swung instinctively a second time with the same fist. The momentum from twisting his hips exacted an even harder punch, and when the officer landed on his knees, young Brian heard the same stomping steps from the night of his arrest, and with them the jingling chains.

They escorted him out of the chow hall, pushing him face-down on the ground, shoving him forward and then back down again, lifting with many hands his two-hundred-pound body by the belt and torpedoing it right out the door.

He lay in the chains, rapidly blinking. The badges and uniforms were multiplying between the flickering black screen
inside his eyelids. They began stripping down Del and his
homeboys and anyone else inside the chow hall during the
assault. Brian had never seen anything like it. Even the man
he'd hit was naked on the wall, his T-shirt balled up into a
bloody red plug in his mouth. While young Brian did not
quite finish his first meal in prison, he felt, fully clothed, that
he'd clearly gotten the better end of things.

III. The First Year

He was escorted off to the hole and would emerge from it a
year later. Only one of the three hundred sixty-five days was
of true significance. Unbeknownst to young Brian, he had
been thrust into the middle of a secret gambling circuit. The
shift of weekend officers called themselves Saturday Night
Special and placed wagers on fights between inmates. The
operation's nickname came from an old Lynyrd Skynyrd
song, but both black and white officers showed a measure of
esprit de corps by not racializing it.

The key to the operation was twofold. The officers of Saturday Night Special needed, firstly, willingly combative par-
ticipants while ensuring, secondly, that no one perished.
Without men who would fight of their own volition, there
was of course no gambling, and without homage to the idea
that the combatants should be at least by the end of the fight
alive, if not standing, an official investigation would undoubtedly ensue, from which members of Saturday Night Special
could conceivably find themselves on the other end of this
very same gambling operation, duking it out with each other
in chains. The solution to this problem was surprisingly sim-

ple: put two known enemies on the yard together and, before they went through the gates, conduct a thorough search of every bodily orifice in which a weapon could be hidden.

It was young Brian's fourth day of his seven-to-life sentence at the California Men's Colony, and third day in the hole. Unlike the last, this cell was weathered and filthy. Young Brian had not been in the original long enough to appreciate the difference, and became accustomed to the filth by the end of the first day. His arrival in the hole was significant, and he could hear the cryptic catcalls being issued down the line. He knew he was being discussed by the other inmates, but for some reason did not spend even a moment breaking down the codes. He fell asleep on his side, the bruises of his escort from the chow hall coming up on his pale white skin.

The officers of Saturday Night Special were especially excited with their new arrival in the Segregated Housing Unit of the California Men's Colony. He was young, naive, and had struck a fellow officer in the chow hall of the East Yard. Their motto was *Nothing breaks down Billy Badass better than Billy More Badass.* They did not hesitate to pit him against Johnson for the show, a black inmate whose nickname, Ringer, came from his volunteering to fight for extra food.

Young Brian Flintcraft awoke. An officer was walking the line. Young Brian came to the door of his cell and pushed his cheek against it. He could see through the crack that the officer was stopping before each cell and asking something. To young Brian, it seemed like the officer assumed the answer to his question, because he did not stop long. Young Brian couldn't hear what was being asked until the officer was two cells down. He said, "Yard, Fitzgerald?"

Fitzgerald said, "No."

Three steps and then, "Yard, McCarthy?"

"Nah."

Three steps to Young Brian's cell. The officer's tag read "Enos" and his face was not friendly. He was an abnormally large man and when he said, "Yard," this time it was not a question.

Young Brian Flintcraft said, "All right."

The officer singled out a key and popped the mail slot. Young Brian pressed his back to the door and put his hands through the slot. Enos immediately cuffed him and then pushed his hands right back through it. Young Brian faced Enos when the door opened and Enos said, "Nah." His index finger made little loops in the air.

Brian turned back around and came out the cell backwards, step by step. Enos grabbed his wrist and pushed him down the hallway from behind. Young Brian Flintcraft looked straight ahead as the cells on either side were passing him. In his peripheral vision, the smudges of gray-white and brown-black faces were pressed to the door watching his progress down the hall. He had to concentrate to kill his curiosity. With discipline, he made it to the end of the hallway without turning his head, most proud because he had done it appearing respectably casual.

The cop told him to get on the wall and he did. His head was down, and when he looked up a white face was staring through the little squared window of his cell door. The wires embedded in the glass did not prevent young Brian from seeing a very curious thing. The man's eyes were empty and the face itself seemed dead, but for the contradiction of movement: the man emphatically shook his head no, as the unfocusing, unmoving eyes remained empty. It seemed like the very same warning in two dramatically different ways. Was there cause and effect between the two extremes, as in, don't go to the yard or you'll end up empty like me? Brian was too young to appreciate the gesture and young enough to think it would have mattered if he had. Enos keyed the door and they went through, as a slew of strange possibilities opened up in young Brian's head.

In the secured hall to the five-by-five-yard yard it was dark, and a lone ray of light crept in through the shatterless glass. Brian saw figures along the wall: officers. One stepped authoritatively from the shadows. He spun Brian around, keying the 'cuffs, while the other, stumpy legs spread and tattooed arms akimbo, said, "Strip down."

Young Brian Flintcraft did as he was told, and it was easy. In the hole, you had a pair of boxers, a T-shirt, and, if you were lucky, slippers. Brian was not lucky, and little time passed before he was naked. One officer checked his ears, his mouth, his ass, and between his fingers and the cracks of the toes. Enos stepped forward and repeated the procedure. He told Brian, "Get dressed."

When the door opened, the first thing Brian saw was a cumbersome shadow on the opposite wall, deep black against the stark sunlight. Within its perimeter, a just-as-black man paced five echoing steps each way, with a head-down revolution. His hairless head glistened from the beads of perspiration coming up on the skin. There were sharpei-like folds along the back of his neck and on one arm a brand of bubbled scar intersecting with the curves of another identical brand. The two J's of keloid ran from the tip of his shoulder and halfway down the arm, and the arm was big, thick. The black threat of three days' back was manifesting itself in the man-animal before young Brian Flintcraft.

He swallowed and said nothing. It was his fourth day in prison, the ninety-first day of his seventeenth year. He felt something climbing the walls of his throat that must have been a kind of survival instinct. He did not know. This was very different, and he did not know. Unexplainable things were happening inside him that could not be checked by the adolescent awareness of his thought. Still, he could not help thinking, *Everything happens so fast in this place.*

Though unaware of the specifics of the setup, he now knew why the man with empty eyes had shaken his head no. The hard part about it was that he couldn't trace the problem back to a flawed decision on his part, unless the flaw had been getting arrested for armed robbery in the first place. Maybe. But after that, young Brian Flintcraft couldn't locate the mistake and attach it to his four-day life thus far in prison.

It was too late, anyway. Ringer Jay Johnson stopped pacing and said, "Fuck you want, man?"

Young Brian said nothing. The instinct was crawling his throat, leashed only by the infinitesimal hope that the encounter need not lead to violence. In the chow hall, the violence there was reaction, his muscles responding reflexively to what the brain interpreted as imminent danger. Perhaps, in a way, he had initiated the incident, instead of letting it play itself out.

But his hands were twitching now and not closing into a fist as they should have been. It was this damned thinking that complicated things. Ringer Jay Johnson pushed his chest out and took a step toward the white boy.

The step was hostile enough to release the instinct in young Brian Flintcraft. He struck first and, without thinking, continued to strike, stepping back with each forward step Ringer Jay Johnson took. Young Brian's arms were much longer, but his young, unaltered vision was the true advantage. Young Brian's aim was the bridge of the nose, and his fists struck the target two out of three times, and then three out of four. Ringer Jay Johnson's head went back and forth, too caught up in its own speed-bag oscillation to stop. He dropped to his knees before five out of six came, and young Brian did not think. He felt the wild instinct pulling him further down the path of the unknown. He grabbed a fold of the black, sharpei-like neck and ripped, opening up a hole with surprising ease, and when he heard the predictable jingling again, this time his arms did not stop. Enos and four other officers of Saturday Night Special got in more than a few extra jabs at the angry, now-soaked-in-blood young Brian Flintcraft, knowing the weekend gambling circuit was coming to permanent closure.

The word got around fast. In that single incident, young Brian Flintcraft had put an end to Saturday Night Special. The whites in the hole passed sycophantic notes of introduction via the white cop who walked the line Tuesday and Thursday nights. A few sent apples and oranges, and another sent a different copy of the same Hemingway book in his last cell. Young Brian met a dozen different white men that first week in the hole, but always through the same face.

Brian was learning the most important law espoused at the California Men's Colony: you stick with your own. Not only that. Those who aren't your own are your enemies. A thousand souls submerged in the law give stage to singular survival. Young Brian Flintcraft was an exceptional seventeen-year-old first-termer, sullen, strong, and silent, big and fast-fisted, indisputably violent, and because the little pocket of fear was always there inside him, fearless. But encapsulated in the law of life was also young Brian Flintcraft, at seventeen, three months and a week, perhaps especially young Brian Flintcraft, the perfectly impressionable age at which to create a prisoner's prisoner.

It was Tuesday. The bruises were now healing, as was young Brian's broken wrist, and now he could write. The white cop was making the rounds, and young Brian felt that now was the time to speak. A week and a half had passed since Saturday Night Special had been disbanded, and he had effectually said nothing thus far to anyone. His motive for speech was simply an inquiry: How much time would he pick up for the fight? And should he write up an inmate request for the time?

Though a part of him felt faultless about the ordeal, he had, after all, struck first and continued to strike long after the notion of self-defense had been eclipsed by pure rage. That was undoubtedly the way the authorities would see it. But when he questioned the white cop, he was succinctly told to forget about it. As near as he could identify, young Brian did, and even a bit thankfully.

Still, the anger in young Brian was sprouting and growing its horns any time he stopped to think about things. There was no sidestepping these issues, for they surrounded his adolescence in ubiquitous iron bars, Pavlovian routine, and shatterless glass. Something was pressurized into birth inside him, a festering kind of hatred that latched itself to the opposing forces of everything he represented, which, at seventeen, three months, and a week, was not much. The opposing forces, as he saw them, were as follows: guards, as he was a convict, and black men, as he was white. It made visible sense enough and had now a physical degree of painful precedence to make the time pass without any mental ambiguity. Prison is many things, after all, but mostly it is the gross simplification of life's complexities.

IV. The First Brother

So he emerged from the hole a year later. Somehow the three bag lunches a day had translated into an even thicker Brian Flintcraft, who was eighteen, very angry, and no longer young.

During the three-hundred-and-sixty-five-day span, he had come out his cell three times a week for an hour. He had taken advantage of every minute, doing push-ups, burpees, and jumping jacks in the five-by-five-yard yard. He had never read, but the apparently popular Hemingway novel lay underneath his pillow every night for height when he slept.

The board had given him an extra two years for the staff assault in the chow hall, but that was the tiny part. His file would follow him wherever he went, and wherever he went were cops. Brian viewed them as the most powerful gang in prison. No one messed with them. Everywhere he saw the same steel-black uniforms and the ostentatious flaunting of guns.

As near as he could figure, someone was going to pay for it. A brother had set him up a year to the day. He came out the hole looking for Del. He didn't look long. Del came to his cell.

"I broughtcha this, brother," he said, like the year in between was yesterday. "I'm still three cells down if you need me."

He put a box down, blocking the cell door. When Brian finally looked up, Del was gone.

Dozens of minutes elapsed before Brian even moved. He was sitting cross-legged on a crack of concrete, his back and much bigger shoulders to the wall, when he recrossed his legs momentously. That was movement. Everything above his waist remained the same. The little calluses on the side of his feet had developed through hours and hours of this very same position in the hole. Merely a different cell of identical dimensions. Only when another white boy stopped on the tier and looked into the box did he say, "Don't touch that," and then he recrossed again.

Well, he was white and Del was white. On the block, on the tiers, at the chow hall, in the hole, distinctions are made. By everyone. Cops. Inmates. In every way. He would have to tolerate Del. More than that. Every day of the week for as long as he remained at the California Men's Colony, he would have to tolerate Del. No choice. Unless Del died. Or he died. Or he went back to the hole. But only a year. He'd be back. Different Del. Same Del. Del was white and he was white. A decision was made long ago. Who is he? Eighteen. Number. Brian Flintcraft. Color. He is nothing. Or: It is nothing.

Brian made his second vow since being locked up, and it took more than a while to formulate: He would never question the idea of race again. Survival has much to do with the elimination of meaningless mental torment, and he would never ask the question again. Minutes before lockdown, Brian finally rose to his feet.

The box was heavy. Like the time all around him, everything inside it was organized. There were twenty neatly stacked cans of tuna fish, a dozen disposable razors, just under forty packets of sealed top ramen, tubed and powdered toothpaste, ten bars of soap, and a relatively recent nudie mag.

The next morning at chow, Del said, "Gotta lotta folks around here respectin' you, brother. A lotta folks."

The other white boy at the table listened closely as Del spoke. This time the chow hall felt different to Brian. It seemed balanced, like he himself sat in threat of someone else's periphery, just as they sat in threat of his. Brian dug into the gravied-down beef stroganoff on his plate, the alien black shadow behind him. Five dozen black men were eating, not a single white boy amongst them.

"Yeah," he said. The words came out as he ate. "Just don't call me brother."

The white boy sitting with them looked over at Brian. It sounded like a challenge. Del coolly forced a fraction of a chuckle. Before anything else, he was a leader and recognized everything and everyone with regard to utility. Brian was simply strong, clearly white, and very angry. Del forced the chuckle again and slapped Brian on the other arm to signify authority.

"All right, all right," he said, making it seem like Brian's statement was unnecessarily repetitive. He looked over at the other white boy at their table. "Hey, Sketch. This man can sling 'em, brother. He got arms and fists those cops can't touch. He's the one broke old Mikey's jaw. Watch out."

Sketch put his fork down. Brian recognized him from the first day. He was older than Brian, but younger. He did everything he was told to do. "All right, then," Sketch said, offering his hand to Brian and taking particular note of the tattooless arms.

They finished their breakfast and a thousand more like it. Brian had acquired a job welding in the iron yard, and after work he trained with the white boxing coach, who had once fought Sonny Liston. Somewhere in between, the bird and the green thunderbolts found their way onto the skin canvas of Brian's arms. After he got his tags, the blacks who trained at the boxing gym no longer greeted him, but Brian took solace in the fact that they had spoken to him very little before, sometimes ignoring him for months at a time. Even in church, worshippers congregated racially.

More tattoos. Spiderwebs and grinning demons ducking behind tombstones. Flintcraft in Old English, and two weeks later, Flintcraft in Old English in flames. Completely green and hollowed eyes of skulls and blocked out numbers denoting years of incarceration and all kinds of generic Nazi insignia that Sketch had found in a history book of the Second

World War. Two years, nine months, and a day had passed since he walked from the hole. Brian's father came to visit.

"I fought those people," he said, pointing at the decorative arms of his son. "You're not even German, boy. You're Irish."

"It's black and white in here, old man. Either this or that. Everyone in prison's a bigot. Niggers, too."

The glass between them was necessary. Including the silence of staring, Brian's first and only visit lasted just beyond six minutes. The father and son's eyes were the same in that both men felt their own anger to be superior. When his father walked off, it was the only occasion since being locked up that Brian felt his time had been unequivocally wasted.

Brian turned twenty-one three months later, and to celebrate he got another tag. The tattoo gun was crude but effective enough to imprint the given image reliably. The ink smuggled from the art class was the problem, as it sometimes faded on the arm. Brian had been for the most part fortunate, though there were some spots along one forearm that needed touching up.

Brian sipped on the applejack Del had made for the occasion. Del and his crew had gathered not so much to admire Brian's latest tag nor celebrate his birthday. Applejack very simply brought the race together, just as pruno brought together the blacks and Budweiser beer the cops. The rotting apples were collected in a Hefty bag over a three-week period, and when the pungent smell came up, so did the alcohol, and no one cared. The process the blacks used for making pruno was virtually identical, except with oranges. But drinking, like everything else, was segregated, and as Brian sipped on his applejack, the ridge of his nose crinkled up like a jailhouse aristocrat.

They all crinkled up their noses and drank. Sketch was the only one not crinkling his nose. He took his work seriously in a young, hopeful kind of way and insisted on remaining clearheaded.

"Try not to move, Bri," he said.

A white boy named Scooter was troubled. After a couple glasses of applejack, he voiced his thoughts. "I got troubles back home."

Another white boy said, "Sancho?"

Scooter said, "Yeah."

The other white boy said, "At least she writes you, brother."

Scooter said, "Oh, she even visits. Got one last Christmas."

Del said cynically, "Did she bring Sancho?" and everyone laughed.

Scooter shook his head. "She might as well have. I asked her, 'How's everything out there, Sally? Doing all right?'" Scooter shook his head and the other white boy smiled. "She tells me, 'Everything's great, Scooter. The kids. Work. Sex. Everything's great, darling.'"

Much laughter. Before it died out, the other white boy said, "She's notchyo girl, Sancho's girl."

Del was watching Sketch and Brian. They both were immersed in the task at hand, and did not participate in the story-telling. Sketch's eyes were unmoving and Brian remained as still as the subject of an eighteenth-century portrait. Del started up his story:

"Once I knew this jaycat over in the county. You know the kind, brother. Jaywalks in front of a police station on Saturday morning so he can eat dinner in jail Saturday night. All he wants out of life is three hots and a cot."

A murmur of laughter came up. Sketch's eyes narrowed and he put the gun to Brian's arm.

"Well, this guy was a piece of work. Used to call him Grasshopper. He was so tore back from all them nights behind the dumpster that his face was like cracked concrete. I mean he was past tore back. He was peeled back, brother."

No one nodded or looked up at Del. The grooves of his own face continued shifting as the tone of his voice became lighter. He had sole authority over the telling of this story.

"Well, anyways, this jaycat decides one day he wants to get a tattoo. Now, we're in jail, brother, and we barely got beds to sleep on, but old Grasshopper has got to get his tattoo. It's like a national emergency. He even asks the cops. Went up to the morning shift lady and said, 'I need a tattoo really bad, madam.'

One of the white boys asked, "What'd she say, Del?"

"What do you think, brother? She said, 'You need a hell of a lot more than that, jaycat. Now get the hell out of my face.' So Grasshopper long-legs it back to the block and we're shooting spades at a table. We're trying to get into the game 'cause we got stakes on every book of cards, and this god-damn jaycat starts crying. I mean he's literally crying. 'Nothing ever goes right in my life, ooooh. I never get anything I want, ooooh. I hate life, ooooh.'"

Sketch was oblivious to the popping chuckles that came up all around him. But his subject paid particular attention to the detailing of his arm while listening with the same attention to the time-killing tale of Del's. Brian suspected somewhere inside him and somehow about him that everything happening at that moment meant very little.

"So we can't get into our game, brother. One of the fellas gets pissed off and tells him to scat, and old Grasshopper starts bawling worse than before. I mean you ever seen an old tore-back dumpster dog cryin'? We all felt kinda bad at first 'cause he's one of our own, brother. But that jaycat kept bawling and bawling. And he stunk, too! You could smell the raunch comin' out his toothless mouth, so finally I said, 'You wanna tag, Grasshopper?'

"He wipes his face and nods with these big old bloodshot dumpster-dog eyes, and I said, 'Oh, you're gonna get a tag, Grasshopper. I'm gonna set you up real good, brother.'"

Some of the white boys had mischief on their faces, and this invigorated Del, reminding him of the same three mischievous white boys shooting spades with him way back when. It didn't occur to him that he hadn't thought of them for well over a decade.

"So I run upstairs to my cell and grab one of them disposable razors. You know, like them Bic razors. I get my lighter and my comb with all the sharpened down teeth. All the dogs are gathered around the back table tryin' to figure out what I got goin', but no one but old Del knows, brother. And that damned Grasshopper was waiting there in the middle like a king."

The red bumps were rising on Brian's arm like beautifully detailed heat rash.

"So I sit next to old Grasshopper and tell one of the fellows to hold his arm down on the table. I get my lighter and I start melting down the handle of the razor and collecting the wax in my coffee cup. You know, it comes out like wax. Five minutes pass and old Grasshopper ain't figured it out yet. He thinks it's some kinda ritual or something, poor bastard. But everybody else has. When it's ready to go, I tell another brother to grab onto his shoulder and press that whining dumpster dog into the seat. Then I get the comb and start poking holes in Grasshopper's arms. He's laughing and yellin', 'Quit it, Del. That tickles.' I told him, "Not for long, you whinin' bastard. Not for long.' His eyes get big and now he knows, but it's too late 'cause the dogs got him pinned to the seat. He starts screamin' just before the wax hits his arm."

A roar of laughter.

"The cops come through and shove Grasshopper's arm in the sink and now he's really got something to cry about. I laughed for a week up in solitary. And you know what's the best part, brother? I saw that jaycat two years later and the wax was still there, like a sky o' stars on his arm." Del laughed and the grooves on his face shifted. He saw that Sketch had paid no attention to the story and said, "Damn, Sketch."

Sketch did not answer. He was concentrating on the pattern in his left hand, as the right hand stenciled with precision. So far, the outline of the iron cross was identical to the original on paper, and now only required the shading for dimension.

Scooter said, "Sketch." Sketch looked up. "You think you're Van Gogh or something?"

Sketch looked down. Brian pulled his arm away, the iron cross pink and swelling. He stroked the other forearm affectionately and Scooter said nothing further. There was violence in Brian's eyes.

As a gesture of authority, Del cruelly took up the clowning. "Gonna cut off your ear, Sketch? Better watch out, brother. They gonna send you up to Vacaville with Manson and all the other crazies."

The other white boy started laughing.

Brian said to the white boy, "Shut the fuck up. And who the hell are you, anyways?"

"'Ey, brother—"

Brian stood and said, "Don't you ever call me that."

Scooter said, "It's cool, Brian."

Del grabbed the other white boy and said, "Let's go, let's go, before brother Brian has a fit," and downing the applejack in an instant, all three left.

Not much time passed before Brian looked down at Sketch. They were the only two left from the party. The violence was still in Brian's eyes. He said, "My arms are everything to me, Sketch. You know that?"

This kind of talk was encouraging to Sketch. He nodded and resumed his work with a new vigor and focus. Tattooing earned a man additional time, no less than a year, but Sketch saw himself as an artist with a cause who could not be stopped.

One afternoon in the iron yard, it was blindingly bright out. Two hundred sixty-two and one-half days had passed since his twenty-first birthday when the black shot-caller said to Brian Flintcraft, "We best talk."

Both men were angry in a vague kind of way, and their scowls seemed interchangeable. Brian was squatting in a corner, and Scooter and another white boy were cross-legged at either side. All three had their backs to the wall, and their bare arms were tattooed sleeves of green. Brian lifted his head, but otherwise did not move.

A little time passed. Shot-callers only crossed the race line for life-and-death reasons, and so a little time passed.

Just as Brian decided to stand and look at him on the level, the black shot-caller turned his back and started to walk. Brian saw the nonthreat in the gesture and caught up with him, though keeping half a man's width in between. Scooter and the other white boy closed the gap on the wall, standing up to watch Brian's back.

"I'm coming atchu wit' respec," the black shot-caller said. He looked down at the racially detailed arms of Brian Flintcraft and the clubs for fists attached at the tagged-down wrists. They walked together and he said, "I know whatchu can do wit' them things, and I'm coming wit' respec."

"Well, what do you want?" asked Brian.

All the workers clustered along the walls were watching and eating lunch. White welders sat and stood with white welders and black welders sat and stood with black welders, as if there were a distinction between the identically brown bag lunches issued at noon.

"Now, I know you ain't calling shots for the whites," the black shot-caller said, "but you the last man I can talk to 'fore somethin' bad pops off."

Brian nodded, and the shot-caller turned on his heels to walk back to the spot. They had taken twelve steps, and it had taken that long. Apparently he knew what he had to say, and it was short.

He said, "Better talk to that Del y'all run wit'. He got himself up in one and won't stay off our bars."

"The pull-up bars?"

"That's our spot and it's always been like that."

Brian said, "I don't know anything about it. I do my time in the gym and welding in this yard."

Just before they hit the wall, the shot-caller said, "Well, you gonna know about it soon, one way or the other. That's your people. You best talk to 'em befo' them bars turn this yard into a battleground, and everyone's up in arms."

That night after training in the gym, Brian walked out to the yard to see Del on the pull-up bars. Normally he ran laps around the track for a few miles, but today it was not safe. Blacks were packed up along one side of the yard and whites along the other. Two very thorough floodlights highlighted the entire yard so that the grass in the middle was gray-black and the encircling concrete gray-white. Only the two squadrons of racially mixed cops were moving in black-and-white pictures through the yard, and except for the jingling chains, everything was quiet and dreary in the floodlit dark surrounding them.

At the bars, more than twenty whites were standing around with their hands in the pockets of their jackets, and not a single man did pull-ups. They were all clustered up, but not arbitrarily. Every angle of the surrounding yard could be seen by one of the men. When Brian approached, they shifted and moved and unconsciously exchanged angles. A few men nodded respectfully. A little spot opened up for him next to Del, and he filled it, taking up a position overlooking his own angle of the yard. He could see the gym he had just come from, and next to it a group of scowling blacks, their superior numbers growing.

For once Del was quiet and tense, and he greeted Brian only with a nod. He transferred his weight from one leg to the other. It took a while before anything was said. Brian spoke first. "Del," he said.

"These niggers," Del said. "They got every little spot on this yard wrapped up."

Brian said, "So we're gonna get down over these bars?"

Del's eyebrows pressed together, as if a single streak of paint ran from the corner of one eye to the corner of the other. Both his deep natural and unnatural frown lines were grooves. A question was the first sign of betrayal.

"You're goddamn right we are," Del said. "We got no place to congregate 'cause we're outnumbered two to one. You know that. They been here longer and there's always been more of 'em. 'S time to do something about it. When this thing pops off, you'll never walk by these bars again without appreciating a single pull-up."

Brian looked around surreptitiously and understood why Del was calling shots for, as the black shot-caller said, *his people.* As untrustworthy as he was, Del's words were merely the voiced version of what Brian saw in the faces of the every other white boy present. He and Del were on this side, blacks on the other; if he wanted to walk the line with any degree of safety, he fought for the birds and thunderbolts on his arms. The flags for survival. He didn't know what they meant, and of course it didn't matter. His second vow three years back was right here, right now. At eighteen, at twenty-one, at riot time, survival meant a clean-sweep removal of ideals.

Brian nodded back at Del, and by the time he came out the hole a year later for ardently engaging in a race riot, he was the number two white boy in the yard behind Del and pull-ups were performed every day by his people.

V. The First Friend

And a bit of time passed.

No visits, no riots, no incidents. Only the clicks of the popping cell in trochaic monometer. Clink. Clank. Clink. Clank. Clink. Clank. Only unquestioned directives over the PA in the same. "Lockdown!" "Chow time!" "Med call!" Day and night in white and black and colorless bricks of foundation being laid for the violence to come. Wordless antipathy thickened in reliable routine, and walls, barriers, and intertwining chains. Two years, eight months, and three days before Old Mac said, "It's called *pugilistica dementia,* and I got got got it."

Old Mac had been technically knocked out once by Sonny Liston. They had fought a lopsided match up in Oakland, but Old Mac took pride in the fact that he never went down. He was a year over forty at the time and coaxed into the match by a loan shark he had owed money. They had stopped the fight in the tenth round, after the pleading screams of his mother could no longer be ignored by the referee. The referee was Old Mac's uncle, who was much older then than Old Mac was now.

Old Mac's age had earned him quasi-immunity from the politics of the California Men's Colony. That is, he wouldn't be relied upon to fight if something popped off. Because of this, Brian Flintcraft spoke as freely with Old Mac as his deeply institutionalized personality would permit. And being the only two whites in the gym, they essentially had no one else to talk to but each other.

"That fight was racial," Old Mac said, wrapping Brian's hand around, inside, then back around the wrist in figure eights. "I know what Jack Johnson felt like, I'll tell ya that much. That whole crowd wanted me dead dead dead."

Brian saw in his peripheral vision the squad of black boxers in the corner. Like Brian and Old Mac, they were getting ready for the big show that night with the Air Force. Brian was the only white fighting for the prison, slotted at heavyweight. The blacks filled in the remaining light-, welter-, middle-, and light heavyweight slots. Brian couldn't wait for the show with the Air Force. He asked, "Who the hell's Jack Johnson?"

Old Mac went on. "Sonny took everything out on this poor white white white man. And now now now, I'm not too sharp. So why you wanna fight, then? Old Sonny's dead and I'm a little punch punch punch drunk. *Pugilistica dementia.* Means battered brain in Eye-talian. It's no good. Why you wanna fight, son?"

"I'm good at it, poor white man."

"You ain't that good, son."

Brian inhaled deeply. The tags on his arm were already glistening with sweat, and his shirtless torso shined. Unlike the black boxers, he had no sparring partner and so his time in the ring was first. Brian would shadowbox for fifteen minutes before moving onto the crazy bags attached to the floor and ceiling where the black boxers stood and jived now. The daily routine was always the same. At the precise moment his time in the ring ended, the group of black boxers would walk clockwise around the ring to avoid crossing paths with Brian Flintcraft. The two paternal trainers focused so deeply on their respective fighter that they, too, abided the politics of the California Men's Colony. But maybe more astonishing was the defying of mathematics. The two never looked into each other's eyes a single time over the span of a thousand thousand geometrical chances.

"Well, whatever, Mac," Brian said. "But I'm gonna kill that flyboy tonight." He flexed his jaw and the veins of his neck strained. A black boxer was skipping rope by the crazy bags. The black coach was head down, snapping his fingers in the rhythm of his stopwatch. Brian added, "Especially if it's Sonny Liston."

Then the buzzer sounded and he climbed through the ropes by himself.

When the battered Team Air Force left from the California Men's Colony that evening, Brian had held true to his prediction. He nearly picked up another charge for attempted murder. Only the weakness of the case prevented the warden from pushing the issue. "How could you allow those killers in the ring and not expect something like this to happen?" the DA inside the warden's head said. "For chrissake, the kid was there for a tune-up before the Olympic trials."

He put Brian back in the hole for inciting through violence the ensuing riot of five hundred men yelling, "Kill him! Kill him! Kill him!" Rather than considering the bright side of things—it was the first time both whites and blacks participated freely together in an activity—the warden canceled the annual box-off with the Air Force, a tradition dating back two decades.

After Brian Flintcraft came out the hole a year later, Old Mac was thoroughly unimpressed. "That's not box box boxing you did up there. That was a mauling."

Brian managed a shrug, which was a lot, and another day passed without incident.

He went before the parole board on his twenty-sixth birthday, and they, too, were unimpressed. The smiles in their drab-white room were whiter than the walls. Thumbed-down condemnations and the occasional conditional congratulations were given in the all-in-one, all-at-once smile. They looked down at the ever-expanding file and up at the arms of institutional art, then into the spiteful blue eyes of Brian Flintcraft. He sagged in the chair, the elbows halfway up the thighs, and looked out the window for wildlife. Even when projecting indifference, he seemed very angry.

"They got deer up here, right?"

Parole denied.

Two more annual meetings ended in the very same way. During the second meeting, he was looking out the window when a member of the board asked, "What are you thinking about, Mr. Flintcraft?"

Brian said nothing.

The big, bright teeth in no way interfered with enunciation. "Perhaps what it's like to walk among the deer?"

Brian looked over. "No," he said. He mentally counted the unanimously blank white faces across the tabletop and repositioned in the chair. A deer outside lowered itself to eat. "Nah," he said, finding the white teeth again. "I was just feeling bad for all the poor niggers that gotta sit before you Nazis."

The next day Brian asked Old Mac for advice. "I don't know how the hell I got here, Mac. Twelve years up in this place, and suddenly I'm pressing thirty. 'M twenty-eight years old, Mac. Feel like fifty inside."

Old Mac spun the wraps in his hand with the affection of a professional trainer. In the other corner of the gym, the black coach was doing the exact same thing. Everything and everyone were being wound up tightly. Old Mac pretended to concentrate very hard on something he had done five times a week for twenty years.

Brian said, "Well, what's on your mind, Mac? I know you gotta say somethin'. Whenever you're not sayin' somethin', I know you gotta say somethin'."

Old Mac remained quiet, rolling Brian's wrist over for a quick, thorough examination and then pushing it away. The other unwrapped hand automatically came up. The five fingers spread so the veins came out, and when the first revolution of wrap went round, the hand balled into a fist. Brian said, "Come on, Mac."

Finally Old Mac said. "You know what your time means with the L, right?"

"Of course I do, Mac. They got me. They can keep me as long as they want. They got me. Parole denied till you die." Brian was a little mad. "Whatcha take me for, Mac?"

Old Mac said, "I take you for a fool." He looked up and there was no fear. "An angry fool fool fool."

"Well, what, Mac?"

Mac went back to the wraps, and stretched the cloth tight across the wrist. He looked over at the black coach in the other corner of the gym, and shook his head. "It's your arms, son. All those silly tag tag tags."

Brian predictably snarled at Old Mac, but that night in the cell he laid his head down on the old book and couldn't help but reflect. He had maintained his second vow so effectively over the years that reflection was an unnatural state of affairs for Brian Flintcraft. He had neither sighed nor wept over floodings of regret. There were no subconscious searchings for fictive nostalgia. Ever. That was strength, autonomy, and survival wrapped up in one. Tonight he felt the control of the topic slipping from him, and squared up mentally.

He caressed the tattoos on his arms. The elaborate conglomeration of design was permanent and unwavering. They would always be there. Beneath the shield of green, the muscular cut could be seen clearly, yet Brian Flintcraft took no special notice. His arms had gotten him everything he needed in prison to survive, and he had no one but himself to thank. They had always been perfectly functional here. For fear of his fighting reputation, no other white man would mess with Brian Flintcraft, and the tattoos meant that no black inmate could say anything disrespectful without the chance of a race riot popping off. These types of rules were simple enough, but the best part was the spiting of Old Man Corrections: what went down on his arms stayed, regardless of any administrative directive to the contrary. Whatever the hell happened, they couldn't cut his arms off.

Five months and a week went by until Brian forged a respectable counterargument facedown and spread naked across the rolling pebbles of gravel, one of a bloody two hundred of both black and white inmates, cops and badges and blue lights flashing in little orbits through the yard:

I gotta get outta here.

VI. The First Book

The block was locked down for three weeks. All movement was frozen until further notice, and everyone ate bag lunches in their cells three times a day. Visits were canceled and telephone privileges postponed. Whites showered on Tuesdays and Thursdays, and blacks showered on Wednesdays and Fridays. A squadron of cops came through each sunrise, shaking down cells, tearing off sheets, tossing mattresses out on the tier, and making things easy for the evening shift duplicating the detail later that night. Confiscated sharpened nails from the iron yard and filed-down toothbrushes ensured the ushering of black and white rabble-rousers to the hole.

Brian used the time to plan. He had six months before his next parole meeting and was determined to follow Mac's advice. When they were finally cleared for yard and job detail, Brian sent out a request to meet with his counselor.

A month became the past. He received a docket for a counseling appointment later that day. He looked down at the time printed in the corner of the pink carbon, and then at his watch. "Later that day" was an hour ago, and Brian hustled himself out of the block to see his counselor.

"This the first time you come to see me," said Mr. Clooney, "and you're late." He wore a badge over his Emmitt Smith football jersey. Two officers were in the room shooting dice.

Brian was standing. He stroked one arm with the hand of the other and said, "Yep."

One of the officers looked up from the dice game. "Get the hell outta here," said the officer. "Who do you think you are? Some big shot?"

Back at the block, Brian filed another request to see Mr. Clooney, and precisely a month later he saw the same Emmitt Smith football jersey and, pinned to it, the same badge. Also, the same two officers were shooting dice.

"Let me get this straight," Mr. Clooney said. In his hand was a binder of inmate files with a Dallas Cowboys bumper sticker wrapped around the outside. He shook his head. "You want me to speak with the warden?"

"Yeah."

"For what now?"

"That program I mentioned." Brian thought about it. "Sir."

One of the dice-shooting officers laughed aloud.

Mr. Clooney said, "Who told you about this?"

Brian shrugged. "I heard around."

"You heard wrong," said Mr. Clooney. He emphatically repeated, "You heard wrong. It's a myth. This state can barely get up enough money to pay staff, let alone finance some tattoo-removal program for inmates. Forget about it."

Brian Flintcraft said, "Okay" and went out the door, the dice still bouncing behind him.

He felt fine now.

He had not felt right in a state of non-anger, calling someone "sir" in the hope of an end served. What more was negotiation than appearing hypocritically peaceful with every angry cell of his body yearning for recognition? Normal to Brian Flintcraft was an angry lull before the violence to come. Normal was no help from anyone with a badge. He would have to summon a solution with the rage in which every other problem was solved at the California Men's Colony. He would have to do things just as he always had.

He tried the reflecting thing again that night in the cell.

He was certainly not afraid to fight Del and Sketch and any other white boy once they saw the disavowal of his arms. He and his green arms would fight to the death if necessary, and everyone on both sides of the line understood that. But Brian was beginning to recognize the painful dichotomy of that gift, for even as the arms saved Brian Flintcraft from harm, they held him down like a rap sheet that never went away. The hatred was welded so deep into his skin and psyche that even something as rooted as the survival principle was predetermined doom. Like his arms, Brian Flintcraft was too functional in prison, and that's why he was still there.

Even a group thumping from his people or a slash across the cheek meant little to Brian Flintcraft. What was physically more painful than the condensing of pure time? It was the other side of the line that mattered; he knew it would be the last straw. That's how the authorities would see it:

Yet another bout of violence, Mr. Flintcraft. So it appears now that you can't even get along with your own people.

He'd told his father that *it's either this or that,* but now he wasn't so sure. He needed to find the grayness of this place. Things change over the tumultuous span of a decade, or at least people change. Who was he kidding? Nothing had changed in that time except one thing. He couldn't say if he was better or worse than the seventeen-year-old boy who had shuffled into the gates that day, but he knew that the fear of unfamiliarity was gone. The place was alive in his mind and in the emptiness of his eyes, and you could see it right there on the skin of his arms.

He tried to sleep. Of late, he was having problems sleeping. The dark had never bothered him before. For quite a while, very little had ever bothered him. Yet it seemed tonight as though the slightest bit of light would warm him.

He raised himself up from the bunk. After "Lights off!" he rolled a strip of toilet paper into an airtight wick and lit it with his lighter. The blackness retreated in a flash and formed a simmering enclosure around his arms. The perimeter of light danced in the converse relationship with a retreating, encroaching, and thus simmering blackness.

Brian was looking for answers in an empty well. Digging for gold in a mud patch. He was no smarter today than ten years back. He was no braver. Function, function, function. What else could he do? It had always been function. It almost could have been nothing else. Survive.

He looked down at the pillow of a novel on his bunk. All was hopeless and futile until the veined and battered book on the bunk spoke to him. Something like rebellious excitement raised the hairs on his arms. He put the wick above the cover of his book-pillow and, for the first time, said the ominous title aloud: "*A Farewell to Arms.*"

There was still something he could do. A new interpretation of the same old book of his life. An answer in the empty well echoing back in *A Farewell to Arms,* the pillow he'd slept on every night for over a decade but never read. It would probably get both sides of the line off his back and leave everything incontestably gray. And he might just get out, too.

A farewell to arms, Brian thought, and then blew out the wick, closing his eyes in the pitch-black.

VII. The First Grayness

This was the iron yard.

Rampant sparks and goggled blacks in one corner, rampant sparks and goggled whites in the other. Deep-voiced directives of opposing dialects; greetings and curt pleasantries kept to their corners. Sweat and sometimes blood, but—so far, this much, what gives?—not today. Jiving cops in the back gaily shooting dice, frowning head freeman pacing the floor in concern in between. Cages and chairs and bars being broken down and built up like a feloniously fabricated jungle gym, and everywhere the visual reminder of ancient ways and old prison films: black and white clutching and scratching at the iron-gray.

Lunch had finished and Sketch came over to speak with Brian. His fondness for Brian Flintcraft had entirely to do with his thick, green arms. Brian was his living canvas, his *ars poetica* in the flesh, proof of a life at least partially unwasted.

Sketch didn't want to talk with Brian like this. He was no counselor. Even to himself, he was known at the California Men's Colony as nothing more nor less than the one-dimensional sketch of an artist. He was merely a recorder whose conduit was a tattoo gun. He spoke in stenciled, olive-green etchings. Sketch was not a troubleshooter and he did not like this. Over the bright orange storm of sparks, he ventured, "Gotta talk to you, Bri."

Brian lifted his goggles and disengaged the gun from a glowing pin of iron. "Yeah?"

"This is hard for me to say, Bri."

Brian's mind flashed back to the book in the cell. It didn't matter. In a bit, there wouldn't be anything to say. "That's all right. I know it ain't you who's talking right now."

"That's right, Bri," said Sketch. "Del wanted me talk to you, Bri."

"Tell brother Del to come talk to me himself."

"We don't see you at the pull-up bars anymore and Del said—"

"Fuck Del."

"Bri—"

"Fuck Del." *The first hour of the first day.* "Treacherous bastard."

"C'mon, Bri. He says you spend too much time with that old man in—"

"Don't say it, Sketch. Don't even think it."

"Everyone respects you, Bri. Especially Del."

The message was delicately laced in warning, and so the anger became Brian Flintcraft, building up and tempered only by the image of the book in his cell. "Shut the fuck up."

"What can you do, anyways? What can you do?"

"What'd I just say?"

Sketch's beheld Brian's arms. He said in a pleading voice, "He just wants to know where you stand on things, Bri. If he can rely on you. He wanted me to ask you, that's all."

Brian said, "I'm gonna show you where I stand on things, Sketch. And make sure you tell brother Del all about it."

Brian left the protective goggles over his forehead. The dragon mouth of his welding-gun fired up. His uncovered eyes were impossibly wide and flaring, and Sketch instinctively took a step back. It didn't take long for the rolling pin to start glowing again. A little time went by, preparing nor comforting no one for the seen and heard deed to come. Sketch actually felt the fierce, forced roar a split second before the brand touched the olive-green skin of the right arm.

"Aaaaaaaaaaaaaaaarrrrrrrrrrrhhhh!"

And it continued as Brian Flintcraft switched hands to repeat the procedure, the race line in the iron yard obliterated in a series of "Damn, nigga!s" and "Damn, boy!s" and "You see that!s".

"Aaaaaaaaaaaaaarrrrrrrhhhhhh!"

And just before the blackness of unconsciousness hit, he saw Sketch's eyes watering up, his life's calling vanishing in a tiny, gray smoke cloud of burnt skin.

VIII. The First Farewell

When Brian Flintcraft returned to the yard from the infirmary a month later, he was a nonentity among both blacks and whites. Blacks secretly admired Brian Flintcraft, but ignored him because he was still four-fifths white. Since the rolling-pin incident, the most anyone had said to him was in the gym. He had gone back to find Old Mac, and the black trainer had told him: "He ain't here. And you can't fight now, anyways, champ."

Brian Flintcraft said, "Thanks," and it felt all right. One of the black boxers working the speed bag nodded when Brian passed.

The whites of the yard avoided him for a different reason. The uniform assessment by Del and his crew was that Brian was not worth going to the hole over, a silly white boy trying to change himself, leave him be. He wasn't ever worth the bird and thunderbolts, anyway. But Del and the sum of his crew privately knew the real reason they left him be, paraphrased best by Scooter. One gray morning in the iron yard, he consoled an unabashedly mourning Sketch, who apparently couldn't eat, sleep, or talk.

Scooter said to Sketch: "Don't think about it. 'Cause Brian Flintcraft is just plain crazy, and not to be messed with."

Old Mac wouldn't talk to Brian for a couple of days either, refusing to even look at his former pupil. He had no one to train in the gym any longer and nothing to look forward to but nostalgia. When he finally got over his anger at Brian Flintcraft, he sent him a simple note of encouragement. On paper it literally said, *I hope I never see you again,* but it was a fabrication of sorts. To a smiling Brian, the note read differently: *I hope I never never never see you again.*

So he went before the parole board two months, three weeks, and six days later on his twenty-ninth birthday. They were still a tandem of five, but one of the smiling white men of the committee had been replaced by a smiling white lady. The meetings always began immediately, but today for some reason they were whispering to each other in an almost circle.

In the excitement of the newness and the dangerous hope accompanying it, Brian had the sensation of goose bumps along his arm. They weren't there of course, but he still felt tingling beneath the layers of scar. He didn't know what else to do but blink and breathe, and when he didn't know what to do beyond that, he looked down at his arms.

They were the same. The uninterrupted scar had little clouds of blue that you could see, watercolor on a canvas of gray skin. As if the blue was caught, or forced to spread and then captured in the moment. The arm was thick but not chiseled like the rest of the body. It appeared swollen and blown from the layers of scar, and yet it sagged, an extra coating of lifeless skin. When the elbow folded at the inside, little ridged blankets formed up. Unlike his face and neck and every other visible exposure of alabaster skin, the two gray arm patches were without freckles. They were a black man's palms, in total contradiction to the rest of his body.

One of the smiles said, "You have an inmate assault in which you broke the inmate's jaw."

Another smile said, "You have a staff assault."

And again, the first: "You have inciting a riot in the gymnasium during an Air Force Exhibition, and participation in a number of race riots."

He turned his arms over proudly so they could see them. The speaker said, "*And now this.*"

The lips of Brian's mouth split. He looked down at his arms, and then back up again. Couldn't they see his arms?

"We think your time with us is just about through, Mr. Flintcraft."

He began the internal process of preparation.

"We wish you luck . . ."

Brian Flintcraft heard the tone, unfiltered by the processed smiles, and institutionally tuned out. He couldn't allow himself to look at their decision in its true light. He had to go back to the old code of no expectation but the permanence of time.

A transfer to Vacaville for mental treatment was just what he'd sought from the parole board. Everything had happened just as he'd anticipated. To be out of the California Men's Colony for good, forever, to never come back.

the good nurse

Tuesday, 0448 hours

One step through the metal detector and I'm momentarily free. There's nothing forbidden on my body except a pack of multicolored Trustex condoms roped around the belt line of my waist. Forty little packaged squares connected to one another like a lei of latex, Scotch-taped right below my belly button. Only now, thinking on it, do I realize a truth: This kind of sneakiness starts at home each Tuesday in the closet of the master bedroom: Huddled, naked, I'll quickly secure the condoms with nimble, panicky fingers, protected in the darkness from Harold's discerning eye in our bed.

Officer Baldwin slides the plastic brown bucket around the detector. It contains my lunch, a *Health* magazine, and two clip-on pens. He's young and three weeks on the job and so he flips cautiously through the magazine as if he's browsing the article titles at a newsstand. He does that twice and hands it over. "Here you go, nurse."

Next he takes the pens, uncaps them, taps the inky ballpoint with an index finger, recaps them. When several correctional officers were indicted for smuggling heroin into the prison, all cautionary measures except the strip search were instituted at the front door.

I say, "It's too early in the morning to work this hard, young man."

He smiles and says, "I don't mind one bit, ma'am."

I pick everything up as the line forms behind me. I hear no words of greeting from anyone, so, without looking back, I start the long walk down the hall to the yard transfer. I can remember my first time here almost a decade ago. Mid-June, 1995. I'd been introduced first to the lieutenant in my yard. He'd warned, "Come to me with any problems you get yourself into," then, taking me by the arm, introduced me to Warden Basil. "You're gonna do just fine here," he'd said. "Don't you worry one bit."

But I hadn't asked for any kind of reassurance from either of them. I was the newly hired lead RN for an experimental, self-sufficient AIDS hospice, and I knew what I had to do. I'd taken the job in the good spirit of healing, and that's what had worried them.

I pass the office of Warden Basil. He's seated in a black leather barber's chair chewing an unlit cigar. He doesn't light up, I assume, because he, too, must follow the rules he's implemented in the institution. He's setting an example. All through the prison there are red three-foot-high No Smoking signs painted on the walls. There's even one here in the administration building, where 99 percent of the people are not incarcerated. The 1 percent on his knees at the feet of Warden Basil is enthusiastically swiping a twisted blue rag across the toe of the right boot with both hands, his bald head shiny-black with rivulets of sweat. He has a lot to be thankful for: a prime position like this pays twelve cents a day, and at the end of three months, he'll have almost twelve dollars cash for purchase on canteen.

I say, "Good morning, warden."

He nods as I pass. "Nurse Carrington."

I wonder if he remembers when we met. I doubt it. He seems to live with such unblinking certainty as to his calling. He is the giver of answers, the prohibiter of actions, the punisher of violations. At nearly every level of his life, encounters are with underlings. That kind of uniform interaction with one's subjects must make long-term memory unnecessary. Memory requires, I think, an even or an upward exchange.

I wonder if Harold remembers when we met. When he first laid eyes on me, I doubt that he even considered me a potential lover. I was, at thirty-nine, eight years his senior, and a foot shorter. I was timid as we danced, standing on my toes, my nervous arms nearly vertical around his neck. I asked him what he liked in women and he said, "Everything."

"That narrows it down," I said.

Then we started swing dancing on the sawdust floor of the Saddlerack Saloon. He whipped me about like a little boy with a cat's tail, and just as I caught my feet he threw me into the air. In that instant, floating, I knew I could never again delude myself into believing that I treasured my independence above all else. The idea was a front for loneliness and sadness. I wanted a man. And if I fell to the ground and broke a leg in the attempt, at least I knew who I was and what I needed. But I landed on my feet and Harold twirled me about for two succeeding songs and I took him home that night and we made love in the not unpleasant blur of drunkenness. From that point forward, it was just a matter of holding on.

When whittled down to its core, I believe that the kindly alias the inmates have given me has more to do with job detail than any truly personal asset. My profession will always begin and end with kindness, and if you're anything exceptional by context, then you're probably, as it is, *un*kind. You won't last long, not even in the E ward of a level II prison. I have never met another nurse whose heart I didn't like. Even Gloria, the current assistant nurse, is kind in time. So the "Good Nurse"—that's me—is simply status quo.

The California Men's Colony is—if there be such a thing— a beautiful penitentiary. The rolling San Luis hills are bright green in the spring, wet as a sponge. Would you believe that deer feed at the base of the East Yard fence line in the moon of the early morn? That just before chow a northbound Caltrain slithers into a cloudy horizon line? It's right there on the ridge for a minute, and then, if you don't pay attention, vanishes. I watch for it every morning, twenty minutes before Gloria arrives. Except for the snoring of a few of the patients, it's quiet enough to appreciate. This morning it's already vanished. I make my first rounds of the day.

"Good Nurse," Roberto whispers, pushing the straw through his box of Ensure. He's always awake early, awaiting my greeting. "You are the kindest woman I have ever known."

I whisper, "It's not true. Try and sit up when you drink."

"*Es verdad*, Good Nurse. The kindest."

"No," I whisper. "I'm just doing my job."

He sits up, frowns, taps twice on the state-issued sheet for emphasis. "You are kinder than my own mother."

I cannot help but think of mine. We shared the same long, Latin nose, dark brown eyes, wavy amber hair. Not much else. The last time I saw her she was yelling wide-eyed for Daddy, who stood, as he always did, right there at her side.

That was ten years ago, plus a month and a week. I remember thinking, knowing, *This is it. My mother is finally too tired.*

"No," I whisper. Roberto puts the Ensure down, shaking his head. I offer gently, knowing it is tough, "You must drink the whole thing, Roberto."

He hits his chest halfheartedly. "*Más duro.*"

But all the strength in the world will not beat what he has. We both are aware of this. He is waiting for the order in my pathetic *gringa* Spanish. He'll then do exactly what I ask, and with the kind of outright duty of a show dog. He's only been here a month, but I learned that trait about Roberto the first day. I say, "*Bebe,* Roberto. *Bebe.*"

At once, he puts his mouth to the straw of the pasty carbo shake, squeezing until it collapses into itself and makes the bubbly sound. I whisper, "*Bueno.*"

"Okay, Good Nurse." He forces a nauseous smile. "Okay. But trust me. You must trust me. She was a crack whore, a *puta.*"

"No, no, Roberto," I say. "She was your mother. Your mother."

"Trust me, Good Nurse. I know her. A whore. A *puta.*"

Wednesday, 0415 hours

Last night, after we fought, I vowed to never talk with Harold again about prison. Those kind of conversations end the same way they start: distant. It's a failure I accept in our relationship for the greater good of other satisfactions, mainly having a relationship. Still, eight hours into the vow, I break it. I guess there's no containing desperation.

"I have a patient that's very bright, very hopeful."

Harold's in bed still, watching me dress for work. I walk towards our bed, button my blouse above him. He used to like this, demand this. He doesn't ask, "Who's this patient?"

so I say, "His name is Roberto. He hates his mother." He doesn't ask "Why?" or "How come you never talk about your mother, Annie?" so I say, "She taught him to manufacture heroin when he was ten."

Harold rolls over and away. I reach for the patch of birthmarks along his neckline, which resemble the Big Dipper without the handle, wondering, "How much longer will I ignore myself for him?"

He mumbles something into his pillow which I cannot hear. At the edge of the bed, I politely wait until he finishes, sit down, tie my shoes into a double knot. In my head I answer, "However long it takes," but say aloud, "Baby. Can you not talk into your pillow?"

"It's not getting any better, Annie."

I know what "it" is, but say anyway, "What isn't?"

"This whole thing."

The worst is when you agree. "What do you want from me, baby?"

"You know, goddamnit. It's the same thing since we first met. It hasn't changed."

In our year together, I've come to more than accept Harold's line of work, antithetical to my own: no inmate in the CMC will ever call Harold the Good DA. He puts them away for good, meaning for a long time, then forgets about them. He's never mentioned a convicted name, not once: to Harold, they're all the same. And it's easier that way. Someday I'll accept that perhaps there is no other way.

I manage, "But you've changed."

"That's right," he says. "I love you now. That's the only difference, Annie. I worry about you at that place."

I am so warm inside I can only nuzzle the birthmarks along the back of his neck with the top of my head. Put my hand into his mussed-up hair and gently muss it up more. It requires from Harold but the tiniest expression of intimacy for me to lose my footing, my training. I become impulsive as an addict, a hungry cub, all for the slightest gesture of tenderness. I know I need Harold more than he does me. Anyone can see that.

Wednesday, 1225 hours

When I'd taken my big stance against the disease ravaging my patients, Harold had just moved in with me. Early 2003. I was an eight-year vet of the CMC, and you can probably guess what happened to my goals of earning healer sainthood. After one week at the prison, I truly learned the meaning of the term "herculean problems." This system is like the proverbial apple and its worm. You have to dig out a little hole in the sturdiness of the core just to survive.

Looking back on it, I know now that I didn't have the courage to go public with the cause; I was too small in the personality to bear the mantle of initiation, to claim the first deed, to risk banishment, termination. Men die, abuse happens, sin lurks and creeps into being, and, sadly, you learn to accept it. Everyone does. Anyway, everyone in a system does. In 1995, I had a heady monthly mortgage to pay and I was looking, with luck, to own my own car within the year. Plus, I wanted a man to lean on and, I believed, a good state job would help. So I obeyed convention.

Meanwhile, my patients were rapidly succumbing to AIDS. Shared needles and unprotected sex assured that the numbers would only increase. In '96, we implemented mandatory testing at Receiving and Release, and it was like rolling over a log and finding a swarming colony of bugs. I'd been ordered to follow the model of self-sustenance of Angola State Prison in Louisiana, and I did. We didn't ask anyone for anything. But it took me eight years and over two hundred dead patients to recognize that the longer I remained conventional, the further I got from an ethical stance.

So I finally decided to smuggle life into the prison each Tuesday. At first, I was admittedly scared for my job. During daylight savings time when the first rays of morning softly lit the parking lot, it was the worst on my conscience. I would pull into my space, *Nurse 1*, unable to even hold my head up. I'd place my feet officially on prison property, grip my lunch tightly by my side. I'd pass the rows of SUVs and raised Toyota trucks and finally look up at the sidewalk to find myself distorted in the silver glare of the shatterless glass doors. I'd breathe in deeply, focus on my chin in the reflection, avoiding my eyes, prepare to nod curtly at colleagues, avoiding dialogue.

After several months, I finally began to feel at ease with my disobedience. Most of the fear was just in my head, and Harold, if he'd known of my stance, probably would have articulated the reasons it was just in my head. There is always—and anyone state-employed knows—room to maneuver in a bureaucracy. You learn that *Nothing is worse in the prison system than outside interference.* All incestuous sin goes on in private. At some point I knew that as long as my patients were processed at a statistically accepted rate, the warden and East Block lieutenant were content enough to look away from infractions of mine, as were same-level colleagues involved in infractions of their own.

So I keep, at all times, several condoms tucked away in the pockets of my uniform, a box stashed in the bottom drawer of my office desk. I keep one at the steel headboard at the base of each bed. My patients are smart about it. They, as it's commonly said in the ward, "keep it all under wraps." A man from each race utilizes a weekly runner for delivery back to the block. Before the runner passes away, he's sure to appoint a replacement. It's all to their advantage: condoms go for a cigarette or a stamp on the yard. Fending off death is like a fringe benefit.

It's a new morning and, as I dress, Harold brings up the same old problem: "If only you were as committed to us law abiders, Annie."

"Please don't do guilt trip."

"Do you know what it's like for me out here?" I put my head on his chest and nod. He shouts, "No, you don't!"

I shake my head, try and grab his hand, ignore the reclamation.

"You're in a pool of sharks. Male sharks."

"There's always an officer within ten seconds of the ward, babe."

"Do you know how long ten seconds is?"

I whisper, "It's the safest position on the staff, Harold. I heal these men."

"Goddamnit," he says. "You're barely five foot one, Annie."

"Baby, you forgot the eight centimeters."

"You know what's going to happen?"

I shake my head again, try again with the hand, but it's too late.

"Callousness sets in."

"What do you mean?"

He looks up at me with deference, momentary role reversal. "Will you quit for me, baby?"

"Harold," I say, "this is a level II prison. It's not that bad. They don't even have cells in our yard, Harold. It's like dorm living."

"What the hell are you talking about, Annie? Damnit! You're so naive sometimes. That's ten times fucking worse!"

"Or," I say, "they're ten times less bad."

"Are there murderers in your yard, Annie? Rapists? Lifers?"

"They're mostly druggies."

"Are they *all* druggies?"

I answer his rhetorical question with silence.

"Will you listen to me, baby girl?"

Más dura, I think. "No."

Harold grabs both my hands. His are soft, clean, moist, effeminate lawyerly hands, the opposite of the hard, dirty, dry, manly hands of my patients. I've never liked Harold's hands. But I make the reclamation this time because I know a speech is coming. He convinces, after all, for a living.

"You don't have to work, babe," it begins. "Okay? I'll support us. Easily. Just stay home however long you want. Don't cook, only if you want. Don't clean, the same. Find a part-time job in town, full-time, no-time, whatever you want. Anything. As long as it's not at that prison. I don't want you spending even one more minute inside that place. Nothing good ever comes out of prison, Annie."

I can't say, "Some good comes out of the CMC," but, "There are some good people in the CMC."

"Bullshit. The inmates, cops. They're all no good."

I wonder what he'd think about my alias on the yard. "And what about the nurses?"

"Will you quit?"

"Baby, I was long at it before you came into my life."

"Well, I'm here now. I've been here." Then he demands, "Will you quit?"

I put his hand on the red alert button around my belt. "See, babe? I'm safe."

"I don't put any faith in fancy beepers. Or an empty promise. What the hell are we talking about here? They'll just sweep up the mess, ten seconds late."

"Can you not talk like that?"

"Last time: Will you quit?"

"Harold," I say, "you can have everything else but that."

"Shit."

I pat his knee. He sullenly pushes my hand away. "That's the one thing I keep, okay, babe?"

Too quickly, he says, "Okay. A big thing. But okay."

He's accepted it. I hate this part the worst. Harold shakes his head with that stubborn resolve which is prelude to either a maxim, a denunciation, a condition, or an ultimatum. I have a bad feeling that it's the last, an ultimatum, and I don't want to think about what's worse.

He says, "All right. That's fine. Okay. That's the agreement you demand. That's fine." He separates from me, stands up, his briefs at eye level. I put my arm around his waist and he grabs my wrists and forces my hands palm to palm, as if I were praying. "You've eliminated any notion of nobility on my part. That's also fine. I can live with it. But if that beeper ever goes off for real, I'm doing the exact opposite of my instinct to care for you. If something happens at that place, I will consider it a breach of contract, and leave."

"Harold," I say. "Baby. Don't talk like that."

"No," he says, squeezing my wrists together. "Listen. No. That's how it is. You made it that way. I'm wishing you well now, ahead of time, if it happens."

Thursday, 1341 hours

Compared to the majority of my patients in the ward, Roberto is still very strong. He is at the beginning stages of the virus. He has no scabs on his skin; he has no fainting spells; the stiffness in his joints is irregular. He can hold down most of his intake. The proof of a relative state of painlessness is that Roberto pays attention to affairs other than his own suffering. He follows world politics very closely, especially the Spanish-speaking nations directly south of our own, and more especially—on the scant chance that it makes international news—his native state of Oaxaca.

I can remember watching Roberto push his wheelbarrow in the fading dusk. The spring of 1996, mid-May. They were all out there, earning five cents a day, laying beds of cement for the structural foundation of the present E Ward Hospice. I stood at the window of my cave of an office in the soon-to-be-obsolete A Ward, and even from a distance through the diamond-shaped holes of a steel mesh screen, I couldn't help but notice Roberto. He was muscular, firm-jawed, of tall Spanish stock, tattooed olive green from the top of his neck down to the arms and out to the fingers. He had the Virgin of Guadalupe spanning the skin of his back. He still has all of those things, of course, stripped of the muscle mass.

Today the Bard snaps me out of my reveries. His real name is Dee Browning III, and he's insisted, for the two-and-a-half months we've cared for him, that we call him the Bard. He can recite and critique the Harlem street poems of Langston Hughes. All of the men tolerate his eccentricities to kill the dwindling time they have left in the ward.

So the Bard's lungs implode in a loud gasp on the bed. It sounds like the echo of a slammed door. His hands seize his deflated, shrunken chest. Everyone in the ward watches, including Roberto. Gloria rushes to the Bard, I rush to the phone, dial Dr. Newman's beeper. He's supposed to be in the North Yard checking patients, but you never know in this system. He might be here in fifty minutes, he might be here next week. Already, Gloria steadies the see-through, heart-shaped oxygen mask to the Bard's mouth, but it's no use. We aren't magicians.

Afterward, no one eats/drinks their Ensures. Not even Roberto. Dr. Newman's nowhere to be found. The gurney's three minutes gone and Gloria takes to cleaning the soiled bed on her knees.

I say, "*Bebe,*" and Roberto shakes his head. I don't say it again. He whispers so quietly I have to bend at the waist to hear him.

"Is that the way I leave this ward, Good Nurse?"

I wipe the perspiration from his forehead.

Thursday, 1809 hours

Before the fireplace in our living room, Harold rubs my stomach. My waist is about three inches larger than when Harold first courted me in the summer of 2003. He plants a kiss on the rim of my belly button. Then he says, "The hole in your belly is too deep."

I force a giggle.

"You should start to work out," he says, "when you're at work."

I want to say, "No one there is too fat," but instead, "Yes, Harold. That's fine."

He says, "I'm worried about your health, that's all. High blood pressure, diabetes."

"I don't have either condition, Harold."

"Not yet you don't," he says.

I want to say to Harold that we need miracles like weight gain in E Ward. My job descriptor could easily be Pusher of High-Carb Drinks on Inmates. The little suede boxes of Ensure are thick and rich as milkshakes, four hundred calories a serving, but, still, they don't come close to cutting it. The carb intake and perpetual inactivity always, in the end, end. You fight attrition knowing that you will lose.

But that's not quite the tough part: the reason there've been twelve assistant nurses and eight doctors during my tenure at the California Men's Colony is you've no time for recovery: The infected men are herded into the ward like malnourished cattle. And usually we get them pretty late. They're stripped to the bone, angular in the cheek, unable to eat even as they're being devoured from the inside out. In the long run, it works mathematically: if one arrives, usually one has left us. We hope for no more than that one-to-one ratio of near death to death.

In the short run, it sometimes hits all at once. Our ward peaks to twice its legal limit: fifty men pushing the bounds of medicine and architecture. The foldout cots are rushed in, the makeshift bunks and the bars, the CO's just barely astride it all, peeking indifferently in the door every fifteen minutes. I have to ask the healthier inmates—those least close to death—to change the soiled bedsheets and boxers of the bedridden. What can you do when the gates of life collapse like a house of cards?

The only thing left at the end, I figure, is kindness, and even that elixir seems to sometimes fail.

Thursday, 1849 hours

I didn't know back then, but I do now: I felt bad for the men. I was able to hide it around correctional officers and Warden Basil and temper it sufficiently around Gloria to function as a team, but I'd been drawn to the job because, in the end, I'm a nurse. I help the accursed, whomever they are, whatever they are, and leave the judgment to someone else. I felt and still feel motherly. Whenever I stop feeling that, I suppose it's time to quit.

Harold does not understand my point of view. "The formula is very simple," he says, as the oak pops and cracks in the faux-brick fireplace. "Do the crime. Do the time. That's life." Yet I know that Harold's job requires that point of view. He would lose his job with my outlook.

When he'd courted me in the summer of 2003, I thought our difference in life perspective would be a definite strength. Yin-yang, symbiosis, opposites attract. At our dinner dates, I learned about a whole other world I'd never known: boxing, *Brown v. Board of Education,* James Dean. Harold would rattle on and on over a dry martini in that eager nervousness of the informer, not quite sure if you were following the tale, and then worried, if you were, about your opinion. In my excitement over discovery, I let him know that I could follow him in his world without any problem. In seeing this, Harold never probed into my own.

Now he says, impatiently, "Let's go to Farmer's Market."

I love Thursday nights in San Luis Obispo. You've the best fruit and vegetables, the best barbecues in the state of California on one half-mile-long street. It's been a tradition of ours to walk it each week. Amongst the hustling mass of farmers, restaurant owners, peddlers, preachers, and breakdancers, it's easy to lose track of your problems. "Yes. Let's."

He says, "And we'll have a drink at Mother's afterward."

"Yes. Definitely."

"I wanna hear you say no," he says.

I cannot say, "You heard it from me this morning, baby," because he's already out the room.

Friday, 0601 hours

Gloria says, "How come no one falls in love with me?"

A few of the patients who've awakened slowly bring the beige plastic sporks of SOS to their mouths. It's a favorite breakfast on the yard—shit on a shingle—because it has real meat. I tabulate the sleepers so as to feed them later. I shrug, say, "Do CO's count?"

"Hell, no!"

I try to smile, then sip my tea. Gloria fills out the ward paperwork for weekly medication. She looks older than her thirty-five years. The deep frown lines, sloped crow's feet, tired, slightly jaundiced eyes are the signs of the drinking life compounded by the prison life. She never makes eye contact in a conversation, as if you were either held within hearing range by a tab and a barstool, or were a convicted rapist. She adds, "I couldn't stand their goddamned badges poking me in my titties, girl."

I smile, blow on my cup of tea. Gloria lifts a tablet of yellow paper. It's the kind inmates buy on canteen. She says, "Are you all right?"

I nod.

She says, "Look what I found in the head."

I try to feign interest.

She says, "A journal of Mercado's."

"Roberto?"

She says, "Yes," and lays it on the table with annoying seduction. I look at the first page, don't pick it up, say, "Are there any violations in it, any threats?"

She shakes her head, rolling her eyes.

I say, "Well?"

She sips on her coffee, squinting. Coffee, milk, juice, water: Gloria squints while drinking, squints while trying to build suspense.

I say again, "Well?"

She flips through it. "Just sappy crap," she says. "Kind lady, *Madre de Dios,* blessing of his life, all that typical shit. He probably left it there on purpose. He knew it'd get back to you somehow."

I say, "Well, it's his business. The CO's conduct searches around here, not us. I'm not going to have him sent off to the hole with an IV in his arm for something so trivial."

"So that's it then?"

I shake my head, think it over. "Well. Why don't you take over his charts, do his calories, Ensures, conduct checkups."

"And add to my workload?"

"I'll take whomever you want in the trade."

"Okay, but no needle work."

"Of course not," I say.

Sometimes we get surplus vaccinations and solutions from the state hospitals. Gloria calls us the Salvation Army of Health Care. Officially, on paper, only Dr. Newman can sign off, implement, insert. In reality, he doesn't care anything at all about it. I say, "That's my business, girl."

Gloria smiles, caresses my arm with the journal. She feels camaraderie with rule breakers. When she first discovered a box of condoms in the ward half a year ago, she kept it a secret for five months until she figured out the scam on her own through unidentified sources. When confronted, I was surprisingly cool. I told her of my mission to save lives and she slapped my hand and said, "Oh, goody, goody, Good Nurse, how could you?" Now she says, "He's gonna miss you, hot mama."

I think she's wrong. A man near death has nearer issues than crushes: bone-dry fatigue, nausea, weight loss, constipation, stiffness of joints. Yet it makes me feel warm inside that the same man, near death, has a little life left to hold onto something so hopeful.

Friday, 1521 hours

I get home from work to start our weekend together and first I think it's robbers. Then I think it's a joke of some kind. Then I know it's a breach of contract: I haven't been hurt yet. Half the house remains. Harold moves so fast sometimes.

Roberto plays his daily card game with Juan and Mateo. Since they've nothing to gamble with except condoms and the dreaded Ensure drinks, I let them play. Juan is an infected patient; Mateo is the condom runner for Mexicans in the yard. He'll leave at noon with a box of latex tucked into his boxer shorts. Sometimes they'll take a walk together around the miniature yard set up for our ward. Other times, they'll ask me if I need any help. I always say yes: One pushes a bucket of suds, the other moves chairs and repositions beds, and the last works the mop.

I ask Juan to give me his right arm for a shot of Epogen, and Mateo says, "In a minute, Good Nurse."

Roberto cuts the deck, holds half the cards in each hand, looks over at Juan. Why he commands such respect from his fellow felons, I will never know. Each day, Juan and Mateo report to his bunk in the far corner of the ward, seem to obey his nods in the games, and interpret silent orders.

Juan looks back at Roberto without lifting his head and says, "All right, all right."

Mateo says, "Hurry up, Juanito. *Estamos esperando, buey.*"

Juan holds his arm out across my waist and, as if the germs of his palm were hygienic, dusts the brown skin on the inside of his elbow. I find a spot between tattoos of a name and a sombrero, dab the cotton swab of alcohol, insert the needle. As the fluid drains into Juan's arm, I hear Roberto start to deal the cards. I detach and deposit the needle in the vial, cap it. I hold the flip side of the cotton to Juan's arm and seal the wound with a Band-Aid. He says, "Thank you, Good Nurse," and takes his dealt hand.

Roberto nods, his own dealt hand fanned against his two palms, says, "*Sí,* thank you very much, Good Nurse."

"You're next, Roberto," I say.

He nods with assurance, lays the cards facedown on his lap, says, "Okay." His arm is more muscular than Juan's but because it's practically solid green with tattoos, I have to make an educated guess at a good spot to insert the needle. I rub his arm softly in tiny circles. Juan and Mateo keep their eyes on their hands.

I start the procedure and Roberto says, "What is that stuff, Good Nurse?"

"Boosts your white blood cells. Adds antibodies."

He nods, says, "Are you doing okay today, Good Nurse?"

I don't know what to say. I utter, "You don't have to make a fist, Roberto."

He lets go. I hope that he doesn't ask again. He says, "You look sick maybe."

"No, no," I say. "I'm doing just fine."

"You have to take a day off maybe. *¿Porque eso trabajo es muy dificil, no?*" He puts his other hand over his heart. "*Aquí es muy dificil en tu corazón.*"

Mateo looks up from his cards and then back down, like he doesn't understand either remedial English or basic Spanish.

Roberto says, "I built this place with my own hands, Good Nurse."

I look down at my tennis shoes so as not to think on the irony. His own bare feet are shaking nervously.

"*Pienso que* it is time for you to maybe change your diet, maybe? Did you eat breakfast, Good Nurse?"

I safely cap the needle. "Roberto," I say, "I don't need anyone *here* worrying about me."

He looks over at the two men intensely, as if they're disobedient children. They fiddle with their hands shruggingly, keep their eyes to themselves. I dab the dot of blood on Roberto's arm. He takes the Band-Aid from me and dresses himself.

I say, "Thank you, Roberto."

Mateo thrusts out the arm of his uninfected body for a shot of Epogen, then slowly lowers it when he realizes the bad taste of the joke.

Monday, 2129 hours

It's only natural, I think, to eventually lose the kindness. Daddy was a doctor who literally drove my mother mad with kindness. She would claw at his neck, spit on his back, choke him with his stethoscope, call him those very epithets she told me not even to think. She did everything to lure him out of passivity, but it never worked while she was alive. When she died of a stroke in '94, there was no time to grieve. I was a month into my thirtieth year, one relative removed from total familial solitude.

When Daddy and I lowered her into the ground, the spell finally went to work: My father actively set out to destroy himself. In just under two years, I watched him build up enough liquor mileage to contract extreme cirrhosis of the liver. He lost his job, our old house. By June of '96, he'd broken five vessels in his cheeks and his face was crimson like a pomegranate. Each week, each day, there was a blood cloud floating in the toilet, blood stuck in the drain of the sink. It took me less than a minute to find dried-up gobs in T-shirts, a blood pool in the plastic liner of the garbage can. Everywhere he'd hide little pockets of discharged blood.

On Monday nights when I'd visit him at his studio, he'd be slumped in the corner of the living room like a dead animal, mumbling consoling words to a picture of my mother. He'd see me and drop off to sleep, as if I were intruding on a private conversation. I'd clean up the mess, reorganize the photo album. I couldn't lift him into the bed, so I'd lay blankets over his shoulders and legs, check his pulse, kiss his cheek. Once he fractured my jaw when I asked him if mother would have approved of her daughter's newly unpaid position: caretaker of her drunken father. That was mean of me, against my nature. I was trying to force his hand, as Dear Abby had advised me, Desperate Nurse, in the Sunday edition of the *Los Angeles Times*.

What makes me most sad is that Daddy's unkindness came in a rare moment of sobriety. It was only 8:30 in the morning, and he was only one beer down. He swung his fist knowing exactly what he was doing. I told the physician the half truth that I'd fallen and landed on my face. He nodded, didn't ask me anything, handed over two weeks' worth of morphine, told me to ice for twenty minutes thrice a day, drink lots of milkshakes. At work the next morning, I was not asked a single question.

So Daddy saw my face and went to AA meetings in the gymnasium of the YMCA. It lasted for thirteen weeks. When the overseer for the sessions accused Daddy of being in denial, he quit. The other members had backed the overseer: no one believed that the cantankerous prune of a doctor—dead of a heart attack in two short months—had not touched a drop of liquor until the ripe old age of 56. No one even believed he was a doctor.

Tuesday, 0454 hours

Tuesday morning arrives like a blessing. Good things are on the horizon. Today I'd attached the rope of condoms around my waist in the vast middle of my master bedroom, the Dixie Chicks at full blast through the house. Harold's absence now means I have more space in which to dress and one less authority to sneak past.

I enter through the gates of the yard, flash my identification badge. Officer Giacomini nods, says nothing. The yard is empty at five in the morning. Families of crows are perched upon the dip and pull-up bars, black triangles in the black shadows of the five o'clock moon. I walk along the aluminum bleachers and drag my left hand in the thin stream of morning dew. It's a wonder that a place with blood-soaked grass and gravel can be so utterly peaceful for a whole half of the day.

I pass under the doorframe of the ward and Filiberta, the night nurse, is big-eyed with worry. She's two months into our program, and she'll last as long as her mother is alive. Two thousand miles away in Manila, Mrs. Maria Dagadon's health care can be directly traced to the California Men's Colony in San Luis Obispo, California. When she passes on, her good Catholic daughter will probably quit. She talks of going back to school and taking up culinary courses, specializing in Mediterranean cuisine. When she talks too regularly about her dreams, I'll say, "Hopefully that won't happen for a long, long time, Fili," reminding her of what's important.

I ask if there were any complications I should be aware of from last night. It's the standard question you're taught the first week on the job. Filiberta emphatically shakes her head up and down, says, "Yes, yes, yes."

I don't say anything.

She says, "One man die."

It's her first. I hold my breath, keep my eyes on her eyes. "Bunton," she adds.

I look out into the ward and see the empty bed in the far corner next to Roberto. He's awake as usual, intensely eyeing the ceiling. Bunton's bed is already cleansed and prepped for the next patient, the sheets folded tightly across the flimsy fold-up mattress. The bed up from Bunton's, nearer our corridors, is also empty. I say, "And Cyphers?"

"No, no, no," she says, a hand over her heart. "He's living. Alive. He's go home this morning."

"Oh," I say. "Good. I guess I missed his release papers."

"Yes, yes, yes."

She's rattled. I don't know what to do about it except dismiss the poor girl. "Okay, Fili. I'll see you later."

She nods, picks up her lunchbox and Thermos, heads straight for the door. Officer Giacomini looks in as she approaches him, nods as she speedwalks by, returns to his post in the yard. I key the lock on the steel file cabinet and finger my way to the B's. Bunton's charts are already gone. He's been officially processed for the last time, right under the bright red "Deceased" header.

Beauty comes in the strangest ways, at the strangest times. This morning it comes from the safety lights. They're suspended in a protective web of steel wires in the four corners of the ward, pushing out thin strands of weak yellow light. They stream against the gray of the concrete walls, the gray of lockers. At the feet of long-gone women stuck to the wall by chewed gum, my patients snore in the frame of darkness, silence rising from the floor beneath their bunks. The whole ward is wrapped in a still sheet of black and cobalt blue.

Maybe beauty comes with memories. The darkness of the early mornings of my childhood looked just like this. Daddy would sit alone in the living room for hours, believing that his family behind him was asleep, free from harm, safe from the madness of weeping. He'd conduct all those arguments with my mother that he couldn't ever initiate in her waking hours. Daddy never discovered his voyeur daughter. I would sit crouched behind the heater, torn by conflicting desire. I'd spy with cotton balls in my ears; I couldn't bear to hear an unkind word from Daddy's mouth, yet I wanted that intimacy of Daddy sharing, even from afar, his most private self. The ritual went on, the angry mime. What a testament of love: Daddy feared making a bad thing worse. When mother died, all that happened to Daddy was that his performance switched times, went public. I know what Daddy feared: I'm one of life's tiptoers, just like him, trying to keep the noise to a minimum.

Nearing the rear of the ward, I force myself to mentally ascend from all this internal sentimentality. Return to duty. Roberto is upright on the bed, back spread out like a canvas, the head dropped, a gloss of light sitting on his slumped, naked shoulders. He must have had a rough night, enduring in the body of another man the early signs of his own near-ing death. I'll ask him if he wants water or maybe some new sheets for his mattress, anything to lift his spirits. That's when I realize that Juan is also awake, sitting at the edge of his bunk across from Roberto's, rubbing his face with both hands. So death keeps you from sleeping in the end. Juan looks up from his bed, stands somewhat feebly, walks toward me, all the while looking back at the door to the yard. I say, "Do you need some air this morning, Juan?" and he says, looking down, "Yes," just as my own air gets caught in my chest.

I think, *Harold. Harold. Harold.*

Tuesday, 0459 hours

A hand yanks at my mouth from behind and Juan thrusts forward and puts a shank to the side of my throat, grabs at my belt and the red button, as I think, *God, God, please, please, please.*

He shoves me backwards by the face and my legs give out as I glide through the shadows on my knees. I can't breath, I can't see why. Another hand clutches at my lower back, lift-ing me, as Juan palms my breasts, and I think, *Should I? Should I? Should I bite the flesh over my mouth?*

In my ear, a whisper, "I kill you if you talk, whore, kill you."

I fall back into the arms of Roberto. He spins me onto the cold concrete floor behind his bunk with another shank or pen at my throat, his face gray in the gray light, teeth gritting, eyes wide open like bottlecaps, and I pull down on his hand and whisper, "Please, please, please."

Roberto pins my hand to the ground, the cold metal at my throat, and I see it out already, poking through the hole in the boxers. "Please, please, please."

He rolls me over to my stomach, pushes my face into the ground, and I hear from above, "*Vas, vas, vas.*" His hand runs down my back, my side. I can't push my hands into my jacket far enough. *Be calm,* I think, *be calm.* I find them deep in the pocket and slap the plastic on the ground—Slap! Slap! Slap!— whisper, "Please, Roberto, please. Please. For me."

He slits the hem of my slacks and I feel them open and let in the rush of air and it slides across my panties first, just as I shout, "*¡Escúchame! ¡Por favor, por yo! ¡Yo! ¡Yo! ¡Escúchame!*"

Roberto suddenly stops. He reaches underneath my stomach, whirls me about, sits astride my waist. *My God, my God,* I think. In the brisk hush of our breathing, he's ripping one open, fumbling with it until it's totally hopeless, and he cannot look me in the face. I hear the chains coming through the door, the orders, the sirens. Maybe he will die today after their momentum drops all his weight on my body. Maybe his last vision will be of me and not his mother. If he will ever cry again, it's coming now, soft as the murderous weapon hanging limp from his groin.

Thursday, 1930 hours

I shrink down like a transient in a snowstorm and weave between families of *paisa* farmers, surfers, couples from the university linked at the arm, turning sideways, slowly making forward space in tiny contortions. Main Street is packed from sidewalk to sidewalk. I pass the lines in front of Mc-Clintock's, Rosa's, Firestone's, and the Lionheart barbecues. The women and children solicit customers with fierce aggression. The last, Toole's Real Good Food, is by far the least popular, and I join the line of three customers.

It doesn't feel too much different to walk Farmer's Market alone. That's both sad and good. Our systems respond with astonishing expedience, the antibodies surge to internal bruising with the speed of light: we've all been thrown into this world out of the same dark void, and our insides don't ever forget. Well before Harold swing-danced into my life, I was accustomed to the pace and angle of loneliness.

The grills are throbbing clouds of smoke. Each barbecue has a big steel crank and chain for heat management, plus a chef with a hanging belly and foot-long tongs. Big plastic banners announce international bragging rights, first claims on certain cuts of meat, family recipes and secret marinades, extraterrestrial sauces. Toole's claim is, "We'll Bite Ya!"

Whenever we walked this strip, Harold always refused to give Toole's business. He'd say, "There's a reason no one eats at that one, Annie. It's demand-supply curve stuff." But the whole chickens, linked sausages, and thick cuts of red meat lining the outer rim of the grill's surface look identical to the meats of the other barbecues. I wonder if it's simply a matter of proximity, that this grill is last in line on the street, bad luck, and therefore attracts fewer customers. I wonder if it has something to do with Toole himself, whoever he is, and—if not yet dead—wherever he is.

I reach the front of the line and say, "I'll have a chicken sandwich."

The chef nods, snips at a breast in the middle of the grill, lays it between two toasted buns. Now that I'm so close to the barbecue, the popping sizzle of the meat possesses my ears. The heat warms my hands. All over, my bruised senses are tingling, coming to life. A small boy pushes his hand out and I give him the money. Then he pushes a paper plate out and says, "Here, lady," and I grab it. The chef drops the sandwich onto the plate, focusing for a split second on my swollen lip, and then quickly looks down at the grill.

I say, "Thank you," and he nods.

I start to walk away and he urgently calls, "No, no. Come back."

I do. This must be Toole.

"Try the sauce. This my specialty. I call it Toole's Revenge."

Before I can protest, he squirts it across the bread and closes the sandwich with his tongs. I say, "Thank you," again and start walking before Toole can offer something else.

I bite into the sandwich, commence down the street. The chicken is hot and tender, the sauce tangy with green peppers. I like the flavor, but I'm no objective source. The arrows of my sympathy have always been pointed in the direction of places like Toole's Real Good Food.

The crowd thins past the barbecues. There's more room on the street, and I can breathe a little easier. At a table of assorted vegetables, I buy a head of broccoli, a bundle of asparagus, and three baby artichokes. The lady says, "Try this one," holding out a tray of sliced carrots for sampling, but I whisper, "I want to keep the bag green" and move to the next table.

A man says, "The name's John, ma'am. John." His country manners make me purchase more than I'd originally planned. At a nearby booth, I buy a caramel apple. I nibble at the golden glaze. Harold used to say, watching me, "Why don't you just bite into it already?"

He called me last night. I didn't pick up, haven't in two days, not even for the appointed trauma specialist. So he left a message on my recorder: In the interest of justice, he'd said, he'd already recused himself from the state's case against me, assigning prosecutorial powers to an assistant district attorney named Espaniola. He'd given Espaniola the whole rundown of our relationship to demonstrate that no link existed between himself and my crime, so I shouldn't waste my time mentioning him. I am now a subject of the world that Harold so ardently believes in: his last words on the recorder were, "What's right is right, what's wrong is wrong. I must say I'm a little ashamed of you. And obviously I was right on a lot of fronts, Anne."

My own attorney says that I needn't worry about anything: Their case is jumbled by poor witnesses and vague circumstances. Juan Maldonado was a convicted thief twelve times over, a fact my attorney will hammer into the ears of the jury if it goes that far. ("And it won't go that far, I assure you, Miss Carrington," she'd insisted. "When something of this magnitude happens, they're forced to act. But in a couple months, they'll come to us with an offer. They just need some kind of plea for their stats. Weekends on the freeway, counseling, slap-on-the-wrist stuff.") And Roberto Padilla, in the winter of 1988, took with a pillow the life of Clara Padilla, his fifty-two year-old mother, as she slept.

What jury, says my attorney, would believe a convicted murderer claiming he didn't force himself on his nurse? A nurse whose philanthropy and decency compelled her to take a job in an AIDS hospice in a men's prison? Moreover, what sane woman would risk her life engaging in consensual sexual relations with an infected patient, or many patients? All that they have, says my attorney, is a question — "Why would any felon stop in mid-rape to put a condom on his penis?"—and a promiscuous, suggestive nickname, the Good Nurse. The law, says my attorney, is a series of believable syllogisms, and they just don't have a strong case for criminality.

The fact that a string of condoms was found around my waist, that Roberto held one in his hand when he'd been apprehended by correctional officers, and that sixty-eight other condoms were produced in the search of the ward conducted after the alleged fornication occurred—all of it will be substantially mitigated, says my attorney, by 1) the testimony of the assistant nurse, Gloria Mackowiak, 2) the slit in the seat of my pants, and 3) the bruises on my chest and my lip. However, since no precedential challenge of lifesaving through prophylactics exists in state penal history, I should prepare to be fired by the California Department of Corrections, who has every legal right.

"Assuming that you want the job back," she'd shrugged.

I'd said, "So many of them will die now. They'll shut the whole thing down."

"Look, Miss Carrington. It's time to think about yourself. They had a choice: Prosecute rape or prosecute misconduct. Look what they decided to do. They know it can go either way. It's CYA. They're cleaning house. They already have those bastards, so why wouldn't they go after you?"

"Okay," I'd said. "I know. I wasn't talking about them. I was worried about the ward."

"We have to worry now about your interests."

"I know."

"You have to understand what's happening, Miss Carrington. These people are out to get you at all costs. Don't cry. I know you've been through a lot, but it's time to get mean back. Take out your pain on them. You can't be kind to snakes."

Thursday, 1952 hours

At a fairly secluded street corner, I finally get through the caramel. I munch on the apple, waiting for the light to turn. I cross the street on the green, and the sidewalk up ahead is empty. I can feel the murmur of the market behind me. I pass the detailed, expansive glass of Mother's Bar and Grill, hear the juke at the door, don't dare look in. I put my head down, but bring it back up when I realize what I've subconsciously done. Don't be ashamed, I tell myself. Don't. I take in a deep breath of air, stride out. Just after the bar, a young girl in a black beanie emerges from Bubblegum Alley and stops me in my tracks.

"Hey, hey," she says.

I step back, point at myself with the apple.

She says, "Yeah, you. You heard about the Cal Poly lady hoops team?"

This year I haven't. It seems very unimportant. I shake my head no.

"Undefeated," she says, blinking rapidly. She seizes my bruised lip with her eyes, wolfishly smiles, nods. "They're gonna be in the college championships."

"That's good," I say.

I start to walk forward, but she's quicker than me. She sidesteps, still smiling, and plants herself in my path. She pulls a ticket from the front of her sweater pocket, twitches her head. The sweater reads, "Stay Out My Business." I look into the empty alley, then right back into her badly dilated eyes. "I can get you into their next game against Stanford," she says. "Just ten bucks."

She reaches into the pocket again, spreads the two tickets out between her thumb and middle finger. They look like a peace sign. She says, twitching, "Eight bucks. I'll throw in another ticket."

I know that she is lying. The women's basketball games have always been free at the school. I try to get angry at her dishonesty, think of my attorney's words, her admonitions. I envision my dead father, drunken forever in the ground, his rotting limbs reaching for the tomb of my mother. I want to get argumentative, like Harold would, speak with conviction on this gross injustice of wasting my time for a fix. I want to tell her, "Little girl, do you know where I work? what I've seen? what I've been through? what it means to be alone?" but the meanness in me is like something of another species growing in my belly: I don't like it because I don't recognize it.

the once-a-week performance

BEFORE THE VISIT EVEN STARTED, HE WAS WORRIED about the zipper. When his parents arrived, he put one hand diagonally across the crotch of his pants and waved with the other. Then he sat back down and waited for them at the table.

They hugged and his mother said, "Son."

"Ma."

"They made us wait two hours."

He looked at his father and said, "Hey, Pops."

"You hungry?"

"Yeah."

His father started toward the vending machines.

"Pops, wait."

His father turned back around.

"I can't walk around too much."

The brows of his father narrowed as his mother sat down, leaning across the table towards her son. The father sat next. "They hurt you?" he asked.

141

"No," the son said. "No. My zipper's busted."

The mother started to giggle, and the father said, "Would you shut up?" A family at the next table looked over until their own son told them scoldingly, "Hey."

The son's hands folded on the surface of the table. His powder-blue issues were ironed down and every button of the shirt buttoned up and the bottom parts tucked into his blue jeans. His collar button made the muscles of his neck strain, and when he swallowed or moved his head, the shoulders of his shirt moved. There was a long, ridged crease along both shirtsleeves covering the tattoos on his arms. His mother liked to play-talk with him and call them "tags."

"Can't you just tell 'em?" the mother asked.

"No," the father said. The son looked off, frozen. "They're not gonna do a thing for you. How long have you been coming here? How long did we wait?"

The mother appeared perplexed. She certainly knew how long they'd been coming, but still wondered how such a simple solution could be ignored. If something was broken, fix it. Like a tourist, she was genuinely interested.

The son said, "They'll send me back to the block, Ma. Make me change. By the time I get back, changed, released, searched, the visit's over. We only got thirty minutes."

The father said again, "How long did we wait?"

"Ohhh," said the mother, nodding at the connection. She looked around the table like a secret had just been told and everyone in the room knew whose it was. The father was mad at the time wasted explaining, and as she sensed it, the mother asked, "Well, how'd you do it, son?"

"I was taking a leak before y'all came, and when I tried to zip up, it got caught."

"Maybe you should keep your hands under the table, son."

"All right, Pops." Both hands went under the table and covered the busted zipper.

The father said, "What do you wanna eat, David? I'll get it for you."

The son raised his brow and dropped his head a bit. One hand came up on the tabletop, and then went back underneath again. Before he gave the long list of food, he said, "Thanks," and just before his father started to walk off, he said again, "Thanks."

They both watched him walk toward the vending machines and get in line. His mother said, "He worries so much about you. He wakes me up at five this morning and says, 'We gotta go, Mom. Those bastards'll put us in late. We'll never see our son. Let's go, Mom. We gotta hit the road.' In the middle of the night, David. He dreams about this place."

"Does he fall asleep when he drives?"

The mother laughed. "We both do."

"It ain't funny, Ma. You need to stop coming. It's too hard on you." He stopped right there, wanting somewhere inside to continue on.

"Tell your father. I tell him only once a month, but he insists."

"Your job is to keep him up, Ma. Make sure he don't nod off."

"You ever been in a car with your father for three hours?"

The son's hands came up on the table and then back down again. "Come on, Ma."

"I keep him up."

"Just talk his ear off," said the son. "Just be yourself."

One of his homeboys walked by and the son said, "Wassup, Jay?"

Jay said, "Wassup, D-Dog?"

Jay sat down at table 19 and waited for his people.

"Who's that?"

"Stop staring." The mother's eyes came back to her son, and they were playful. When he first got locked up, she'd said, "Don't lose your sense of humor," and he'd smiled at her naivete. "See," she'd said, the water of her eyes starting up. "See, you're smiling."

"The homeboys make fun of me 'cause of my visits," he said. "Call me Once-a-Week David."

The mother began laughing, then automatically put her hand to her mouth. She leaned towards her son and said, "I love you, D-Dog. I know you keep it all inside for us. I know these visits are hard on you, too."

"It just ain't reality, Ma, you know what I'm saying? It's like show-and-tell day. I can't go back to that hole smiling."

"Your father says the alternative's harder."

Immediately, he thought of all the homeboys back at the block getting visits every other Christmas. There were thirty-five tables for 2,500 men in this always half-full visiting room of the one and two yards. Except at Christmas, it never approached its capacity. During every visit he felt caught between two opposite poles, and today was no different: familial pride on the one side, fraternal empathy for the forgotten on the other. One dutifully came from the outside every week and the other came from the incarcerated element all around him. Which of the two was stronger, he didn't know. But both were inside him, vying for space. He left his hands in his lap and said, "You're right, Ma. I'll keep the show going."

"I know," she said.

In the unshrinking line of the vending machines, his father stood strong and silent. He was taller than the other parents, and his shoulders were wide and well developed. He stood tall and his face was placid, and he looked like a former inmate in civilian clothes. In his palm was a Ziploc bag of loose coins, held up in plain view. From the first visit, no one from either side of the line had to tell him that rolled quarters were potential weapons and thus not allowed. The son said, "He's got this place figured out better than me."

The mother nodded and said, "He's your biggest fan."

The son couldn't help smiling a bit. *I got a fan to cool off the flames . . .*

Officer Quintana activated the PA with his thumb. When it crackled, everyone looked toward the desk at the entrance of the visiting room. Kids stopped playing, couples reclaimed their hands, and those with poor vision unfolded their glasses and fastened them to their ears. Most of the inmates dropped their heads, some of the lifers looked off to the ten-by-ten-foot patio outside. When all movement ceased, Officer Quintana put his mouth to the microphone.

"Visiting will be over in thirty minutes. Thirty minutes. Bring all board and card games back to the counter. Picture-taking is done."

"He's a friendly one," the mother whispered. She hadn't seen him before. The son looked down at his hands folded in his lap. "He's a piece of shit."

"Don't say that, son."

"Okay, Mom. Won't say it."

The father came back with the three cans of cranberry juice and three hamburgers. "The bar-b-que chicken was out," he said. "I knew we should've gotten here earlier."

"It's all right, Pops. I'll eat the burgers."

They both got up and walked over to the microwave together. The son held his left hand low over the fly of his pants and, to make it less obvious, kept the free arm motionless instead of swinging it. Officer Quintana was watching him from the desk, just as he watched anyone else crossing the floor of his visiting room.

Father and son got in line behind an older *paisa* lady visiting her son. She wore the same ankle-length velvet dress from last week, and the rosary was still resting there on the slope of her breasts. The wrinkles around her eyes had depth and meaning. She nodded at the father, said something kind in Spanish, and he nodded back respectfully. They waited in line in silence and, when the little bell sounded, put the three burgers inside.

"This damn thing's overheating," the father said.

A minute passed and then another, and only two minutes left until the feast. The son grabbed a napkin from the condiment table. He chose his condiments precisely: two packets of catsup and one packet of mustard. He enjoyed the variation in the visit room, which absolutely did not exist in the chow hall. One hamburger would be eaten plain, and he would savor the flavor of real meat. The second would be eaten with catsup only, the taste buds still conscious of meat not processed, the first step toward the true completeness of a deluxe real-meat hamburger with catsup and mustard. By the time he got to the third hamburger, he always felt spoiled and undeserving.

The light on the microwave went out.

"Damn thing died," his father said. He tried once more just for good measure. "I knew we should've gotten here earlier."

The middle of the patties of meat was cold. The son said, "They're good, Pops. They're good."

At the table, the mother rapidly fired questions while he ate: "Have they locked you down this week? What about the Mexicans? Are they still at war with each other? Did Sharon write you back? What'd you eat for breakfast today? How's that lady you work for in the library— Mrs. . . . . Gilliam? Are you cold at night, son? Where's that guy Jay's family at? Don't they know the schedule by now?"

She just as rapidly answered many of them. "Well, I guess we couldn't visit you if they locked you down, huh? And you did call home twice this week. And you would have told me if Sharon wrote. I know you. Nope. I can see it all over your face. She didn't, nope. Oh, that's right, you don't eat breakfast today. You like to save up for our feasts together, don't you? That food is rotten. I hate that food, son. Oh, here comes that Jay's girl now. She's kinda cute. Done up, too. What's that Officer Quintana saying to her?"

The son ate with one hand, his busted zipper protected with the other. He kept eating and said, "They're gonna get married today."

"What?"

The father said, "They're getting married, don't you listen?"

"Well, where's the priest?"

They all three looked towards the entrance of the visiting room and the door opened.

The son said, eating, "There he is."

"What's that Officer Quintana saying now? Oooh, I don't like him. Look at how he's talking."

The priest went back out.

"Oh my god! He sent the priest off. He just kicked the priest out."

The father said, "They do what they want. This is their house."

The son nodded. In a very strange thought that he squashed immediately, he wished his father was inside with him. He switched hands eating, protecting the fly, over and under the tabletop. "It's too late for the ceremony, Ma. They gotta do it at the beginning."

"They still have fifteen minutes!"

The father smiled for the first time. "Shhhh," he said.

She heard it and said, "All you say is 'I do,' right, Daddy?"

The father smiled again, and chewing on his half-frozen deluxe hamburger, the son felt spoiled. He ate ravenously, tasting with all of his being and somehow not thinking of things. He was the efficient, eat-now-while-you-can-before-they-lock-you-down man of his father's living vision of manhood, and to his loving mother, the little boy who was still in there somewhere.

At last, the three hamburgers were gone and there was silence. The father turned serious.

He said, "Try to keep your head up and your hands clean, son."

Immediately: "Sometimes it's tough in here. This room ain't the real thing."

"I know, I know." The father looked over at Officer Quintana sitting at the desk, and then all around him at the bland white, yellowing walls. "This place is tough. Just remember we'll be back next week. Getcha out of there for a little bit."

"Let's go outside while we can," the mother said. She jumped to her feet and they feigned indifference, following.

The air was warm and temperate even as the evening came down on them. The cut of the mountain range behind the town of Avenal was blackening and the dust of the land in between the two settling, and though they could see it from the ten-by-ten-foot patio, it seemed distant and far. It had been a toxic dump for so long, this strange wasteland, that nothing grew on its own accord and no one built houses anywhere near the prison for reasons having nothing to do with the prison itself.

"Yeah," said the father. "I believe that. This land here was cheap. That's how the State of California works. Believe it."

"You don't know that, Daddy."

"Would you buy a house out here?"

The mother looked around like she'd never seen the sights of Avenal State Penitentiary before. "No!" she cried.

The son smiled. The father nodded. "That's right," he said. "The only people that come to Avenal are the ones that don't want to be here."

The son put his head down, and then told his father an additional fact. "This is the biggest prison in the world. Seven thousand mutherfuckers in here."

"My God!" the mother said.

"See, that's how this state is. There're more citizens locked up in this town than there are outside."

"You don't know that, Daddy."

The son looked off to the void where the mountains had been. They were now black and indecipherable as the flat toxic dust plain below and the vast sky wrapping itself around all of it. Things always turned dark fast. "I'm telling you," said the father. "That's how they get extra money from the state. When you got five thousand people, they give you money for five thousand people. When you get twelve thousand people, you get money for twelve thousand. Did that shit-for-a-town back there look like there was twelve thousand people?"

The mother said nothing.

"But what'd the sign say? 'Welcome to the town of Avenal, population twelve thousand.'"

The shatterless glass door of the patio opened and the mother's eyes brightened. She whispered, "There they are."

Jay and his bride-to-be huddled in the opposite corner of the patio. Ten minutes were left. They held hands tightly and her tears shined from the new moon. Suddenly a wind swept through the little space, but it was warm and brought no dust. The mother put her nose in the air and looked over at the couple.

"I want to congratulate them," the mother said.

The son said, "No."

"I know," the mother said, pushing his hand away. "I know all about this place."

Then she went inside and waited at their table. The couple looked back together. The almost-groom separated from his almost-bride and walked over. Out of respect, the father went inside to give them both time together.

Jay said, "Excuse me, D-Dog."

D-Dog said politely, "Wassup, homie."

Jay said, "'Ey, man, I didn't mean to cut into your time and all," as D-Dog nodded, "but your fly's down, homie. Zip that shit up. I saw Quintana watching you, and he ain't no joke."

"Damn thing's busted, man. That's why I been hidin' out."

"Oh, all right, all right."

"But good lookin' out, homie."

"Yeah," said Jay, and walked back to his almost-bride nonchalantly. D-Dog went inside through the doors, his hand covering the busted zipper.

At the table, the son patted hers with his free hand. "They're not married yet, anyway, Ma. Probably next visit."

She patted it back and looked up at the clock.

The son said, "You didn't have to go inside, Pops."

"You just don't like hearing him talk like that, huh, Daddy?"

The father quickly said, "No, that's the language of the land." He looked back at his wife as if she'd betrayed a secret between them. A little time passed, but when the father spoke again the undercurrent of urgency made it feel immediate.

"Not much time left."

They all three looked up at the clock.

The father said, "We got two minutes."

The mother started stroking her son's hand.

The father said, "You need anything, son? Need money on your books?"

"No, I'm good, Pops."

"Got stamps and letters, stuff to write with?"

"Yeah, Pops, I'm good." He smiled up at his Pops. "I got everything I need."

"All right, son," he said. "We'll be back next Sunday. Just keep your cool, son. You'll be outta here before you know it."

They looked up at the clock. The second hand kept rotating.

"Talk about something pleasant," the mom said.

"We'll be back next week."

"Do you still have your glasses, son?"

"Yeah, Ma. They're back at the block. Thanks."

"'Member when I snuck 'em in for you?"

"Yeah."

"Those cops hadn't the slightest idea. 'Member that, Daddy?"

"Yeah," the father said, patting her hand. "You did good, Mom."

The mother laughed. "I couldn't see, David. I've never worn glasses in my entire life. Your father had to hold my hand the whole way and guide me."

The son said, "Yeah."

"We had a good visit, huh, D-Dog?"

"Yeah, Ma."

"See, at least we made you forget about that silly zipper."

He lied just as he always had, nodding and looking up at the clock. "Next week," he said.

The unnecessary official announcement was made over the intercom. Everyone knew. "Visiting is over. All visitors make a single-file line at the door."

Officer Quintana rose to his feet. He was the only person in the room not being given a hug or waiting for one. He went from table to table and separated and scolded and gently moved mothers by the small of the back. A line formed up on opposite ends of the room. Many were waving, and in the visitor's line some women were crying, while in the other a few men squatted in their powder-blue issues and didn't bother looking over at all.

He hugged his mother and shook his father's hand, turning without looking into their eyes. In the line, his mother waved frantically and made a smiley face with her index fingers. To calm her down he waved back halfheartedly, neglecting the busted zipper of his blue jeans. His father looked over at Officer Quintana roughly pushing the chairs under the tables. The father pointed to his own slacks very slyly. The son's hand automatically came down, and his Pops nodded across the room.

Officer Quintana said, "Let's go. Gimme three."

They watched him off into the chamber leading back to the yard. When the door closed and they could no longer see him, their son was promptly shoved against the wall. The other two inmates were already stripping down, bent at the waist, trying not to look at each other.

Their tiniest movement made sound and echoed and they did not hear the collision because his back had hit solid, flat brick coated in yellow plaster. When they were finally naked, they looked up and heard Officer Quintana say, "You fuckin' puke. You think I don't know what's goin' on in there."

His hand went down to his pants in guilt, but the cop-hand was still on his chest.

"How long you think I been working here? You think you can take advantage of me?"

The two naked inmates were watching without watching, neatly stacking and folding and refolding their clothes. The idea of helping was nonexistent. No man helps another man naked.

"You think you're original? You think you're the first to try that shit? What do you take me for?"

He thought of his father and the visit. Wasn't he just talking to Pops, his number one fan, a minute ago? They were out there in line now waiting for the bus back to the parking lot, gathering up energy for the three-hour drive home. He felt unmanly pinned against the wall. But he wanted the visits to end in the way that they should, shaking hands with Pops and hugging Ma at the gates. That's why they came every week. He wanted the visits to end for good, and so he thought long-term, and boxed himself up in nothingness.

Officer Quintana said, "You're lucky I didn't make a scene in front of all those people. I should have ended your visit and charged you."

"You can't charge me for shit."

"Oh, you'll catch a charge now, wiseass. I guarantee you. Insurrection, flashing, unlawful sexual exhibi—"

"What?"

"I was watching you the whole time. Do that shit on your own time. You jack off in my visiting room and you catch a charge."

One of the inmates looked up conspiratorially, leaving himself entirely exposed. The other shook his head and looked away. Officer Quintana's hand came off, eyeing the two already naked men accusingly.

He said, "I was with my Pops, Quintana. And the lady was my Ma."

Officer Quintana started to speak when suddenly their son broke out laughing. The hand shot back to his chest, yet he didn't stop. He could see Ma in his mind at the performance next week, leaning across the table for the juicy details.

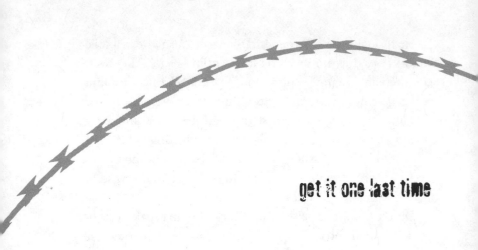

get it one last time

WHAT YOU REMEMBER ABOUT PLACES LIKE THIS IS THE first time. I'd gotten out the pen on a Friday afternoon and had forty-eight hours to report to my parole officer. I hustled out to the East San Jose Parole Unit that night, but everything was closed. So I went home and tried to sleep and came back Saturday, Sunday, but everything was shut down over the weekend, too. I was going back to the pen on a violation, was ready.

I rolled into the Unit Monday morning, absorbing the whole setup without even consciously trying, that's what institutionalization does to you: You've always got your radars going, like an insect. There were little framed signs up, the kind you find in convalescent homes: "Footsteps in the Sand" and "Chicken Soup (for Convicts)." Bullshit to keep you from thinking about the loaded deck of the system.

And an educational pitch from Bill Cosby. Touting a book by James Baldwin with the word "READ" at the bottom of the poster. Bill Gates, too. Really absurd stuff. The Microsoft billionaire is gonna save us cons from twenty-five to life peeking over the cover of *The Old Man and the Sea,* the eyes behind his specs zany with money. I'd read that good book twenty-six times in three years because they didn't have anything else to read in the East Block of San Quentin save Louis L'Amour and Sidney Sheldon, but I think it's a fair prediction that I won't be making too many pretty pennies on Hemingway, not now or ever.

And the ceiling sixteen feet up. An opera balcony jutting out from the wall eight feet from the ceiling. First consideration, anywhere you go in the system, is always the safety of the staff. If some pissed-off homeboy came stomping through the Unit toting weapons and swearing vengeance, the staff had a good distance on him, could appraise the situation from up top, rally and proceed accordingly, militaristically sound stuff. And then it doesn't hurt their cause either to assess your felonious ass from the highest soapbox in California, state-appointed Peters at the Gates of Heaven and absolute clout with God.

One Agent Abbott was assigned to me, and I waited there in the lobby for two-and-a-half hours. I thought for sure he was getting the paperwork ready to send me back. When he finally came out of his office and peeked over the balcony, it was hard not to laugh. He was so short, he barely got his head over the rail. He said, "Ulufale," and I said suspiciously, "Yeah," and he came down the steps and out the door to the lobby.

He was just over five feet tall, a little bearded midget. He grabbed my arms and said, "Hey, hey, hey. You're a big one, aren't ya?" I followed him up to his office. At his desk, he said, "What are you, Samoan?" I nodded. "They let you grow your hair out like that, huh? Don't want to tie it down into cornrows or braids?" I shook my head. "Hey, hey, hey. I dig

Afros just like anybody else." He never said a word about the forty-eight hours and I naturally kept my mouth shut.

Abbott's claim to fame was his second uncle Jack Henry. Norman Mailer had gotten second uncle Jack Henry, a lifer, out of Sing Sing by writing a letter to both the governor of New York and the parole board on his behalf. Some probationary pardon was granted, some gift. One week later, second uncle Jack Henry then went and killed one of his bunkees in a halfway house, so his second nephew's big joke was always, "Now don't go stabbing anyone in the windpipe like second uncle Jack Henry, huh, huh, huh. All it got him was a sentence and a period, huh, huh, huh, get it, huh? Big scholar was killer second uncle Jack Henry." I'd read his second uncle Jack Henry Abbott's book once in the county jail awaiting trial and, probably to Agent Abbott's liking, could see no similarities whatsoever between the relatives.

Abbott would show up at my studio at seven o'clock Saturday morning and talk about Britney Spears's bubbly white ass until lunchtime. A lecture on all her videos and records, her hometown in some forgotten-now-resurrected map dot in the South, and her favorite food. How she helps kids and was a Mouseketeer and believes to her soul in the Almighty. Then after the feigned innocence of the fan club bullshit, as if by behaving humbly and being properly enamored of Britney he might one day earn himself into her life and her pants, as if she'd even be *interested* in one of these badged bastards to begin with, he'd get truly vulgar like the dog of the state that he is, saying how he'd love to eat a Big Mac off her ass, a Big Mac and super-size fries, how he'd love to eat her ass period. I never heard language like that before, and I did three years in Quentin. That bearded midget pervert went on for hours with that shit, me nodding in a kiss-ass cloud of half sleep. Then just like that he'd say, "Duty calls, gotta hit it, huh, huh, huh, get it?" and bounce out the door for the dollar meals at McDonald's. I always felt sympathy for the server ringing up his burger and fries. That's how I am, see: I don't forget what it's like to be down, whatever pinstriped monkey suit they got you wearing.

Now at sundown thin lines of brown light refract into the lobby and I'm waiting on Agent Hernandez. It's been a little longer than an hour and a half. When I came into the Unit at three o'clock, the secretary languidly clacked out Hernandez's alert number with her little dragons and said, "He'll be down. Sit down." She's got fingernails longer than her fingers and color coordinated with her eye shadow. Turquoise slop around her eyes, like a clown.

Three years of reporting to this joint and she never once gave me eye contact. Not even today when I'm sporting a T-shirt, shorts, and slippers. The only aspect I can find a semblance of peace in is that she treats every parolee like that, no respect for anyone on this side of things.

If doing time meant nothing to me, I could've lit into her on a rainy day. I know her story, the old reformation bit. I could've asked about the two tattooed teardrops beneath her eye, what they represented in prison, and why she didn't learn her lesson after the first term. Could've asked about the two upper canines she smoked away with the pipe, how she managed to kick crank—or if she ever did—and if she planned to devote any of the lump sum she made working for the cops to some much-needed dental work. If I was cruel, I could've asked if she'd be signing up for the laser tattoo-removal program in ten-step rehab. If she feels any guilt being on the other side and not doing a damned thing for us. Not even saying hello. If that ever bugged her.

But I didn't say a word, not once. Hell, I never even stood in front of the desk long enough to make her look up and say my name ("Do you want something, Ulufale?"). I just signed in on the roll sheet and said my PO's name and sat down in the lobby, my hands folded in my lap.

Today there's a brotha waiting, too, right across from me. He's got that hard-time look where nothing in the world can faze you. A true hard-timer's got nowhere to go or be, and as long as there's a roof over his head and it ain't leaking, he's lucky. He's got the patience blocked and molded by time. That's this brotha. Every molecule and fiber of his body is geared to wait. And he couldn't get at a shred of self if he tried. They take your pride first, that's where it all starts.

From top to bottom, the brotha sports Raiders paraphernalia, Raiders beanie, Raiders T-shirt, Raiders jacket, and, somehow, Raiders hightops. A mini-Raiders helmet on the top of the tongue where the laces are tied. He's reading his leather-bound pocket-sized New Testament out loud. He's gotten through the first two books of Matthew and now he's on chapter 3, just when John the Baptist appears on the scene. He doesn't care about my earspace: If I say anything about reading quietly, he's gonna prove he cares about my soul and offer up some text like old Herod offered the prophet's head on a platter. He's just waiting for one word, one little nudge from me to let loose. So I sit still, look up at the clock under the rail of the pulpit. Four fifty-six.

Some white boy rolls into the joint in a blurry blue-gray flannel, signs in on the roll sheet, and says to the secretary, "Abbott."

She's got a miniature television going on her desk. There's still half an hour of daylight outside, and she's polluting the world with an episode of Jerry Springer.

The white boy says, "He wanted me in today for a test."

"I'll call him down in a minute," she says, turquoise eyes on the screen.

"I'm a little late."

"He'll be right out," she says. "Don't worry about it."

"I ain't worried," he says, his upper teeth digging into his lower lip.

He sits down next to me, right under the Bill Gates betterment ad. He's a blessing in disguise, this white boy. The brotha-prophet marks his place, closes the pocket Bible, stands up and leans against the wall, right next to the Cosby-Baldwin betterment ad. He doesn't want anything to do with the white boy. So twisted in the head he plays the race games out here on the streets, only recruits God's children if they got some brown in their skin or a 'fro on their head like me, a full-blooded Samoan. Back in the block, we shower, eat, and walk the yard with brothas, and brothas *only*, but I don't play that shit anymore: As of two days past, I'm off parole. A free Samoan American citizen with voting rights restored and all privileges thereof including free speech and talking with whomever the fuck I want to, white boys, *eses*, and brotha-prophets.

I say, "That chump Abbott was my PO for eight months back in '99."

The white boy nods, looks over at the brotha-prophet.

I say, "Had three more PO's after Abbott. He wakin' you up every morning?"

"Yeah," he says in a subdued whisper. "Weekends, too."

"Damn," I say. "That chump's just looking for a friend."

"Yeah," the white boy says, "talks too much, too."

I think he might be insinuating something, so I put a halt on the bonding. Despite the restored free speech, I also got my pride to consider. To the institutionalized man who silently endures forever, a big mouth is a sign of weakness. But I can feel the freedom bubbling up inside and I just can't keep it down. It's the principle of deprivation at work: I didn't talk for years, see. "Oh, he's gonna ramble on for the rest of your time. It's gonna be the two of you and Britney till you discharge."

"Who the hell's that?"

"Britney Spears," I say.

"Ain't Abbott," he says. "You got the wrong PO, brother."

"Just over five feet tall, beard?"

"Yeah, but this guy's crazy for J. Lo."

"No, no, no," I say, recognizing immediately what Abbott's all about. "He loves that ass, homie. That chump loves ass. White girl, Puerto Rican, don't matter."

The brotha-prophet shakes his head piously, the white boy half smiles, still a little doubtful. Both silent. The brotha-prophet walks off and leaves his framed homeboys, Cosby and Baldwin, stands by the entrance of the door. He leafs through a rainbow-colored pamphlet that Seventh-Day Adventists were handing out on the street corner. It's no good to talk too loud in this place, and I understand it: Who wants to get pinched by association? Smiles, nods, and sniggers qualify for indictment in the ruthless cyclops eye of the State of California.

So I whisper like we're in a funeral parlor. "I ain't takin' no more of their shit, homie."

The white boy nods and hunches over towards me, appreciating the reduction in volume.

"I discharged two days back, homie. I called these bastards a month ahead of time, see, 'cause I knew they'd be late on my papers. Left a half-dozen messages with them, but you know how it is."

"Yeah," the white boy whispers, half-nodding. "Once I was doing three months for a violation up in Avenal. I get my papers and the date's three weeks off, too early. I tell them about the miscalculation 'cause I don't trust them a bit, even way back when. Especially. I'd rather do my time straight than get caught off guard. You build up hope and then get chopped at the exit. So I say to the counselor, 'Sir. By my figures, you're releasing me three weeks too early.'"

"Yeah," I whisper, "yeah."

"He's got the Cowboys-Redskins game going. He nods me off, saying, 'It must be good time, half time, third time, what else?' I say, just after he yells, 'Touchdown!' 'You don't get good time on a violation, sir. I haven't worked a day since I been here. Will you look this up for me?' He says, 'Yeah, yeah. Go ahead,' and I split. But you know what happened next."

The white boy's shaking a little, his teeth returning to the lower lip. He needs a fix, that's easy to see, nervous about his impending drug test.

"So the so-called release date comes and they tell me, 'Pack your shit, Jameson, you're going home.' Now what am I supposed to do? I'm telling you, brother, I got right to the gates— right to the gates—seconds from hugging my girl and my mother, and the cops grab me."

"They ran a check at the gate?"

"Yeah. That counselor never looked up a thing." The white boy looks around and then says almost dreamily, "I damn near picked up another charge for assault. Had to ommm my way out of not striking a cop just once, brother."

I whisper, "Or twice."

He smiles and I know I've got an ally on the level, someone who still has a little self left, despite what he's been through. It's almost like being back in the block, rapping with your bunkie after p.m. shutdown.

"'S the same thing here, homie," I whisper. "I been looking forward to discharge for three years. Been walking inside the pedestrian lines a thousand days plus. You know how it is. Never straying. Tuning out their lectures AOAP."

"As often as possible."

"These bastards want me here, any time, any day, I'm here, bang. They come knocking at my door in the antemeridian, weekends, Christmas, birthdays, I'm there, no problem. Never complain. Say I gotta piss in the bottle once a week, done. I'm putting pure 100 percent drug-free urine into the cup. Counselor, group therapy, fines, lawsuits, stay in the county lines, all that shit: done. I'm accountable, homie. Did my time."

"That's right."

"But where are these bastards when they owe you papers? Do they give you that shit on time? They catch you slippin', an argument with the neighbor, the woman, they send you back. Jaywalkin', sneezin', same thing. But do they do what's right? Are they straight up?"

The white boy shrugs, whispers, "Take it easy, brother. Ain't worth it."

"That's the point," I whisper. "I'm off parole. It's either worth it now or never. I told these bastards my release date four times, man. *Four times.* I have to tell them. Once a week for the last month, and they still screw up. I know the system: You're not out till you're out on paper. You gotta have the papers."

"I know what you're saying, brother," the white boy whispers. He sits up in his seat so it appears that everything I just whispered requires deep consideration. He's got prideless grooves in his face, beat-yourself-up frowns bunched in the middle of the forehead, two big slopes from the nostrils to the corner of the lips.

"But you know what," I say. The white boy puts an index finger up and kisses it. I remember, nod, and whisper, "I ain't trippin' on the fuckup, homie. Who the fuck am I to trip? Everyone fucks up, even these bastards. I just want someone to claim it and apologize, whether it's Hernandez, Abbott, or that bitch behind the desk. I want some fairness, goddamnit, some fairness."

The white boy's still biting on his lower lip, says, "You're scared, aren't you?"

"Huh?"

"You're scared."

"Hell, yeah, I'm scared," I whisper, looking over at the brotha-prophet under the frame of the door. He forgot about me years ago, minutes ago, same difference. "I'm scared these bastards are brewing something up back there. Went into the annals and found new charges to send me back. Nothing in the world ever cleans up your conscience. I done shit way back when, maybe they found something new at the last minute."

"No, brother."

"I never sketched like I have the last two days. What are they doing on me? What's the holdup, homie?"

He whispers, "I don't know, brother. Probably just late, caught in paperwork. But just try to take it easy. Don't let your mind run wild."

"'M past that."

"You don't want things to get any worse."

"Goddamnit," I say. "That's the point. I'm a *free* man: From here on out, things only get better, right?"

"Yeah, yeah, yeah," says the white boy. His lips are twitching now, fiending for something. He doesn't whisper any more: "That's right, brother. Good luck, man. Excuse me."

He gets up and blinks respectfully, walks over to the window and says, "'M gonna grab a smoke outside."

The secretary gives no response, eyeballs glued to her talk show. She doesn't know what it's like anymore to be nervous. When the insides sketch like the moments before a verdict. You push your chest out at the state, and you're gonna get it, rule number one. But she pushed all the gettin' it back into the gray-matter recesses of what's left of a crank-addict brain: she's on their side now, throwing her infinitesimal secretarial duties into the wrong side of the equation.

"Damn," I say out loud, "I hate that bitch."

The brotha-prophet shakes his head without looking at me. It's all about the rainbow pamphlet, the pulpit, and the brotha-prophet. He's like a mascot up in this joint, a standing fixture. He ain't moving for a long, long time. I think, *That brotha could pitch camp in a ditch of shit, and read his propaganda unfazed.* I hear from above, "Ulufale."

I look up to the pulpit and there's the bottom of Abbott's beard, fluffed out in spots, tended to. The mischievous, perverted, wiseass smile behind it, like a raw oyster hiding in a bed of seaweed. Abbott's munching on fries, what else? He says playfully, "What's up? I thought you discharged by now. Don't tell me you're back already."

A true free man would be amazed at his excess faith in the system. They just don't get it, these bastards. I say, "I've been calling for the last four weeks, and nobody's gotten back to me."

"Who's your PO?"

I look out the door, casually. The white boy's making smoke, fingers twitching. "Hernandez."

"What?" he says, moving his eyes downward from my chest to my waist to my feet, and back up. He smiles. "Going to the beach, Ulufale?"

I can't think of anything to say except, "Hernandez," and then, "No. I'm here to see Hernandez."

The oyster smile widens and I suddenly realize I've been standing at attention. Abbott says, "'Ey. Who's down there with you?"

"A white guy and a brotha," I say, sitting down right beneath Gates and Hemingway.

"Jameson!"

I don't say a word.

"Jameson! 'Ey," Abbott says to me. "Is he sleeping? Outside?"

I know he's looking for the white boy, but I can't be overtly cooperative with these bastards any more. "Who?"

"Jameson."

I look over at the brotha-prophet and, the same tone as Abbott, say, "'Ey. Are you Jameson?"

The brotha-prophet shakes his head in contempt, like condemnation on judgment day, returns to the rainbow propaganda.

Abbott shouts, "Jameson!"

On the patio, the white boy flicks his cigarette and comes rushing in. I feel a little guilty. Just as Abbott says to me, "Go outside and tell him to bring his ass in here," the white boy says, "'M right here, Abbott, right here."

"Goddamnit," Abbott says. He's smiling, chomping fries. "What the hell you doing out there, Jameson?"

"I needed a smoke."

"Legal, I hope," says Abbott.

"Yeah, yeah, yeah."

Abbott looks down at me, smiling and chomping. The white boy has now crossed the race line and united with the brotha-prophet in one obvious aspect: Jameson doesn't know me. He's got the slave posture down, humpbacked yet looking up at the pulpit, brow reaching for the top of his head.

"Why you late?"

"I got caught up at work. Boss made me scrub the floors over again."

Abbott puts a fry halfway into his mouth, eats it in three bites. Then he grabs a cluster and stuffs them into his mouth. "So why'd you go outside?"

"I needed a smoke."

"Not of the Indonesian persuasion, of course," adds Abbott.

"No, no, no," Jameson says. Then, "No."

Abbott lifts his head to the roof and starts to bounce and roar. I know he's smoked weed before, I can hear it in his laughter. Probably in the not so distant past, probably yesterday. He keeps on rolling, no piss test for Abbott. The little skin holes peeking through the beard on his double chin look like the torn fur of a stray cat after losing a scrap in the alley. Jameson follows Abbott's lead and lets out a fraction of a laugh, like a yelp. Only the brotha-prophet and the secretary are unfazed by the ranting, drawn into their own virtual unrealities, unconscious. In as deep a bass I've got, I say, looking up, "I need to speak to Hernandez at once."

Abbott stops laughing and puts his fries on the waist-high rail. He's breathing postmarathon hard, the little frown for me, contemplative. He looks down and says, "What?"

"I said I need to speak with Hernandez immediately."

The tongue comes out of the mouth, an eel from its tunnel, squirms on the bed of beard. He says, "Stay right there. I'll be right down."

"Good."

This is what I want: Someone from the state dealing with me on the level, where I don't have to strain my neck looking up. The brotha-prophet has his eyes closed in worship, shaking his Raiders-clad head at the tonal impropriety of my voice. Jameson's a lost cause, too, lips shaking so violently he's gotta contain it in a just-as-violent overbite.

I say to the brotha-prophet, "Can't see God's sunset with your eyes closed, homie."

"Just fine like this," he says.

The door opens up and it ain't Abbott. It's another PO, big as me, but unnaturally. This one likes D-bol–filled needles piercing his ass cheeks, steroid freak. He looks like a grape about to bust. Maybe Hispanic, maybe Melanesian, can't tell anymore when the skin's purple and bloated. He's got knee-high snakeskin boots and a big silver-plated belt buckle. His polo shirt looks like it's about to sever at the seams, two sizes small, one sneeze or cough and his pecs are ripping out the fabric like the Incredible Hulk.

But I ain't trippin', seen bigger, better forty-pull-up-worth homeboys back in East Block with nothing to lose but their life sentences. Seen guns, too, owned and fired them, German-manufactured Walther PPKs just like the one attached to his waist. He's got the cowboy look without the ten-gallon hat and his wild wild west. Without the even risk, too, the fair-fight draw.

I stand up for even eye level. That midget Abbott comes out the door next, along with Isumu, my old PO back in February–March 2000 till she got switched from violent cases to arsonists. I remember the crazy look in her eye when she told me about the move, how amped she was. I've seen cats on PCP look like librarians next to her look: She's got it now, that straight insane look, that's why I remember it all. I shake my head, realizing that all three PO's have business with me, step to the side of the cowboy. I say to Abbott, the gentleman I *originally* had words with, "I came to see Hernandez."

"Hey, hey, hey, Ulufale," says Abbott, stroking his spotty beard. He's got his gat showing, too, the holster angled in towards his body on a little shelf roll of fat. "What's the problem now?"

I say, "I've been calling Hernandez for the past month, and he hasn't gotten back to me once. It's very unprofessional. I expect more from him."

Abbott smiles through his beard, shakes his head, says, "Look, Ulufale. You're a smart kid. Never had a problem with you when you were mine. Why you want to get heated like this?"

"I'm not heated," I say. "I'm calm. I'm free."

"You want to stay that way?" asks the cowboy.

"I'll register my disappointment with Hernandez in person."

"Ha!" gasps the cowboy. "Send a note to the governor, son."

Isumu grits her teeth, triggering her eyes to grow bigger. She's like a little bulldog waiting for the command to kill. Almost like I never met her before, never earned a little space in her memory.

Abbott reaches out and taps my elbow. He says in a soft tone, the same soft tone he used to describe the holy nature of Britney's ass, "Maybe you had a bad day, huh? Got lectured at work, a fight with your woman—take off. Go ahead. Go home and come back another day."

I shake my head. "I came today and I'll see Hernandez *now*."

"Are you stupid?" the cowboy says, repositioning in front of me. There's one crazy yard between us. "Answer me that. Are you stupid? Do you see what kind of chance you're getting here?"

"I don't need a chance from any of y'all," I say. I straighten up, feel the breath in my throat. That crank-addict secretary is watching us now: She turns Springer down and I can hear the chair squeak as she leans back and repositions herself. I hear the wind from the door, too, and I know either Jameson, the brotha-prophet, or both, are out it. I turn and see the answer: It's just the crank-addict secretary, me, and the three cops now. Outside on the patio, Jameson and the brotha-prophet are on opposite rails, looking into the Unit. I turn away from the glare of their desperate faces and say to the cowboy, "I earned my chance myself. I'm a free man."

"Your attitude needs refinement," says the cowboy. The Cosby-Baldwin *READ* poster frames the purple, steroided veins on his temple and Abbott's slug mouth. I move my eyes to the other side and it's the same thing, another veiny cowboy temple, except for Isumu's own maddened eyes.

"You're wrong," I say, steadily. "I'm here to see Hernandez. That's the business at hand. I've left at least four messages with him and he ain't gotten back to me once." After a pause, I add, "So maybe I'm not the one with the problem."

"What?" says the cowboy, purpling.

"Hernandez is in the field," Abbott says. His voice is changed now, deeper. "He's out in the streets, so it's best you take off." I look over at the secretary and she shrugs. From the beginning, Hernandez was never even in the building.

"Well," I say. "I guess I'll have to get my discharge papers from one of y'all."

Abbott says, "You don't need papers. Once you dis—"

"Look," says the cowboy. Isumu takes a half step forward, her hand on the pair of cuffs on her belt. "I want you to listen to me really closely, okay? What you're gonna do first is stop talking. You're gonna listen. Then you're gonna turn around and walk out the door. Like we say. After you've come to your senses, you can return to thank the three of us promptly. Get it?"

Abbott says, the same deep voice, "You don't need papers, Ulufale. You think it's a goddamned degree? Once you discharge, you're off the fucking computer."

All my time in the system, I never heard that once: You always gotta have the papers: There's no other way. The con's on with these three cops. I say, "My life's starting today, Abbott."

"Start it tomorrow," says the cowboy.

"I can't leave without something in my hand."

"You're gonna leave," says the cowboy, "with something *around* your hands."

Isumu smiles a little, eyes big as quarters. Suddenly I hear the secretary's voice. "Ulufale," she says.

I turn around. She hasn't risen from the chair. Just leaning forward with her elbows on the desk. I turn back around and the three POs haven't moved. The cowboy's gonna blow up or pop or shoot. Isumu's got his back. Abbott's got hers. I'd rather look at the secretary. Her turquoise eyes are closed, as if she can't stand the sight of me. Everyone but the cops've got their eyes closed. She asks, "Will you listen to them?"

"'Ey," says the cowboy. "I don't care if you discharged your number or not. You're gonna turn around and split, either of your own volition or in chains. Feel me, tough guy?"

Outside on the patio, litter's blowing in a little circle at Jameson's feet. He's lightly kicking at it, head down. In the last brown of day, he's missin'. The brotha-prophet's reading his rainbow pamphlet, or pretending to, and it's damned good of him not to watch, goddamned good. The crank-addict secretary touches her teardrop and half nods adamantly. I feel everything collapse inside and for a half nod of a moment, anyway, I forgive her for selling out.

The cowboy says, "Do you get it or don't you?"

"I get it."

"Then get out of here."

I do what I'm told one last time in the Unit. Two of the three bastards are frozen, the other, Abbott, nodding his head at my exit. Not a glance at the secretary, I'm tight-lipped out the door. She says, "You don't need the papers once you're off."

The litter floats on the walk. I pass Jameson and the brotha-prophet, no eye contact between them, no eye contact between us. I hear Jameson offer from behind, "Think about tomorrow, brother."

That took courage, no doubt about it. The last time I needed those words was in the chow hall in Quentin when I couldn't get the food in my mouth. It was my baptismal prison meal, six years past. There were gunners up above on the rail and a deep grumble of five hundred men dressed just like me. But I wasn't like them. Not yet, anyway. I had a lot of time to change. The plastic spork didn't find my mouth in three tries. Luckily, no one saw it, faces in the menudo. I switched to my left hand and the same thing happened. I couldn't keep still. My hands shook like a drunk. Finally, I pushed the plate forward and away and folded my hands on my lap like a schoolboy. The cop walking line said, "Get up then," and I stood and followed him out the door. I was shivering all over the place and the grumble grew into an echo in my head. I had to tell myself to *think about tomorrow*, that each step is like a little promise of goodness to come. So two thousand tomorrows pass like an echo.

I reach the corner of First and Hedding, steady-handed as a mime. There's no full circle back to menudo in Quentin: I'm steady out the system, head up. I nod at the Seventh-Day Adventists packing it in. They're folding the legs of a table as evening sets, and all the filth they fear therein. They hold out a rainbow pamphlet and another handout and say, "Bless you," and I shake my head. "No. No." I push the button and wait for the flashing green hand and the beep. Haven't jaywalked in half a decade, will keep the streak going tonight. Cross the street within the lines, hustle to the bus stop, slippers slapping in the dusk.

They're probably high-fivin' right now back in the Unit, but what those bastards don't know is that meshing with freedom will be the easiest thing I've ever done. Maybe one day the big bad cowboy gets pinched for steroids, who knows? Maybe perv Abbott gets bitch-slapped with sexual harassment, finds himself peeking over the counter at a downtown San Jose hardware store hawking nuts and bolts.

Maybe Isumu gets checked by a lifer-to-be on PCP, two big black shiners under the eyebrows, her vision permanently altered. Maybe they lose some stock on the market, a tire blows out. Stuck in the rain. Or homeless. They'll know who to come to for advice.

In the recycled air of the free world, up into the warm stench of County Transit line 22, I'm one step ahead of everyone else. The tiniest triumph is sweetest for those who've lived defeat: I know you don't dictate fate. Not one convincing word against that mutherfucker, ever. Just gotta sit down on the bus and wait. When you can do that, it'll eat everything else up, like a virus. The reward's no expectation, no hope. Just a keen understanding of what it means to mess with things like pride when there's nothing left inside but the newly cleaned slate.

guts and viscera in the chicken farm

IN THE EARLY MORNING JUST BEFORE CHOW, THE stench filtered in through the vents and hung low over the homies snoring on their bunks. As it crawled along the walls, the cement wettened and awakened, sweating its own hidden toxins into the air and then taking on the newcomer to battle for space. It would eventually win out around noon when the slaughtering had been an hour done, but for the first five or six hours of day a man did not smell mildew in Building 230. Always, if wanting to eat, he awoke to the foul reek of evaporating chicken filth.

Of course, the homies improvised methods to counter the smell. The dope fiends slept during the day and tweaked at night. With the help of coffee shots the night went by fast, and became more a state of mind than a time of day. The wealthier addicts used speed. They demonstrated surprising frugality, saving coffee shots for the unpredictable times when visits were canceled, freezing all smuggling, or the predictable tossing of the lockers. While the plastic-wrapped dope floated in a Lysol bottle and the floor became an ant farm of sniffing cops, the fiends gathered and organized by the hot water sink, coffee bags in hand. Since no man could leave his bunk at night, dope fiends never got off their beds. Their olfactories still processed the smell of chickenshit, but their minds could no longer perceive that the rankness was bad.

Lifers had a different method, safer but requiring time to get used to. They had the time, so there was no real issue. Before lying down to sleep, two foam earplugs were compressed and reshaped into the appropriate size. This was done in a simple rolling motion between the thumb and index finger. Then the tiny orange corks were squeezed into the nostril to expand. At first most men had difficulty with the newness of the impostor in their nose, but eventually the practice became habit. Some couldn't sleep without them, a few learned to walk breathing through their mouths and never removed them, even during the day. They pitched shoes in the dust open-mouthed and studied law in the library with the lips forming a tiny O over their chins.

By sunup when all the selected tools of prevention were in the throes of service back in the block, Bernardo Sotelo was walking point at his chicken farm. He was the head freeman at Avenal State Penitentiary, the biggest and flattest prison in the world. The hexagon of concrete and wire had six yards of twelve hundred men, some of whom worked at the chicken farm. It sat in dust on the western periphery of two yard, condemned land the state of California bought cheap and built cheaper. Nothing was alive on its own accord at Avenal, not grass in the yard, not weeds on the roadside. You had to persuade life, get creative. Take charge and make it. Mr. Sotelo and his five thousand rotating chickens knew this, and in a way, they learned it from Mr. Willem.

The two had met four years ago because it was inevitable. Bernardo Sotelo was offered the official job of head freeman at Avenal State Penitentiary, an enticing enough title but a misnomer. Through the years the job had evolved into something more along the lines of head chicken farmer. On paper his duties stretched into laundry and canteen. On the real, he never saw either place. Justifying a budget was hardly a tricky thing at Avenal State Penitentiary, and something needing no disguise. What was more inconspicuous than public inaccessibility? Bernardo Sotelo humbly accepted the position, and the seven Sotelos picked up and moved from Bakersfield to Fresno. A pig farmer by trade, he envisioned little trouble in performing his duties.

The vision lasted almost a day. Things were going well at his chicken farm until Bernardo Sotelo noticed something. It was quiet. Save the squawking birds, there was complete silence in the building. Bernardo Sotelo had never been around a more untalkative group of men in his life. Especially at a chicken farm. He was by no means ignorant and had expected a different way of doing things in prison, but not a single man spoke. Not to each other, and not to him. It was like he wasn't there. It appeared as if things were being run very smoothly, but verbal communication was nonexistent. No questions or directives, just furtive nods. When the fellas got demonstrative, there was brow-raising and finger-pointing.

This annoyed Bernardo Sotelo for two reasons. One: technically, it was his chicken farm, and one likes to be acknowledged. Two: two days prior, he had been briefed by the sergeant to "expect anything from these scumbags, especially connivance. Believe nothing and establish control early on.

Once a single man detects an ounce of weakness, exploitation will occur. Trust me."

And Bernardo Sotelo did. He looked around at his newly acquired crew in their bloody powder-blue issues and thought, *They're up to something.*

He adjusted the identification badge on the front pocket of his flannel and dragged four fingers through his hair. There was a day in his life when he couldn't do that. As a boy, the grime was perpetually encrusted in the palms of his hands. He used to wear a baseball cap over his head, and under that a hair net. They'd start in the fields when the sun came up and finish when it went back down again. At home he'd bathe and put on a clean baseball cap so soot couldn't pass from hands to hair. Everybody had stained and callused hands, but filthy, unkempt hair was taking it to the next level of dispossesion.

Without anyone noticing, Bernardo Sotelo took a deep breath. He was walking across the floor at a steady pace when the air seeped out. He approached a pale-white peckerwood sitting on an empty milk crate. The 'wood was named Johnson, and his beefy hands caressed each other on the flat of his lap. When the new head freeman was virtually standing in front of him, he turned his hands over but did not look up.

"Why are you sitting here, Johnson?" asked Bernardo Sotelo. He had chosen Johnson for a reason: Johnson was the only worker whose name he remembered. Except for the "h," it was the same as the warden's.

Johnson looked up and lifted the red, freckled mitts from his lap. When he stood he was taller than the head freeman by half a foot. His blank stare befuddled Bernardo Sotelo more than his size. The head freeman knew there was something beneath that look worth exposing. He felt a surge of authority rise up in his chest. It canceled out the fear, like an adrenaline rush. He said, "Now why are you standing here, Johnson?"

Johnson did not answer immediately. The homies called him Bear, and for good reason. He always looked like he was coming out of hibernation. Plus he was big. He slowly curled his lip up. Bernardo Sotelo believed he saw a trace of mockery in the gesture. Out of the old nervous habit, he dragged the same four fingers across the top of his head. Johnson spoke and made a conversation out of it.

"Bathroom," he said simply.

Just then a door swung open and another peckerwood came rushing out. He fumbled with his work shirt and his fly was halfway open. Bear was watching the door as a favor, though coincidentally he did have to piss. Naturally Bernardo Sotelo knew none of this. He could only catch a glance of the worker who flashed by him head down. He turned back to Johnson.

"All right, Johnson," he said.

Bernardo Sotelo struggled with himself. At all times of the day there was a line outside the facility restroom. His intuition told him there was a reason for this, and that it was not a good reason. He checked for evidence of deals: latex gloves and balloons, errant smoke floating up from under the door. He eyed the pockets of the homies going in and out, and listened for rapid, multiple flushings of the toilet. Bernardo Sotelo knew something was going on. Yet whoever went in always came out, and alone.

The head freeman kept a watchful eye over the procedural doings of his chicken farm, but in his peripheral vision he kept the line of men for the john. Once he considered installing a hidden video cam like the one they'd been using over in New England, but couldn't think of a way to get the prison to pay. He'd have to use his own money, and he couldn't do that. Also, he was a little reluctant doing anything which he'd never been explicitly told he could do. He was sure of the support from the staff verbally, but on paper was another matter.

Still his men did not speak, and the line to the john remained. A week had passed and by now he had learned many names. He knew reputations and could relay with passable truth the details of the crimes of his more notable workers. All of these things he discovered without asking a single question. He was picking up on the finer nuances of prison life, such as addressing lifers as "mister" and never approaching a man from the rear. He once made the mistake of crossing up on the same assembly line northern and southern Chicanos, but not twice. He learned fast and read Warden Jonson's pamphlet only out of duty:

1. The lines: Mexicans from Southern California loathe Mexicans from Northern California, and vice versa. 2. The reason: A stolen boot back in the '60's. 3. In the event of a riot: Norteños fight with blacks, and sureños with whites.

Simple enough. The warden further said don't cater to the boys, but minimize problems by foreseeing problems. Bernardo Sotelo arranged his crew accordingly, using complete bias and perfect judgment. He understood that efficiency suffered when lines were drawn up by the homies that weren't already drawn. Inmate initiative was a bad thing.

There were several queens at the chicken farm, and on the seventh day Bernardo Sotelo approached the one he considered the friendliest. His name was Marge or Margaret, and he, like Bear, towered over the new head freeman. Big Marge had the biggest tits in Avenal. Somehow he had received from the streets a doctor's written order that each day during med call estrogen tablets were to be distributed to him at levels consistent with his size. As a result, in less than a few months Marge's round and manly belly shelved above it two lactating, oval breasts. They dripped constantly, and Marge was visibly proud. He had something on the other queens, and that explained his friendliness. Bernardo Sotelo believed him to be the least threatening of the resources available for information. He dragged his hands across his head and looked up at Big Marge.

The head freeman fumbled for words. "Excuse me, Mr. . . . um . . . I mean . . . Mrs. . . . well, yes . . ."

James Matthew Margherita was a lifer. He pushed his two barely restrained medical miracles out for examination by the head freeman. Ruby-red Kool-Aid outlined his pursed lips and blood pricked from the thumb was spread and dried on his cheek for rouge. Big Marge didn't wear eyeliner. And Big Marge didn't break the code of silence. Rapidly he blinked three or four times, a flicker of femininity. The ostentatious gesture made Bernardo Sotelo's stuttering worse.

"Yes . . . well . . . Mr. . . . you know . . . Mrs. . . . I was just wondering about . . . the line . . ."

The head freeman turned and hurried off to his office.

Bernardo Sotelo slammed the door and raked at his hair with both hands. Outside his office things were the same. Except for the chickens, all was quiet. No one had seen anything, but inside his head he heard laughter, waves and waves of it. Motionlessly he stood, his face flushed a bit, his back to the door. When only the monotony of screeching birds was left to hear, he turned and faced his chicken farm.

Through the shatterless glass of his office, Bernardo Sotelo saw Mr. Willem for the first time, though he had been there all along. It was surprising that the head freeman hadn't noticed him, because Mr. Willem's job detail as executioner was the most important in the chicken farm. He saw each and every bird just once, but he was the only man who saw each and every bird.

A dozen bloody things were happening around Mr. Willem, but he seemed to be separate from the others. He was working just like everyone else, but something was different. He wasn't noticeably large like Marge or Johnson, but his frame was sturdy, as though his feet were somehow connected to the ground.

Bernardo Sotelo could see in his mind the oil-drilling contraptions outside the gates of Avenal. The big steel hammers went up and down, tearing into the earth of his mind, soundless. Then the image stretched itself and he saw himself again in the fields, the baseball cap, his mother. The head freeman watched Mr. Willem work in wonder.

He slowly opened the door of the office and crept amongst his workers. There were a few passing glances at the head freeman, but nothing more. Everyone was working now, or at least pretending to, and despite their silence a steady buzz of action could be heard above the birds. Bernardo Sotelo looked over the men for a minute, arms akimbo. Then he approached Mr. Willem from the side and stopped a couple yards short of invading personal space. His hands searched for his hips, but the more natural he tried to appear, the more nervous he felt inside, and so at last he decided to just stand and watch as he had done behind the glass of his office.

Mr. Willem was hard at work. At sunup his day was half finished, and the chicken farm was bright now, active. Endorphins had kicked in hours ago. His two bloodstained hands were past getting into the groove; they danced, deathly, precise. The nimble ripping of the little carcasses was something Bernardo Sotelo could appreciate. Mr. Willem sliced into flesh, spilling guts and milking the blood dry with his hands. Despite the ravenous beauty of it all, the movement was mechanical. It was the blood and guts that gave it flavor.

Someone whistled from behind, and Bernardo Sotelo turned. Head down, everyone was working, or pretending to, and so he turned back around. Mr. Willem was wiping the sweat and blood from his brow with the sleeve of his forearm. He dropped his hands and they were dead at his side. Then Mr. Willem returned the head freeman's stare, but harder, as if he'd been interrupted and awaited an explanation. Whistles were issued by the homies for a reason. Yet there seemed to be an evenness in temperament to which the new head freeman could relate. Bernardo Sotelo found nothing to say, and so Mr. Willem stooped to his birds and the bloodstained hands came to life again.

The head freeman said, "Excuse me."

Mr. Willem stopped and stood and once again dragged his arm across his forehead. He seemed annoyed that there wasn't much salt or grime or anything else to wipe at. The head freeman matched the gesture, digging into his head, across it. He felt an almost obsequious respect rise up in his chest. Bernardo Sotelo looked down at the ground and said, "I thought I might ask you something."

Mr. Willem's hands pressed together palm on palm, as if he were giving a holy lesson. "*You*," he said, "don't ask *me* anything." Then Mr. Willem went back to work without any hesitation or thought.

The head freeman's chest filled with air and he struggled to let it out. He'd never been on the other end of such undeserved insolence, and he'd been working with pigs and chickens for the last twenty-five years. Automatically, his hand went for his whistle to alert the cop, but he checked himself. Bernardo Sotelo had a better idea. In a bureaucracy, paperwork always hurts you the most. He turned on his heels, plotting simple vengeance.

In his office, the pink slip was nearly finished when Bernardo Sotelo read

REASON:

He quickly checked the box to the immediate left of "Insurrective behavior" and then summoned Mr. Willem into his office. He made it a point to remain at his desk when he yelled out Mr. Willem's name.

He was just on the verge of roaring louder and deeper, "Willem," when Mr. Willem appeared under the bridge of the door. His head was shiny black, and after he lifted his sleeve to wipe at it, the same little beads of sweat came up again. This time the head freeman did not match the gesture. His hands were flat on the desk and full of anger.

"Close the door," he said.

The door closed and Mr. Willem stood at attention. The hands were lifeless at his side and his eyes were uninvolved except for the blinking. Bernardo Sotelo leaned forward in his chair and said, "I'm gonna tell you this one time, you understand?"

Mr. Willem nodded, looked down, looked up.

"This," Bernardo Sotelo said, "is *my* chicken farm."

Mr. Willem did not shift or move. There was a kind of cooperation in the nothingness that the head freeman did not miss out on. Was this the same insolent worker who five minutes earlier was not to be questioned? The inconsistency of this strange man only made the head freeman angrier.

"My chicken farm," he said.

He jumped to his feet and charged past Mr. Willem into his chicken farm. Already there was a tiny line forming up at the john. From the moment Mr. Willem set foot in the office, the mysterious lure of the bathroom went into effect. Johnson was sitting there on the milk crate rotating his thumbs around and around. Two other peckerwoods stood behind Bear, and the one closest to the door arched on the balls of his feet. The anticipation on his face froze as Bernardo Sotelo slammed into the bathroom door.

The peckerwood inside said, "Goddammit, Bear." His ass was white and when he turned and saw the head freeman, his face lost color and matched it. Frantically, he grabbed at the belt of his work pants and slid in, hiding his erect penis as best as he could. His hands went to the buttons instinctively and when he zipped up a small tragedy was avoided by less than a centimeter. He tucked himself in and tucked in his shirt, and then shot his head up. "What?" he said.

Bear's thumbs were still in unconscious motion, but the other two peckerwoods leaned and shifted on their feet. One walked off, but Bernardo Sotelo had registered the face and frame. He pushed his chest out a bit. "Get out," he said. "All of you."

One did so immediately, and after the guilty peckerwood said, "Don't want to be in this mutherfucker anyways," he walked off, too. That was the most anyone had said to Bernardo Sotelo since he had claimed his chicken farm.

Bear looked up at the head freeman, finally registering something. "Bathroom," he said, and then he stood and somehow found his way around the head freeman. He headed back to work in a slow and certain manner.

Without any investigation of the john, Bernardo Sotelo closed the door and returned to his office. There was a satisfaction in his chest, almost a victory of sorts. Bernardo

Sotelo did not believe in prophecy, but he knew that never again would he have to worry about the magnet in the john. It was one less concern in his chicken farm.

The head freeman leaned back in his chair and put both hands behind his head. Mr. Willem was back at work, apparently oblivious to the major political events that had just occurred. He was partially hunched, but the ecstatic flight of his hands suggested bodily comfort, and one forgot. By now the anger had subsided and Bernardo Sotelo breathed normally, watching Mr. Willem. His hands were like the shadows of birds, twin angels of death. They swooped in and out and then back in again. The strange beauty of the process seemed to parallel the man himself, and this made the head freeman reach for the pink disciplinary slip on the desk. He looked down at it, thinking out loud the five words that had started it all: "*You* don't ask *me* anything." In disbelief, his mouth opened up a bit, and then when the realization came, it clamped shut. He looked up at Mr. Willem, and then a cutting glance to the newly vacant space around the john.

My God, thought the head freeman. He crumpled the pink slip dead in his hand and tossed it into the garbage can. *That's the first time anyone here's ever helped me.*

From then on, the men of Bernardo Sotelo's chicken farm ended their silent ways. Any time the rare need for speech came about, they opened their mouths and spoke without reservation. The pointing and brow-raising became signs of emphasis. Without the issuing of any official directive from the head freeman, Johnson removed his milk crates and the line to the john vanished. A few of the homies still used the two-by-two for self-gratification, but they moved fast and never posted a lookout as they'd done before. The new head freeman could barge in at any moment.

Four years passed and Bernardo Sotelo established a reputation for hard efficiency. There was the inevitable outburst from a disgruntled homie every other week, but nothing the head freeman couldn't handle himself. He was direct, in charge, and if the old doubt began creeping into his psyche, he disguised it cleverly with an order. True to Mr. Willem's words of wisdom, Bernardo Sotelo never asked an inmate for anything, and only occasionally were the cops summoned en masse. The two regulars always had a good dice tournament going in the back of the chicken farm, farthest from the feathers, blood, and guts. Their rule was the same as any other man at Avenal State Penitentiary, badge or no badge: Do not disturb.

The forgotten fixture of Bernardo Sotelo's chicken farm was Mr. Willem. He had the highest pay number available, but no one ever guessed who the three cents an hour went to because chest-thumping invariably accompanied those types of positions, and Mr. Willem never boasted. His numbers were right there in the books, but somehow the hardest-working man at the chicken farm went unnoticed, even by the head freeman. Mr. Willem was very simply an assumption. He had never missed a day in the four years since Bernardo Sotelo's arrival, and he was always on time. Of the men who had maintained the boycott of silence during that long baptismal week at Avenal, Mr. Willem was the only worker who still did not speak.

But one never doubted that Mr. Willem was alive. He was no dope fiend, no dead man walking. Mr. Willem was forgotten until a new hiree was brought into the chicken farm. The hiree was given a soiled apron and work issues and a pair of worn-down steel-toes, and then immediately ushered to watch the mystical hands in flight. With a lack of emotion, they'd say, "This the man you wanna talk to." The hiree would sit and watch and a bit longer before the novice eyes could see something. He'd follow about for a couple of days, and then at last go on his own way convinced that with enough time at Bernardo Sotelo's chicken farm, he too would perform like Mr. Willem. A few workdays later and the time with Mr. Willem was a distant memory, not even something to shoot for.

Today Bernardo Sotelo sat in his office and, for some reason, watched his best worker. There was nothing new in what he saw. Yet as Mr. Willem tended to his daily duties just outside the head freeman's office, Bernardo Sotelo had to remind himself that it was the same old thing. It was easy getting swept up in the silent authority of the deathly dance of Mr. Willem's hands, as if he too were being led to the slaughter. This simultaneously disturbed and enthralled the head freeman. The chickens corralled around their executioner almost affectionately, *and in a way,* thought Bernardo Sotelo, *that is the ultimate homage.*

Suddenly the head freeman turned from the glass. *Never again,* he thought. *I won't ever do it again.*

Tomorrow came too fast, and the head freeman was unable to abide the thought. As determined as he was, he broke the promise. Every time he looked out in the direction of Mr. Willem's work area, all self-control subsided and he became the spectator. A few times he circumvented the area in what appeared like a random, casual stroll, but inside he knew the reason the pattern existed. It bothered him deeply.

Why do I care about this man? What do I know about him? He's my best worker, the best I've ever seen. He ain't a scrub like the rest. Let him do his thing.

The irony in the thought irked the head freeman. Mr. Willem was the one worker never requiring supervision, and yet for the last two days the eyes of Bernardo Sotelo had remained fixed upon the laboring fixture. The head freeman impulsively stood, dragged the single habitual finger across his head, and imperiously advanced to the door. He called out, "Mr. Willem!"

Mr. Willem looked back, released a bird, wiped his hands, walked. As he neared, the head freeman's hand went to his head, and remained. "Come in," he said.

Mr. Willem stepped inside the door of the office and planted himself, standing. His apron was the soft brown of autumn, his hands the black of night. The blood had stained itself so deeply into his blue jeans that they, too, were black, only to be equaled by the second pair of work issues in his locker back at the block. He looked up and then back down again. "Close the door," said the head freeman.

The door closed and Bernardo Sotelo pointed to a magazine on the desk. "That," he said, "has got a lot of good stuff in it. You'd like a magazine like that."

His best worker looked at it briefly, the latest issue of *American Farmer,* then back to the floor. The hands hung black and obsolete at his side, but the head freeman could not make out the outline of fingers. The backdrop of blue jeans was just as black, blacker. The enigma that was Mr. Willem had a magnetic effect on anyone courageous enough to look. Since one felt himself being drawn in deeper and deeper, few bothered putting themselves in that position to begin with. Bernardo Sotelo's head dropped to his steel-toed workboots and he thought, *What is it with this guy?*

"You know," said the head freeman, "there was a day when I, too, couldn't say a word to anyone." His eyes narrowed like a conspirator's. "I know what it's like to be on the other end of things."

Mr. Willem did not blink or nod or show any type of confirming tic or gesture, and this made the head freeman speak again. He looked out of the shatterless glass at his workers. "Yeah," he said, "I spent fourteen hours a day in those fields. My brothers all ran off, but I stayed. I just passed the time dreaming about the day mama'd say, '*Mijo,* look at you. In charge. My little *jefe.* Look at you.'" Bernardo Sotelo raked his hands over the slickened sphere of his head once, then again, as he looked up at Mr. Willem. "It finally happened," he said, "but mama didn't say a thing."

There was a jumpstart in Mr. Willem's hands, a sign of life, and the head freeman misinterpreted the stir as empathetic support. He said, "Sometimes I look around and I can't believe I'm here. Had a hard time at it. Came a long ways. A hell of a time, but here I am."

Mr. Willem did not move, but he could see the chickens in his peripheral vision.

"You know I had this hat," continued the head freeman. "No. I had two. One I wore in the fields. One I wore at home. I used to think, 'Damn. One of these days I won't need a hat. I'll have a different crown, something real.'" The head freeman stopped speaking. "Mr. Willem."

Mr. Willem looked up.

"I wanna help you like you helped me, Mr. Willem. Look at me, how far I've come. I understand down and out, but I realized my dream. Will you let me help you, Mr. Willem?"

"With what, sir?"

"People like you remind me of the old days, how it was. When I watch you work, I can feel the soot on my hands, the grime on my fingers. You, too, can realize your—"

"Excuse me, sir," said Mr. Willem. He raised his head and his piercing black eyes met the head freeman's for the first time. Bernardo Sotelo's own eyes widened, excited at the prospect of a conversation involving his life and the guiding of another man's life. Almost in the intonation of an order, Mr.

Willem said, "We gotta get those chickens out before work change."

An empty silence filled the room. Bernardo Sotelo came back from the nostalgic intangibilities of yesteryear and into the real. Somehow he felt Mr. Willem's commitment to the job was an insult to his mother. Still, he could say nothing because he had freely exposed himself, even after understanding the risk. He knew well how things worked at Avenal State Penitentiary because he was an integral part of how things worked at Avenal State Penitentiary. And anyway, Mr. Willem was right: They had a job to do, and there was nothing between them worthy of discussion.

But even if there was, what then? Along what impossible path could something like friendship blossom between two men divided between the lines? Because that's what Bernardo Sotelo wanted, someone to share in the secret of his success, someone to whom the secret could be passed. He wasn't, in truth, even sure what the secret was except the sticking it out, the enduring, but he'd like to talk about it. There was an inhumane loneliness to giving orders all day long. That made perfect sense, but it didn't make things any better to Bernardo Sotelo, or Mr. Willem's silence any less disrespectful.

The head freeman rapidly nodded thrice, the first time to get headway, the next as a reminder of what he could never do again, the last to take possession of the thought. "That's right," he said. "Get back to work, Mr. Willem. Hurry up. You've less than an hour before work change."

Mr. Willem went out the door and the head freeman couldn't help himself. Again he sat and watched his worker work. The chickens rallied about their executioner confidently, as if cooperation erased all chance of certain death. Mr. Willem cut in and out and through the birds, grasping, clutching, slitting, each motion the living gift of precision, lifting the wordless, bloody vision of slaughter as close to a litany of words as possible. A kind of envy rose up, then an admiration, and then the envy again. The head freeman wrapped his hands around the *American Farmer* magazine, squashing the emotion in his chest, and then took to his chicken farm.

He passed Mr. Willem in the silence perfected through four years of solemn authority. The eyes were far beyond the area, impersonal, careful not to focus on anyone or anything. Without a word said the section behind him vanished, and Mr. Willem with it. He entered the next, packaging, populated by the whites of his crew. He walked by Bear at the end of an assembly line.

Carefully articulating each syllable, Bear said, "Good morning, Mr. Sotelo."

The head freeman half-nodded, the eyes well beyond the speaker, and muttered, "Johnson."

Everyone appeared occupied and hard at work; another typical day at Bernardo Sotelo's chicken farm. He came to the inmate locker-room, where Big Marge, his clerk, tabulated production statistics on a tiny desk bolted to the ground. The desk had been donated by the local elementary school, along with fourteen copies of *The Pastures of Heaven.* Everyone trusted Big Marge with the position of watchkeeper of personal property, and so Bernardo Sotelo had made him his clerk. Big Marge admitted to difficulties with the written word, but was a self-proclaimed whiz with addition, subtraction, and anything related to that type of mathematical calculation. Big Marge even did fractions. He automatically rose from the desk and said, "Mr. Sotelo."

"Mr. Margherita. Clear out and finish your work in my office."

"Sir?"

"Get out."

There was a moment's pause, like an accusation, but not much. Big Marge looked down at the magazine tucked into the waistline of the head freeman, and then pranced through the door. In one hand he held delivery figures for the week, while he rested the other hand on the slope of his hip like a cowboy at a duel waiting to pull his gun. His breasts bounced when he walked, as did his stomach. In the ear of the first worker out of earshot of the head freeman, Big Marge whispered, "Guess he's doin' a search, sweetie," and then made his way to the office.

The head freeman circled the room several times before peering out the door at the dice game going on behind the building. The two cops didn't look up. The dice hit the board and bounced around and Bernardo Sotelo heard "All day long" as he closed the door. Moving to the middle of the room, he dragged his hand across the top of his head. He looked inside himself once and once about him, searching in vain for something he did not find. Instead, he found the locker assigned to

Willem J23486

and without looking about this time, opened the steel state-issued lunchbox resting above it.

IN J POD of Building 230, two lifers were discussing the latest.

"You heard about Old Will?"

"Nah."

"Cops stripped him down at work change. Caught 'im with contraband."

"What'd they get?"

"A mag."

"Nudie?"

"Nah," the first lifer said. He shook his head. "A farming mag.'"

"A what?"

"A farming mag.'"

"Man, shut up."

"'M serious. Ya-Ya works that shift. Told me everything."

"What's that fool thinkin'? He been working with chicken-shit for ten years, right?"

"Yeah."

"Well?"

"Ya-Ya said Old Will just stood there. Didn't say nothin'. Cop opened up his box and told him, 'Put your threads on, homie, and don't come back.'"

"Damn. And here I thought Old Will lived for the chicken farm. Heard a gang o' stories 'bout that mu'fucka."

"Yeah."

They both turned their heads and saw Mr. Willem at his locker on the other side of the pod. They could see the broad width of his back and shoulders beneath the black shine of his head. The palms of his hands were pink from the soap and wash, and the calluses had been trimmed by a friend with a razor. There was no bodily evidence that Mr. Willem had ever been a part of the chicken farm. The second lifer asked, "You gave him some plugs?"

"Yeah, but he don't want 'em."

"What?"

"Says he likes the smell."

"What'd you say, nigga?"

"I said he likes it, homie. You know the old saying, 'Can't help a lifer do life.'"

"I know it, live it, but I still don't want chickenshit crawl-ing up my nose 'fore chow."

"Yeah. Well."

They both looked up at the vents where the unrelenting stink came in every morning, and then back over to the other side of the pod. Mr. Willem reclined on his bunk and lay his hands flat at either side. The second lifer shook his head.

"But all right then," he said. "'S his coffin."

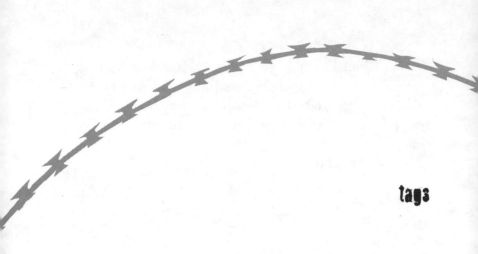

tags

EVERYONE HAS TAGS. RAMBO HAS R-CRIP ON HIS NECK, by the ear. He's from Long Beach. He wears the crest of the University of Tonga on his arm and tells everyone in two yard he went there, even cops. Around his traps he has a tagged wreath of puka shells, an ink-green lei that fades near his chest because the ink was cheap shit Face stole from art class. Rambo never did a tour in Vietnam, but he's done two terms in California, the first in Chino State Penitentiary, the second in Avenal State Penitentiary. He's fired machine guns before, too, AR-15s and MP5s out the sliding steel door of a 1984 Dodge van.

Except for B-Dub in Three-Block, Rambo's the biggest mutherfucker in two yard. Six-foot four, 280, no fat on Rambo. Sometimes he pushes his weight around, but I knew the first day we kicked it together he was afraid. He was watching me smoke the heavy bag and he said, "Hey, Pika, let's cruise the

194

yard, *uso.*" So under all the muscles, he wanted to be seen with my knuckles. Just like everyone else, he's got a little pocket of fear. That first week he told some of his crip homeboys, pointing at me, "This mu'fucka put eighteen hands on you 'fore you even cover your face, cuz." I'd say, "Nah, I'm mellow," and Rambo'd shout, "Next world champion, two yard, Avenal."

Face is tagged up, too. He's got a teardrop beneath his eye, a killing he never told anyone but me about. I never wanted to hear the story from the very start, but I heard it anyway, just like I hear everyone's story. Face wears his name across his arm in cursive—*Leapaga*—and it looks very professional, as if it was done in the streets at a tattoo convention. In a combination between standard Old English and typical Polynesian block, he wears *SAMOAN* across his chest, and underneath that, in the same cursive on his arm, is the name of his daughter, *Tali*.

Even when the Central Valley sky blankets two yard, Face is laughing. He's a fool. Every other mutherfucker fighting for air, straight suffocating under the covers, and Face be laughing for days. Any bullshit the cops are up to, any drama from Mexican factions in the yard, all of it's one big joke. He don't care if anyone sees the gap in his mouth. Face was smoking his enemies in the streets, that's what he always says, and smoking away his upper front teeth in some back-alley crank house, that's what we all know. Face is a dope fiend. Twenty-six years old, looks like he's forty. He confesses under heavy prodding from the homeboys and some *lelei* in his system, he confesses laughing.

He gets *lelei* from his girl on visits. He passes it around to us no charge, then sells what's left over at a good profit to Asians and brothas. So he's the main man on the yard for weed. Everyone but white boys and southern Mexicans goes through Face when they want out of this place through a cannabis cloud of smoke.

Face has a system with his girl. Before getting searched on the visit, she rubber bands the baggie of weed to her braid and pushes it up to her scalp, then slides it down the braid in the women's head, pastes it to the back of Face's neck under the jheri curls when they kiss before the visit ends. He always says, laughing, "My weed's clean, *uso!* From Lani's head to my head. None of that smuggling in the snatch or the asshole like Mexicans!"

Face is from Hunter's Point, Frisco, and claims 415. That means he's always making catcalls in the middle of the yard, a little tribute to the Point.

"Hootie-hoo!"

Some brotha from South San Francisco'll yell back on the other side of the yard, "Hootie-hoo!"

Tut'll say something like, "'Ey, Face. Who you down for, cuz? The Point or the *usos?*"

"The *usos,* cuz. You know!"

"*Salapu* with that shit then. Shut up, fool. Chill with that hootie-hoo shit, cuz."

Laughing, Face'll rip off another one, and some other brothas'll hootie-hoo back.

Tut'll say, "You turning this yard into a zoo, cuz," and Face be laughing, *lelei* smoke blowing out his black hole into the black Avenal night.

Tut has more tags than all the homeboys combined. He's doing double-life for homicide. Pure green ink from his neck to his belly, all Tut's work done inside the walls. Authentic shit. When you look at Tut, it's like reading a book, story after story on his skin. Spearfishers deepsea hunting for octopus. Taro farmers knee-deep in mud. Dead and living family members' names, dates, and faces to match, thinly detailed tuberose slithering down the list. Tut's a living, breathing mural of time.

He crossed states, too. Locked up at thirteen, booked for armed robbery in Halawa Heights, Hawaii. Whenever the homeboys complain about Avenal, Tut'll talk about butchering cows in Ko'olau Boys Home on the Ko'olau Range, the green mountain slopes steep like walls and disappearing like vapor into God's clouds. You never see the top. Tut killed eight cows a day, chopped the head off right at that midpoint between the ears where a cow'll twist its head for a tickle, the little bell ringing at its neck. Tut says it always took three or four strokes, thick like firewood, could never do it clean, not once. He'd kick the head into a ditch and watch the green ground turn red wherever it was still green, still bloodless. Tut can't eat meat, even eighteen years later. It's all about kipper snacks with Tut, sardines, oysters, and all that good canned shit from the sea.

"Gettin' back to our ocean roots," Tut says, covering up the real reason.

Face blows smoke into the sky, then sings it, "Back to our ro-oo-oots, nigga. Back to our ro-oots."

I FOUND THE PICTURE in an old Samoan mythology book Pops bought at the University of Hawaii bookstore. He'd sent it in my quarterly package, following, bless his heart, the eight pages of prison regulations to a tee.

Tut had seen it and said, "What's that crazy shit, *uso?*"

"Maoris," I said. The picture took up the whole page. "They're landing in Samoa to take the island."

"Mu'fuckas," Tut said. I smiled. Tut nodded, put an index finger above his eyebrow. "That's gotta go up on my head, *uso.*"

I said, "Yeah, yeah," raising my yet-to-be-tagged brow.

Now Frankie's saying it's sin of the worst kind to get a tag when you ain't a real high chief elected by the village elders. "It's no good. Wrong. Bad luck. Only *matai* get *tatau*. Only high chief have *pe'a*."

I ask him, "Are you for real, homie?"

Frankie Aulaumea's one of those fobs who got off the boat in Carson and, a couple days later, broke off some loudmouth American in an eight-second fistfight, straight paralyzed the cat with his bare hands. So he pretty much walked right down the ramp of the boat into the LA County Jail. Got no lawyer, no money. Frankie thinks it don't matter. The *mea'uli* called him a name, the *mea'uli* put his black middle finger in his face, the *mea'uli* got *fasi'*d, just what he deserved. Punched twice in the mouth and, for emphasis and a reminder to never disrespect again, kicked once in the ribs on the ground, swollen, unconscious, leaking face in the gravel. That's how things are settled back in his east coast village of Amouli, Tutuila, the territory of American Samoa, straight Old Testament law Polynesian style, a black eye for an insult, done. So Frankie thinks it's all good, poetic justice served, cross-legged on the floor of the filthy, airless LA County Jail, chewing on his American cheese-and-mayonnaise sandwich while niggas hoot and holler around him, shout, "Don't say nothin' nigga! That fool'll snap your bones like a rubber band!"

Seventy-hours later, the public pretender walks into the lawyer-client cell, skips on the compulsory translator after Frankie nods to "Ow-lamb-ee" and nods again to "Can you speak English?" The public pretender gives the facts. Confess and he'll plea bargain a fifteen-year sentence down to eight years with half time. You'll get a strike for the assault. INS gets you afterward, a separate immigration issue, nothing I can do about it, you'll have to deal with it then. The guy's in a wheelchair, this the best you'll get. Okay? Good. Just say "Yes" when we get into the courtroom and I tap your shoulder. Frankie the Fob, blinking that stupid fresh-off-the-boat blink with the extended overly humble pause, pleads guilty, "Yes," no contest, "Yes," *tōfā soifua,* good-bye and God bless for fifteen hundred days behind bars, Ow-lamb-ee.

For the most part, Frankie doesn't talk to the homeboys, kicks it on his own in two yard. Pisses Tut off a good bit. Tut always asks me why I shoot the shit with Frankie, and I give him the truth: "I was born here, *uso.* East San Jo. He learns me a gang of stories about our people back home."

"Yeah?"

"I like his stories, man. And we can't forget our own people, *uso.*"

"I got family back there, too, homie. Used to go back every summer."

"Nah. I'm talking about Frankie, man. Right here. Can't forget about him, can we?"

Tut can't say a word to that because Frankie follows the basic rules the dumbest cat can pick up on in the pen: he eats on our side of the chow hall, he showers at our spigot, works out in our little spot at the bars. But he does his thing without ever acknowledging the car. He doesn't talk to Rambo because Rambo's Tongan. "Tonga. No good. Tonga kill Samoan. Three hundred years. I kill Tonga." He doesn't talk to Face because "*Kele kaukala kama.* He talk too much. Like black. *Mea'uli.*" He even skips out on Tut, our shotcaller, because Tut's all tagged down and, as I said before, only the high chief traditionally gets tags in Samoa. Sometimes Frankie looks bad for our car, our people. Like if Frankie don't respect our car, and he's supposedly riding with it, why should anyone else respect it? The cats in two yard pick up on little shit like that, and if need be, exploit it.

For some reason, Frankie talks to me. All I got is my last name—Fusufusu—on my neck and a tribal band on my forearm.

So I tell him, "It's changed now, right? Everyone gets tags? Even in Samoa. My cousin in Pago Pago has tags. All the way down his arm to the tips of his fingers. So what," I say, "whatchu got against it? Plus," I say, "Tut's our shotcaller, our high chief, our *matai* on the yard. You make us look weak, homie."

Frankie says, "Listen, Pika. You know what *matai* is?"

I nod.

"No," he says. "*Leai. Matai* don't break laws. He make laws."

I nod so he'll keep talking.

"And *matai* is master with story. Tut tell story?"

I shake my head. "*Leai.*"

"He not *matai.*"

I say, "'Ey, man. I'm talking about tags, homie. Stick to the story, *uso.*"

"Listen. You said tag? What is that? Tag? I talk about *tatau.* The *pe'a. Loa tatau?*"

"You mean tattoo?"

"*Tatau!*"

I shake my head again. "Nah, I don't know no *tatau.*"

Frankie puts his face up to the concrete roof of the block and laughs out loud. I look around right quickly. No one but the peckerwood librarian caught it, a harmless mutherfucker who reads Virginia Woolf all day on his bunk. Frankie asks-accuses, "*Tama Samoa?*"

I say, "Yeah, mu'fucker. That's right. I'm Samoan. What?"

"Listen," he says, pointing at his ear. "No talk."

TO REALLY APPRECIATE TAGS, you gotta go back to the days when American, British, and German missionaries rolled into Samoa in the nineteenth century: They brought medicine to cure the measles, mumps, and influenza they brought. Plus lots of Bibles and priests. Things were changing like never before. Tagaloa, the great Samoan god, died within a decade. Not so great, I guess. Tagaloa went down hard. But it wasn't all bad. Later, when the twentieth century hit, they also brought delicious buckets of corned beef, and radios and televisions. Put up phone lines. Set up hospitals. Built beautiful churches. *Misi Katoliko* battled for Catholic space and influence with the London Missionary Society, *La Mo Sa*. It was all about doctrine: Put an end to that unspeakable practice to which Captain Cook fell victim. By the turn of the century, no one ate anyone else.

But not every Samoan vice was flushed down the drain of the Pacific. Thank God for that hardened foreign element, sailors, cons, and that certain American author who wrote about a hardcore vengeful whale. One tradition was kept, even as the all-Samoan congregation of both Saint Malia's and First Congregational Samoan Church denounced the savagery. This was the ancient practice of *tatau*, a rite of passage reserved for a newly appointed high-talking chief, the *matai*.

FACE FINISHES DRILLING into Tut's forehead. He cut the picture in half so it'd fit temple to temple. He eliminated all the backdrop of ocean, sky, sun, birds. The bottom of the picture is what he wanted. Just the Maoris coming up the beachfront. Tut, too. Tut had said, "I don't want none of that sky and birds shit on my head, *uso*."

Face sang, sharpening the needle on the gun, "None of that skyyyyy shit, nigga. None of that sky-yyy shit."

I'm waiting on my visit from Moms. Just got back from giving blood to the FBI, DNA in case I escape or get out some day and jack someone's house. Tut sits up, a red-and-purple rash across his forehead. Face gives him a beanie, and Tut pulls it low on his brow to cover the tag.

"What do you think, homie?" Tut asks Frankie.

"No good. Very bad for you. Bad luck."

Tut smiles. "I'm a convict, man. I ride with that bitch my whole life." Then he looks at me, like it's hopeless to rap with Frankie. "I'm gonna catch some z's, man. These tags wore me down."

He walks off and I know it confirms Frankie's belief that Tut's weak, doesn't deserve the ink. Over the yard PA, the cop says my name: "Fusufusu."

"All right, yo. I'll see y'all."

"*Tōfā*, Pika," says Frankie.

"Hustle me back a Pepsi," says Face.

I wait at the door of my dorm. Padilla says, "Let's go."

He escorts me across the yard in the torch of a Central Valley sun, telling me about all the big fights coming up, Bernard Hopkins, Johnny Tapia, James Page, what I'm missing locked up, why did I get locked up anyway, don't I see the errors in my ways, and even though I wanna say, "All those mutherfuckers you root for on Saturday night pay-per-view been locked up, too, bitch," I just nod really contemplatively at his therapeutic Dr. Phil wisdom, say, "Yeah," nod again when he pops the gate and says for the hundred and eighth time in the past two years, "Walk directly to the door. Do not knock on the door. Do not pound on the door. Wait for the officer inside the yellow line." For safe and humble measure, nod one last time, not even a trace of a mumble.

I walk a hundred yards under towering barbed wire and between two full-blooming rows of white lilies along the fence line. Some white boy lifer's project, planting and tending flowers until he dies. Every nanosecond of growth recorded from above for potential evidence, the only real proof of a life. I wait outside the door, keep my hands out my pockets and visible, peek in the window, see Moms at the table already, her own free hands folded on the surface, still.

I recheck my sleeves, make sure everything's fastened up like a straitjacket. I do not knock on the door, I do not pound on the door. Take my eyes off the camera, suspicious of myself, look out at two yard. Already it's filling with mutherfuckers doing their programs, slapping handballs on the concrete wall, rolling cherry-red dice palms down.

Inside I hug Moms and she asks me, "Did you get the book from your Daddy?"

I say, "Yeah, yeah," nodding for emphasis.

"Did you read all the tales and myths and did you like it?"

I say, "Yeah. Read it plenty times, Moms. Thanks again."

"What about the others? Your friends? Did they like it?"

"Yeah. All the *usos* send their love," I lie.

"*O'ai?*"

"Who? All of them, Moms. Especially Frankie."

"He's okay for you? What's his family name?"

"Aulaumea. He's from Tutuila. American Samoa."

She clicks her tongue, good Catholic from Western Samoa.

"Nah, Moms, he's okay. Lotsa good guys in here. They all said make sure you tell your Moms *fa'afetai lava*. Thank you for your hospitality."

"Good," she says. "Good. Are you doing your prayers? Your rosaries."

I nod, lie with my mouth closed.

"No *tatau*, right? Clean skin? You promise?"

All she can see are my hands and my face. I'm buttoned to the neck and the wrist, wrapped in fabric like a mutherfuckin' mummy. I nod with my eyebrows, "Promise. No ink."

"You should unbutton. It's too hot."

"Can't, Mom. Dress code," I lie.

Moms says, "How is your friend again?"

"*O'ai?*" I got no clue who she's talking about. I say it, tell the truth for once. "I ain't got no friends in here, Moms."

"Your Protestant friend from Tutuila. Aulaumea."

"This California, Moms. To hell with Tutuila." Aulaumea, too.

"Are you reading your Bible? Remembering your lessons? Keeping the rules?"

I put my head in my palm. "I got amnesia, Moms."

"What is that? Hah? Amnesia?"

She's worried. "Nah, Moms. Just playing."

"Are you sick?"

"*Leai.* I'm okay. Don't worry."

"Keep praying to our God in heaven. Remember your rules. And be good to your people."

THE YARD'S COOL in the early evening. It's me, Frankie, Face, Rambo, and B-Dub, Rambo's homeboy from the streets. I'm rolling dice on the wall, squatting like a Filipino, Frankie watching listlessly from above. Rambo and B-Dub are both drunk. They're leaning on the wall, talking nonsense. Rambo has his hair all blown out like Don King, and B-dub's is tied down into cornrows. They're like a before and after, blown-out chaos and rowed-down order. The two biggest mutherfuckers in the yard, getting straight faded on pruno.

I tell Frankie, nodding at Rambo, "'*Ōgā kama lea.*"

Frankie makes a clicking sound with his mouth, shakes his head. "*Valea kama.*"

"Come on," Face says. He understands the words of condemnation that Rambo, being Tongan or drunk, misses, and that B-dub, being a brotha, pays no attention to at all. "Roll, Pika."

I throw the dice, watch them bounce.

B-dub and Rambo have been brewing this batch of pruno for the past month in the chow hall kitchen. Letting it ferment with bread for yeast, tossing in oranges and grapefruit, rind and all, sugar packets, Kool-Aid. Letting fruit and sugar sour into alcohol. B-dub stored it in a big black Hefty bag in the vent by the cooler. The whole week prior, Face would fuck with him and say, "I don't want no two yard rats in my liquor, nigga," and B-dub'd say, "Awww, hell no. An orange a day keep B-dub dub kickin'! Gonna party Long Beach style, nigga! None of this Nor-Cal shit."

I take the dice from Face, give them a shake. I hear my name. Rambo's looking down at me, smiling. I nod back and he swallows half a cup of pruno. He puts his face to the sky, lets out a *fa'umu,* Samoan war cry, "Shheeeee-hoo!"

"All of a sudden," I say, "Rambo's Samoan."

He gets loud whenever Tut ain't around to keep him in check, starts pushing his chest out on the homies. Especially when he kicks it with other Long Beach crips. I say, "*Sole.* Keep it down, *uso. Salapu* with that shit, homie. Gon' bring heat from the *leo leos.*"

Rambo slaps B-dub in the arm. "Fuck them cops," he says.

B-dub, the brotha, lets out a Samoan war cry of his own: "Sheee-hoo!"

Frankie curls his lip, shakes his head. He don't want to be around the homeboys, listen to Rambo and B-dub's nonsense. But it's a mellow Sunday night, Fourth of July, and Frankie's just defended his two yard pull-up title, whooping out a tough thirty eight. Beat a little box of a brotha named Droopy by three. I was yelling out, "*Fa'a mālosi,* Frankie! Pull strong, *uso!*" And so I told him afterwards, "'Ey, come kick it with the *usos* for a minute. You made us look good on the yard, homie. Celebrate."

So he came, watched Face finish Tut's tag, listened to Rambo and B-Dub's clowning.

He's still here. I stay on the wall, shooting dice, thinking bad things, say, "Wanna shoot some, Frankie?"

"*Leai*," he says, looking back at the block, itching to leave.

So me and Face square off. Face says, "Gimme the money," and throws a seven. He looks over at me and massages his cheeks. He says "I am pretty. *Māgaia kama lea.*"

"Shit," I say, "Let me see you smile, Muhammad Ali. Let me see those pearly whites, Face."

Frankie smiles, eyes on the dice.

Face says, "You cold, Pika, you know I'm missing a canine," throws another seven. "What now, Pika? Gimme your money, dog. Give me that *kupe.*"

I take the *sikaleki* out from behind my ear, lay it under Face's knee. He drags it slowly beneath his nose like a commercial, says, "Ahhhh. Nicotine."

Frankie says, "Smell like shit."

Face says, "What?"

"All right, all right," I say. "My roll."

I grab the dice, toss them against the block wall knuckles up.

"Damn," says Face. Frankie smiles. "How you gonna throw a seven on me, Pika? I own that number. *Fitu*'s mine, nigga. Fours and threes, fives and twos, sixes and ones, that's mine, nigga."

"Don't ask," I say. "Just pay."

He rolls me the smoke and I shake the dice in my hand. "Big Gulps. Slurpees. All day long, Pika's gettin' served at 7-Eleven."

I roll a four and three, say in my best *palagi* announcer voice, "That is precisely what I'd spoken of earlier, young man. The chap is simply unconscious."

"Shit," Face says.

Frankie smiles.

"The bank's broke, Pika. Busted."

"You know I'm a credit man, Face."

Face sings, "I'm a creddddd-it man!" like that fat diamond merchant on TV back in the day.

I say, "Play on your word, Face."

"I'm broke, fool."

"No word?"

"Don't gloat. You got it all, Pika. Kool-Aid. Soap. And paper. Been wiping my ass with socks for a week."

"Whyn'tchu sell some of that *lelei?*"

"Ah, hell no!" says Face. "That's my greenroom, my lifeline, my Kona Coast, nigga."

Frankie squats against the wall. The game's done. He's whistling under his breath. I stand up, move down next to him, squat, look up at Face. He's slapping hands with B-dub. Other crews are walking the yard, cops under the goalpost watching Mexicans play soccer, shouting, "*¡Bola! ¡Bola! ¡Bola! ¡Paisa!*" The hand jive ends in a big hug, Face holding up Rambo's homeboy with his shoulder. Rambo and B-dub making fools of themselves, these two hardcore Long Beach crips.

B-dub looks down at Frankie like he's a lost dog. I know what's coming, say nonchalantly, "'Ey, Frankie, let's bounce, man."

Frankie stands up and B-Dub says, nodding at Frankie, "Yo, who's this nigga?"

I look over at the cops. Three on the wall of the visit room, checking out the lining of leather on each other's gloves. B-dub separates from Face and sloppy swim-moves over his shoulder, and just like that, he's all up in Frankie's business, breathing pruno into his face. I look over at the cops: still occupied, trying on each other's gloves. Rambo's smiling, slaps

Face on the arm. I step between them, just as Frankie spits on the ground at B-dub's feet.

"Chill, man. Chill," I say to Frankie. I'm trippin' on Rambo and Face, stepping back from the show like two cowardly civilians.

B-dub throws his cup of pruno on the side. "Wassup, cuz? LBC, nigga. Fob, mu'fucka."

"*Alu'ai kai, mea'uli,*" Frankie says. "Eat shit."

"'Ey, Rambo," I say. "Talk to your homeboy, man."

"Nah, Pika," he says. "Hell no. Not this time."

"Who's your blood, Rambo? Who's your people? Tell him to step off, homie."

Rambo looks off at the yard, answering my question. This the USA, where the old bonds get broken down. A couple other crips spot up on the wall across the way, already feeling the tension, watching us. I look 'em down like *This a Polynesian thing, don't even sweat it, walk on and do your own time,* but they keep right on peeping, unmoved by my eyes. Another little crew of crips are walking towards us, like sharks on blood.

I'm right between 'em. B-dub says, "Mu'fucka, you better recognize. B-dub slingin' them things. I'll drop ya' ass like doom, nigga."

"Fuck you, *mea'uli,*" Frankie says. "Nigger."

"Oh," says B-dub, nodding. "It's like that, huh?" He takes a step back, looks Frankie up and down, nods again. "Okay, cuz. You gon' get what's comin' now. Never sleep, never walk this yard. You better go volunteer with white boys, fob, 'cause you a dead man."

B-dub walks off, the crips on the wall rising, crips coming out the grass and pull-up bars, materializing dark out the darkness, like black dots out the Black Hole. It ain't the back of Rambo's 'fro that makes me worry, he's playing that crips shit from the streets, leaving his own blood on the wall, fuck Rambo. It's Face that worries me, quiet for the first time, not laughing or jiving. His 415 un-crip ass just looking off at the yard like he don't know us. That's when I know I gotta get as much out of Frankie as I can.

THE *MATAI* WAS anointed with sharpened boar's teeth digging into his skin like the fangs of a snake, hammered with a tap tap tap of the *matofi* board. Thousands of little holes for the soot of the candle nut to color. He had to take the pain, wince in silence. Laid up for two weeks minimum, straight paralyzed immobile, mutherfuckers carrying him like the king that he was to salt his skin in the ocean water. Sometimes it didn't matter: One in fifteen *matai*s died from infection.

The *matai* had to be a poet. Had to speak in metaphors, allusions, high formal Samoan. Had to fire out in a *kava*-influenced trance the very stories encrypted onto his flesh. That all Polynesians came from Samoa. That all the voyages from Samoa populated greater Polynesia. That the root of every Pacific-island mutherfucker who lives or ever lived is or was from *him*. No women allowed, just like the pen. Only the council of cross-legged men on the finely woven *fala* heard the stories on his skin. From the belly to the top of the knee, garnished with flowers and basketry, quad, ham, ass, belly, back, all the way around the midsection, Army tank green. Copper skin gone forever on one-third of the body.

THE TAG TURNS out cool, straight institutional art. On one temple, a beachhead sparkle with green dots. The dots are fallen coconuts. The beachhead slopes into a mass of solid green ink—the ocean—with little waves breaking on the shoreline. Damned pretty. Damned sneaky. If you focus on just the beach and the water, you'll miss the whole point of the tag. You'll think, *This poor mutherfucker tattooed some beach he's never gon' visit on the front of his brain.* Then you'll shake your head feeling bad for Tut, and that's when you see the ghost faces on the other temple.

The little ghosts have tags on *their* faces. Little spirals on the cheek that loop up around the eye and claw down the nose in hooks. All four ghosts have wheel-eyes, round in Maori fury, and all four ghosts have machetes in one hand pointing toward the beach, a paddle in the other. Everything else is black, but you know by the way they're lined up, the ghosts are seated in one of the old-fashioned canoes, the *va'a* floating through the blackness to occupy the beach.

Before he walks the yard on this, the first night of his best tag, Tut pulls his wiry hair back into a wiry bun so everyone can see it. The work took some time for Face to finish, and he's telling every mutherfucker around, including cops, about his skills with the gun. Tut, Face, Rambo, and me, circling the yard. Handball courts, infirmary, equipment area, softball · field. We pass peckerwoods, norteños, niggas, sureños, nazi low-riders, bulldogs, skinheads, skins, v-boys, paisas, all of them, and there's Face shouting about Tut's new tag. At the pull-up bars, Frankie don't even look over.

"Frankie's skin is clean," Face says. "Like his conscience."

Frankie's right in between niggas and white boys, like a buffer of brown. I say, waving him over to join us, "*Sole. Uō kākou.*"

Frankie turns his head, lips in a downward frown, lifts his eyebrows and his head, turns back around. Shuns my invitation to walk the yard, I can't blame him. He throws up his grip, starts up his program. We pass him and he's still at it, through the teens and into the twenties.

Face says, "That fool was born in a coconut tree. Muther-fuckin' monkey."

I say, "Frankie can whoop 'em out all right."

Tut puts his mouth down to a *sikaleki*, covers it with his palm, hits it with flame. The little fire lights up the pattern on his forehead like a tarot card. He blows smoke through his teeth. It drifts past the tag and out the bun of his hair.

"I'm gonna go talk to him, man," I tell Tut. "Don't even trip."

"Tell him wassup, Pika," says Face. "Give 'im the low-down, nigga."

"Yeah," says Tut. "Tell that fob he ain't shit."

EVEN COPS WEAR tags in two yard. Cops are the worst, the biggest, baddest gang in the pen. They have easy access to all them street artists, skip getting cut up from some makeshift tattoo gadget passed around by lifers for a fee. They wear *CELLBLOCK* on their forearms, gun-towers on their biceps. Some of the Mexicans put their last name, Escalante, Martinez, in slanty cursive on the side of their necks. They show it off to each other, or a trustee, or anyone. Don't have to sneak it on the bunk in the back of the pod. They get whatever they want done in some downtown Chinese tattoo parlor; just the same as in the yard, they get whatever they want.

White boys wear some wicked tags. Twin lightning bolts of the old SS, ghouls and goblins with eyes of fire. Cemeteries across the back, the old Gaelic across the arm. Fuck you right in the middle of their forehead. Elaborate iron crosses and encircled swastikas; some mutherfuckers put that shit right on their faces like a stop sign.

Mexicans are into Roman numerology. Northerners claim and tag XIV, southerners XIII. Hand, neck, face, arm, chest, cheek, earlobe, forehead, eyelid, back of the head, inside of the lip, straight Roman numerology. *Teines*, too. Sexy *teines* with sloping hips and big, round, perky tits. She'll have a sombrero on her head and a dagger in her mouth, like that sticker on a Raiders helmet. And all Mexicans slam their names across their backs, whatever they claim, shoulder blade to shoulder blade.

Brothas are fixated with cash, cold cold *kupe*. Dollar sign across the chest, maybe branded on the arm, *It's All About the Money* and *Gimme Dollar* all over their bodies. And dissing women, too, straight misogyny with brothas. *Don't Trust No Bitch,* and when they're feeling polite, *Don't Trust No Woman.* They balance the gender scale out. *Don't Trust No Man Either.* Crips and bloods have their thing, too, but since they ride together in the pen and unite against white boys and southern Mexicans, a brotha tends to bypass immaterial work done on the streets.

It takes just one little peek around two yard to see that every cat but Frankie Aulaumea's got tags.

IT HAPPENS THE next day. Little Buzz, the blood trustee at work exchange, tells me all about it. He don't have to say a word. I orchestrated the whole thing with Tut. A battery tag, of sorts. Planned it out when nearly the whole damned yard was gone for their weekly NA meeting. Tut'd been catching hard flak from crips, like, "Wassup with your nigga, Tut? That mu'fuckin' Nazi in disguise. Your car looks sloppy with that mu'fuckin fob bustin' out 'nigger' on niggas."

So Frankie got done, and that's it. No use talkin' about nothing. Even though I caught some good, authentic tales about tags, I don't owe Frankie shit. Or you can look at what went down like this: I saved that fob's life.

Tut and Rambo wanted Frankie stuck in the yard like a pig. Face shrugged and said, "End that nigga, he ain't one of us." But I took their hit down a notch, said, "I got a better idea, *uso*."

So some dope fiend from San Bernardino put a battery in a sock and lumped Frankie in the head when he was sleeping. Before it went down, I specifically told the nigga to make sure Frankie was on his back, not sleeping on his side, and to hit the target square, anywhere between the bottom of Frankie's nose and his chin. If he fucked up and drove the bone in Frankie's nose into his brain or lumped the temple as he slept on his side, we'd kill his ass. I told him that, said, "You'd better do the deed sober, nigga. Better get your aim on." But if he did right, did what the contract said, he had a pack of Camel *sikalekis* coming and free Kona coast *lelei* for a year.

In one swing, he broke Frankie's jaw and knocked out a tooth. Frankie nearly died choking on it. He rolled off the top bunk, fell five feet to the floor. The cops gave him the Heimlich maneuver, the tooth zipped out his mouth like a grain of rice, then they took him coughing in chains to the infirmary. Stripped every cat in the pod down to their boxers, and tossed all the lockers. They called back Tut from laundry, Rambo from the kitchen, and stepped in front the swing of the seventy-five-pound heavy bag when I was working it in the yard. They said, "Come with us, champ," and I did.

Nothing happened. We don't know Frankie, and he don't know us either. Maybe it's sad, like kissing an old relative for the last time, but it's the truth. Maybe I can't look Moms in the face at the next visit, but that's the way it is. The minute you set foot on American soil, your story's changed.

"We're West Coast," Tut says to Sergeant Dixon. "We don't kick it with fobs like Frankie."

We were all shot back to the block after the interrogations and threats from the cops. We returned to our business at hand, one less useless *uso* representing our car.

Over a shot of coffee, Tut tells me a story.

"There's a flatland planet called two yard where nothing ever moves."

Oh, shit, I think. *He's getting outer space on me.*

"The time sits inside your stomach, rotting. That's the purpose of the tag, homie. You put condemnation right out there for everyone in the world to see. Wear it like a badge on your skin, let the lead leak into your blood like heroin."

I'm mesmerized, more than a little impressed. I hit the bunk at shutdown thinking Tut might be a storyteller after all, a natural-born *matai,* green skin, pain, and stories at his endless disposal.

I dream of a boat at sea with Frankie at the helm. He's pushing into waves that shouldn't be pushed into. I wake in the middle of the night and see Tut. He's standing at the foot of my bunk, face ghost-white. I pop up, pull my hands out, think the worst.

"I feel like shit, *uso,*" he says. Then he walks off.

It's Wednesday morning and the tag goes straight to Tut's head. His cheeks are sallow, he's got no appetite. All day long I'm watching him turn down top ramen and kipper snacks, sleeping through chow call. We roll into Thursday and it's worse. In two days, he's shed fifteen pounds through sweat and not eating. It's like he went off with the skins and had visions in their smoke-filled peyote teepee. Friday, and he's straight trippin', talking about curses and hexes, all that Old World voodoo none of us believe in anymore. I tell him, "Put up a request to visit the infirmary." He says, "I did. The *leo leo* said I have to wait, just like everyone else." I hustle ice water from a connection in the kitchen, bring it back to Tut. He drinks it down, slouches into the corner toilet, pukes it back up. Afterward, he smokes a *sikaleki* in the yard, and I swear he looks like one of those nicotine fiends in a lung cancer ad, eyes and pores and teeth gone chicken-skin yellow. All in three days. Saturday comes and he passes out on the towels in laundry detail. They finally push him off to the infirmary.

Little Buzz comes back with the news: Tut caught hepatitis B from the infected needle of the gun. The cops wrote him up for an infraction while the doc pumped loads of liquid sugar into his weakened green arm. And propped on a cloud of pillows two bunks down, unafraid and tattooless, Frankie the fob was laughing through grit teeth, the metal bridle taut across his jaw like barbed wire.

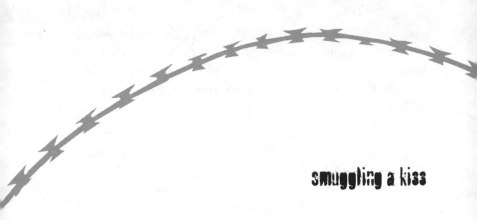

smuggling a kiss

SHE WIPED THE STEEL SEAT BEFORE SITTING. USUALLY there were amoeba-shaped urine splotches on the rim and occasionally the ruddy brown red of blood, but today there was only a soft rust from the steel, and the rosebud of toilet paper remained mostly white. She noticed it, but wasted no energy pondering the difference, and sat.

Her abdominals tightened and she felt it sliding down. She had remarkable muscle control along her uterine wall. Though she had never given birth, the muscles had undergone extensive training during her days as a performance artist firing paintballs at a naked white canvas onstage. That was a while back, but the muscle memory was still there. She could very easily force it all the way down and out, but it would serve no purpose floating in the toilet. Instead she inserted two fingers into herself.

The balloon was still a little wet from her insides, but reasonably intact. She stretched its tip to double-check for damage. Before she could assess the chance of leakage, she heard the pitter-patter of tiny footsteps. The balloon fit perfectly between her lower gum line and cheek, like a prophylactic pouch of tobacco.

The door opened. She did not cover herself. "Yes?"

The cop went back out.

"Little midget," she said.

She rose off the toilet, took a step towards the sink and then stopped. There was no use cleaning it off now.

Well, she thought, stepping out of the bathroom with her head up, *if he wants a taste of my pussy so bad, he'll sure as hell get it.*

In the never-ending line at the vending machines, no one paid her any attention. Grandmothers and girlfriends were vying for position, planning their purchases based upon the ever-depleting items for sale. They had little Ziploc bags or transparent plastic purses where twenty dollars in quarters could be seen clearly. Everyone watched the family in the front of the line, and when they were finished, everyone watched the next family.

She passed the cop at the desk who had barged into the bathroom earlier. The cop's tag read "Gertstein," and she was by far the smallest person in the visiting room. The fact was exacerbated by the hulking shadowlike presence behind her. Next to the shiny badge his tag read "Reno." His protective eye followed his partner wherever she went, except the ladies' room. Both Gertstein and Reno watched her suspiciously. She did not look down.

At their table, he said, "You had to walk right by the cop, didn't you?"

"Where'm I supposed to walk, Brian? I didn't see you get up and unroll the red carpet for me."

"You could have walked along the back wall, Sally."

"Oh," she said.

She raised one eyebrow, but the other did not move. The frown lines started at one side of her forehead and ended above the ridge of the nose, as if she had Botoxed one half of her face. The skin was pale white and the dark, stenciled eyebrows made it almost phantom pale. You could fit quarters into the bags under her eyes. She was tired, but the little exhalation she let out was sarcastic.

"All right, all right," he said immediately. "I don't wanna fight. Just keep talking. Those fuckers are watching us, so just keep talking."

She put her elbows on the table and then pushed the bones of her chin out so that it fit onto the two fists pressed one against the other. A white form-fitting sweater outlined every detail it covered, and her hair brushed the points of her shoulders when she moved. She rapidly blinked three or four times, and then puckered her painted-on lipstick lips. They appeared bigger to Brian not because they had grown, but because the rest of her face had shrunk. He twitched a bit but caught it. "Don't get stupid," he said softly.

She half-smiled. "I love you, too."

Through the shatterless glass, she saw the sun opening up on the shadows of the enclosed ten-by-ten-yard patio. A lifer was outside with his wife. Together they made a 90-degree angle standing, not side by side, but not face to face either. He was fixed intently on her midsection and she was looking away, as if he weren't standing there at all. Her leather jacket was open like a street hustler's, covering them both, and you could not see the hem of her knee-length dress.

Sally asked her husband, "How do they get away with that?"

Brian didn't look back. He said, "Have you been eating?"

"They do that every time I come here," she said. "And that bitch with a badge pretends like she can't see anything.

Let's watch her. I bet she doesn't look outside until they're finished."

She watched the front desk, more than mesmerized, but he did not look up. He shook his head. "Are you stupid? You think it's a game, bitch?"

"Is that my name?" she said. "I'm 'bitch'? I was christened 'bitch'?"

Her pale, emaciated face still did not face his, and she seemed to be leaning away from Brian. She did the eyebrow thing again, and it seemed to require too much energy. When she turned, she could see the couple inside the black leather jacket outside. One of the lifer's shoulders was going up and down, and even through the thick, shatterless glass she could see him breathing heavily.

"Unbelievable," she said. "And yet that bitch with a badge has to follow me into the bathroom."

He said, "You gotta take care of yourself. How the hell can I trust you?"

She said, watching the couple outside, "Doesn't she have any pride?"

He said again, "Hey. I'm talking to you. Hey."

She heard the tone and finally met his eyes. He saw something familiar, which, with a little more time, he could identify. "You can't do shit to me here, Brian. Your threats are nothing. I've got that midget bitch over there to protect me."

"Who the hell said anything about threats? Keep it down."

The tongue went in for a bit, searched around, and came back out again. His jaw tightened when he saw the sealed heroin-filled balloon on its tip. "Are you stupid?" he said.

The tongue pocketed the pouch perfectly between cheek and teeth. Though the skin was wrapped too tightly around the jaw, the balloon was back by the molars of her mouth and you could not see even the faintest sign of it. "I wouldn't say that," she said, dreamy-voiced.

"Say it with your tongue in your mouth."

"I'd say I'm smart."

He looked into her dancing eyes and saw the vague, familiar something again. He said, "Hey."

"I got my ace in the hole, sweetheart."

"Hey."

"It's called swallow the pill and leave on the bus. They won't look through my shit like they will yours."

Her anemic fingers were twitching in her lap. All around the room, people were inexplicably chatting and crying in their own little world, and she turned to see why. Through the blur of her watering eyes, they seemed so healthy and alive.

He said, "Are you high?"

She turned around but didn't answer and he said, "I can't believe this. You're fuckin' high."

"Fuck you, Brian."

"Goddamnit. How many times have I told—"

"You don't tell me anything," she said.

He looked up at the cops at their table and then back at his wife. "Are you stupid?" he asked.

"Fuck you."

Atop the table, one fist fit inside the palm, and there were flames crawling out his sleeve along the wrist. They were army-jeep green and exquisitely detailed and she had always hated them. The tattoos represented the things about him she could never know. *Well,* she thought, *not knowing is a two-way street.*

He asked very calmly, "Do you know what happened to Scooter last week, Sally?"

"I hate when you do that."

He said very calmly, "Do what, Sally?"

"Talk about these people like I know 'em. I don't know any Scooter. Who the hell would name their son Scooter?"

"He named himself Scooter."

"Well, who the hell would name himself Scooter? Can't you talk about something else?"

The fist switched places. "What am I supposed to talk about, Sally?"

"All right, all right," she said.

"Scooter is my homeboy." She rolled her eyes. Somehow they were as white as her face. This surprised Brian. "How'd you get your eyes so white?"

"Don't change the topic," she said. "Tell me about your *home*boy."

"He caught his third strike last week in here for possession, Sally. They struck him out. Do you understand? This ain't a fucking game. Twenty-five to life is a long time."

She gripped the insides of her thighs and rocked a bit in the chair, as if she were gathering up strength. Finally, she said, "Well, why don't we just quit then? Why don't we end this?"

Brian said, "I'm worried about you, sweetheart."

"Bullshit."

She looked up at the cops at the desk and felt the breath catch in her throat. Including the visitors, there were nearly fifty people in the room, but she felt like the only one being watched. Though fewer than fifteen tables were occupied, throughout the room a thousand infants collaborated in a single piercing scream. Her all-white eyes jumped back and forth and her semihushed voice was panicky. "Can we just get it over with already? I wanna get the hell outta here."

"Just calm down," he said. "We gotta do this right. I gotta live with these cops. If they suspect—"

"But I feel—"

"Calm down."

"Okay, okay, okay," she said. "Talk about something else."

"Did you double up the balloon?"

The horror in her eyes was the answer.

"Goddamnit, Sally. How many times have I told you?"

She saw him OD'd and laid out dead in his cell.

"If that shit busts in my stomach, I'm—"

"Sorry, sorry, sorry."

He looked up instinctively at the cops. Luckily, they did not look back. "Okay," he said exclusively to himself.

"Talk about something else."

"Okay," he said again, this time including her. He automatically considered the one in ten chance of the bursting balloon. Sally had forgotten to double up the last four months, so now it was about one in six. *Fuck it,* he thought. *If you gotta go, die numb.*

Suddenly calm and self-assured, he said, "Well, 'member Johnny?"

She cooperatively nodded in a grudging way.

"He got out last week."

"Good for Johnny."

"Didn't think he'd make it when he first got locked up. He was just a kid. Used to call him Babyface. He grew up fast, and then just like that, he was gone."

She was calmer now, too, and the babies had died in her head. "Is that what you do in here: grow up?"

"Oh," he said, forgetting her highness. "It's like that, huh?"

"That's right, it's like that," she said. "It's always been like that."

He grabbed her hand and it startled her. He could see the old submissive haziness coming up, and now he more than held the hand. "And what are you doing out there these days,

Sally? Firing bullets out your pussy? You and all those fake wannabe artists you hang around with. Suck the dope off you like leeches. I betcha pack a wallop now, huh, girl?"

She reclaimed her hand, the lavender blood cells already coming up on the skin. "I been packing something."

Her cryptic statement floated vindictively in the air, yet he went on, stroking the tattoos on his wrist. "Those damned pimps. Do you know how many real artists will die in here forgotten?"

She rolled her white eyes at the schoolyard challenge. This same strange outburst was paraphrased more and more often during their visits. "Cry me up a river," she said.

"They'd out-art those pimps anytime, anywhere."

"No, Brian. Not anytime. Not anywhere. Isn't that what you're always telling me?"

"You think you're highbrow because you hang with those pimps? You're an embarrassment, don'tchu know that?" He unbuttoned the wrist of his shirt and rolled the sleeve to the elbow, pointing at the elaborate conglomeration of ink on his arm. "That's art," he said.

"Want this 'bitch' to put up the cash for an exhibition?"

He said, "I am your cash."

She felt a surge of rationality and, despite her highness, ventured into the unknown. "I'm sure all these thoughts are comforting, aren't they, Brian? When you're back in that hovel tonight digging through your feces for the magical balloon, just think of your wife, sacrificing her dignity out there in the free world." The couple of the black leather jacket outside walked back in, arm in arm. "Now they," she said, "are performance artists. Should we stand up and clap, Brian?"

"You got no control," he said. "And you probably couldn't stand anyways. We're lucky you got this far. Look at yourself. Trying to hold your head up like it's nothing. I know who you are, your highness. You can't hide underneath the cockiness."

"Who wants to hide? I've always loved the big—"

"Who're you fucking out there?" he demanded. The cryptic statement from before had finally registered.

She smiled. "'Member Johnny? Old Babyface?"

"You're a fiend."

"And you're a pimp."

To his annoyance, it came again, the coquettish smile, with depleted bags under her eyes, the seductive, coquettish smile. He squeezed her hand and a cop, the short female one named Gertstein, got up from the desk. Somehow Sally remained cynically composed. "Oh, Babyface grew up, all right. He sure as hell grew."

"Just chill," he said. "Just chill."

"I'm through with this, Brian."

Gertstein made her rounds every ten minutes. Though the cumulative path was less than fifty yards, the journey took longer than five minutes. Gertstein's steps were of course short, and as they were made with the deliberation of a minesweeper, the combination of the two took time. She walked self-assuredly. At whatever point in the room she found herself, Gertstein knew that there was a direct tangential relationship between her path and the eyes of her partner Reno. At the front desk, his head rotated as slowly as she walked, and even separated, the two seemed together.

She circled the perimeter along the drab yellow wall, hitting its corners at the microwave station and then approaching Sally and Brian at table 16. The husband caressed the frail, twitching hands of his wife, and Gertstein watched without watching from behind. A dozen yards in front at the front desk, Reno saw the same from a different angle. Though everything appeared normal, something caught Gertstein's attention at the table. She made a mental note for future reference. She thought: *That woman doesn't like me,* then made her way to the vending machines and lastly the bathrooms in back.

When Gertstein was out of range, Sally said, "I hate that bitch. I'm never coming back to this place, Brian."

"Listen to me, Sally." He began to massage the fabric over the forearm, considered rolling it up to touch skin, and then thought better of it. The inevitable tracks on her arm would be the visible counterpoint to his upcoming speech. "Listen to me, babe."

"I can't do this any more, Brian. I'm so tired of it all."

"Sally," he said. "Let me tell you a story, babe."

The pockets under her eyes started filling with tears. "Brian—"

"I don't care about him, babe. I know you're lonely out there. It's all right."

"We don't get along anymore. We're up and down all the time. We should end this, Brian."

"I ain't got much longer, Sally. I'll be out in under a year."

The wife raised her head to the roof. He could see the protruding veins around her Adam's apple like little branches beneath the skin of her neck. "We won't make it. My god, Brian. How the hell did we get to this point?"

"It'll be all right, babe."

"I can't even imagine you in normal clothes anymore. I wouldn't know what to do if I saw you outside of this miserable room."

"Sally, look over there."

"Sometimes I hate you, Brian. I hate all of it. I hate myself."

"Look over there, babe."

"No. You look at me, Brian. It's killing me."

"Look."

She turned to where his eyes pointed. She didn't know why. Maybe to see the screaming babies, all of whom had died. Definitely to preserve energy. She turned to take a break.

A few tables away, there were no babies. Instead, the very large back of a very large man outframed his very small chair. Amazingly, his monumental size was of secondary distinction: The jheri curls of his head were pasted down and lathered up so completely that every strand of hair just seemed flat stuck. It was a fantastic sight. Across from him sat a woman whose sweater was tighter than Sally's.

Brian said, "Dry your eyes, babe."

The sight piqued her limited interest, and Sally managed "What's with the hair?"

Brian smiled. He said, "You're funny, Sal. You never lose your edge. Dry your eyes."

She almost smiled back and wiped at her gaunt, angular cheeks with a forearm. Brian thought, *She's coming down now. And I can see it.*

"You know why his hair's like that?" he asked.

Her mind found a memory and it provided her with all the remaining internal energy she harbored. She said, "Remember when we went and saw that boxing match together?"

He nodded as uninterferingly as possible.

"That guy reminds me of it."

Brian's eyebrows narrowed. He admittedly did not have the abstract artistic mind she had, and could not make the connection. And anyway, he wanted her to keep talking. His hand found hers and he asked, "How, babe?"

"That poor fighter. The short bald one. With the big tattoo of his name across his back. He was getting beat every round and his face was lumping and when he came back after the bell, his corner just put more and more Vaseline over the cuts and bruises, 'member? They just kept wiping it on until he couldn't see. Like one big fix. And you couldn't see, either. You were high, 'member, and you kept asking me, 'Sal, is his face blurry, or is this bad shit I'm on?'"

He smiled and she said, "Now it's my turn. Is his hair blurry, Brian, or is this bad shit I'm on?" She smiled and did not make the effort to reclaim her hand.

He said, "I remember, Sal," looking over at the table. The gargantuan plane of back beneath the pasted-down hair had still not moved.

"That's Fats," he said. "Old Fatu. He's my story, Sal. Runs weed for the Samoans. Grows those jheri curls long for a reason. Gets about half a jar of pomade before every visit and wipes it all over his head. When she comes, he sticks the bag of weed right underneath those curls along the upper neckline. Don't have to kiss nobody, don't have to swallow shit. Gets naked in the room, cops check his ears, check his ass, he gets dressed, and back to the yard. Cops just think it's a fashion statement, to look good for his girl." He waited dramatically before continuing. Finally he asked, "And you know what he told me himself, Sal?"

Some color came to Sally's face. Even in her highness, she admired ingenuity.

"He couldn't get any of it done without her."

She whispered proudly, "That's right."

"I love you, Sal."

Her eyes fell to the ground.

"Wait till I get out, Sal. Just wait. I'm gonna set you up. Just watch, babe." He looked up quickly at the cops and not at his wife. They were there together, just as they had always been. Sally's chin dropped to her chest, following her eyes. He couldn't afford to lose her. "I got hookups all over the place. I got a hundred people owing me. Before it's all over, they're gonna know about my girl. If someone has to die, this world's gonna know about you, Sal. You know that, babe? You got more talent than anyone I know."

"I don't feel like it, Brian. I don't feel like it."

"You do," he insisted. He forced the sudden real-life flash of missed meals and railroad tracks along the forearm and all-night whoring from his institutionally me-tracked mind. He had to convince himself, too, and so he said, "Look at me, babe."

Her eyes closed. All around her the vacuum of voices echoed in support. He said it again. "Look at me, Sally."

Slowly she opened them, but did indeed look back and whatever little fraction left of her was absolutely his, and he knew it. He did not give her back. "You're the most beautiful woman in the world, and you're mine. You keep me alive in here, Sal. You. Those cops can't touch me, Sal, and it's all because of you." At the front desk, they were waiting for the good-bye show, and he knew that, too. His voice was matrimonially soft and confident. "You're mine, Sal."

He reached over and closed both lids of her eyes with an index finger. Husband leaned toward wife, numb and without feeling. She collapsed into his arms. The lips of her absurd mouth automatically opened in acquiescence. Everyone like Brian and Sally was doing their thing in the room, and no one but the cops watched or cared. And when at last they kissed, he sucked the balloon viciously into his own mouth, hoping it would split on its way down his throat.

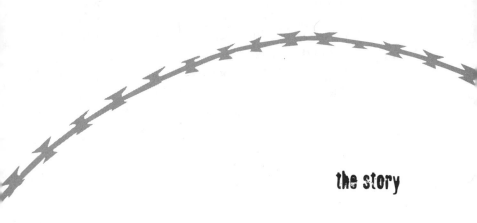

the story

I AM READING THE PAPER UNDER THE DIM LAMP IN THE corner of our bedroom, thinking on domestic violence. A Mexican woman was beaten to death in an older borough of Fresno, and no one quite knows why it happened. By all accounts, her husband has been a stellar neighbor, quiet, kind, gratuitous with pleasantries, an all-around likable man. None of it makes sense. He's worked hard, two jobs for eight years, gravedigger during the day, dishwasher at night, a typically diligent, dutiful south-of-the-border immigrant of this valley. The prosecutor declares that nothing will prevent him from rendering justice, not race, not the past; crime is, and therefore punishment is, color-blind.

"There is no reason for something like this to happen," he says.

Our grandfather clock chimes in midnight from the hallway and I decide I need a drink. This is not common for me: I am not quite sure why I need one tonight. I do enjoy the burning sensation of whiskey as it kisses the membranes of the tongue and throat, and contrary to its eventual numbing effect on the head, I wake up for a few minutes. Stupid things to ponder, for sure, when the phone rings.

I accept a collect call from the county jail, say, "Yes, yes, of course."

The kitchen light flashes on and my wife is squinting from the gleam, slightly shivering body in the hallway, leering head in the kitchen.

She whispers, "Albert, who is it?"

Suddenly in the ear of the phone I hear the breathlessness of my boy, who sounds like he's caught in the middle of a wind tunnel. There is a scratchy undertone which is probably the recording mark of some four-eyed monkey monitoring the call in a room of spyware. Finn's telling me about the pending charges and the arresting officer and I stop him just as he's about to indict himself with details.

"These conversations are all taped," I say, and he goes quiet for a second.

The random background noise makes me think of the random ejaculations of the city, and I can envision with no difficulty the crew of cranksters and hustling cons and hostile CO's lurking in the periphery of my son. Orbiting, enemy planets. Looking at my wife, I put my index finger to my lips.

She mouths, "It's Finn."

"Don't cry, son," I say into the phone, softly, but with authority. "I'll be down there tomorrow with an attorney. Don't cry now, not there."

He starts into the details again, out of breath with passion, and I hang up on him, knowing that he won't be granted a second call, hoping that the abrupt rudeness shocks him into shutting up. My wife grabs my hand, awaiting the story.

Now, I fear, it becomes a game of rationalization.

I CAME TO this valley in the autumn of 1988 with a pregnant girl in the passenger seat of my K car and the promise of a job as a correctional officer at Avenal State Penitentiary. I was a year past twenty, but felt much older. I'd been told repeatedly since boyhood that I was beyond my years, and I viewed my commitment to this girl as the result of the mindset and maturity of someone in his thirties. The girl had refused to listen to her friends, who'd advised swift termination of the pregnancy, and the least I could do, I figured, was to shun the position of my own friends, who'd said it wasn't my responsibility. The girl would become my wife. We had the sexual compatibility consistent with our ages, but what made our thing special, especially then, was a shared fearlessness in the face of unsupportive social forces. Very few people rooted for us, unofficially and officially. We didn't know much about life, of course, but we both believed that we were diligently digging for the nuggets of a nuptial gold mine, and that all these people were merely envious miners of the heart's copper and tin.

For the first several years of our young marriage, we attached those reveries of grandiosity to our son, Finn. Those most standard of dreams parents have for their children (which a nonparent might accurately describe as bias), we invariably had: basic developmental progress of the boy was a minor miracle to us. Any sound he'd hiccough had the harmonious effect of symphonies on our ears; when he first talked, we saw visions of a civilization-saving politician, a Tom Jefferson or an Abe Lincoln, at bare minimum an attorney of the verbal likes of Clarence Darrow; his first step was that of a world-class sprinter.

At nursery school, we waited for some kind of progress report from Miss Nurry affirming what we knew. It never came. But not only that. Any time she'd mention Finn, which wasn't often, he was the quiet accessory to a story, an enabler of another child's shining moment, usually a watcher, occasionally the victim of circumstance or childish cruelty. Eventually we came around to the truth: Finn was middle-of-the-road, a normal child, nothing special. When the good teachers at Avenal Elementary School, no doubt seizing upon their training in positive energy courses, would tell us some favorable anecdote about him, we knew it was a fabrication; they'd told us an equally unconvincing version of the same thing the year before.

I review these things now for an obvious reason. Look: I work at a prison, for Christ's sake. That is, I think, a bad way to raise a son. You have two options when it comes to the truths you learn behind bars: share the gory stories without holding back, or internalize the job in your guts. I chose the latter, believing I had the immunosystem to process the place cleanly. My goal was to present a clean picture to my family of freedom, to be a kind, goodhearted father in the living room of his house, Mr. Rogers in the late evening through early morning. And for the other half of the day to undergo, on the way to work, a voluntary bout of schizophrenia, to grow the figurative fangs of the prison guard who ruled in a household of murderers. But I know—we *all* know—that that kind of transition leaves behind evidence of the other life, like muddy tracks through the kitchen.

FINN SAYS over the phone, "They're talking about twelve years."

I don't wince at the news. I am prepared for the worst, and this isn't—though it's damned close—the worst. We're split by the institutional glass crisscrossed with steel mesh. Steel disk of a stool beneath me, padded walls leaking air like some amateurish gas chamber, steel counter etched with claims of rival gang members. This is my son now, slight in a gown of orange issues, his white skin lucid in the bright lights. This is my seventeen-year-old son charged with second-degree murder.

I say, "When your mother comes in here, don't talk about the case, okay?"

"I know that," he says.

She's waiting just outside this phone booth, horrified at the surroundings, but hiding it well. It is more than the fear of a mother, though it is mostly that. The weekly tours of corporate sponsors and university groups here give visitors the same look of shock, all without a relative, a lover, or a friend to visit. It's a discovery of the cancer which you've known all along to be there. But for Shannon it's worse: today, it's me, not her son, who has been accused in her head. This whole thing's too circular for cheap concepts like irony: Shannon wonders if her son's day-old ordeal is just a matter of regeneration, natural consequences that all sons of correctional officers must eventually face.

I'd told her this morning, "It's best if you don't come, darling."

"I'm coming," she'd said, already dressed, walking past me without eye contact.

I'd thought, *Maybe it's good not to spare her this. Finn will need the determined finality of motherhood on his side.*

"All right, darling."

I say to Finn, looking down at the counter for just a moment, "How are you holding up in there, son?"

"Fine," he says. "I'm fine."

"Maybe you should consider protective custody."

Finn's eyebrows come together: he's insulted. He knows enough to recognize an avenue of cowardice. Still, he has no clue how fast it happens in here, how radically different one moment can be from the next. The judge and the prosecutor and the cops will say otherwise about Finn, but he's just a kid, and this macho defiance on his face is the proof. What does it matter in the end, I want to say, if the whole deal ends like that?

I say, "Son. Look. If you get sent upstate, there are going to be some people in there who will eventually know what I do for a living."

He says, "Well, that's you, not me."

"That's not how they see it. It takes one person, one stupid grudge."

"I don't care," he says, on the brink of tears.

Here's what I've learned about Finn over the years: if you tell him enough times about the sense of something, the sense of it withers in what he considers to be the presumption of your suggestion. That you've the nerve to suggest anything. And I've seen him oppose the suggestion, or do the exact opposite of it, even as he acknowledges its sense, even as he perhaps agrees with your observation. It is the ultimate form of hubris, flouting the hands of fate, the lessons of fathers. I mean, I know what evil lurks in the dark corridors of the human heart. Only that someone who lies down nightly in the shadowy confines of a cell knows it better than me.

So even something like this—"Don't talk about the details with your mother"—is potentially hazardous. Just to spite a goodhearted plea from his father, Finn will send his own mother out the box crying into her hands.

To avoid any problems, I say, "The attorney will be in to talk to you, son," and—to show him I love him—"take care," as I hang up the phone.

IN THE EARLY YEARS, we had our problems. I brought the prison home. The induced schizophrenia, I'm afraid, never worked. My wife was constantly scared and, I fear, by the age of ten, Finn was scarred for good. The themes in our house—love, loyalty, goodheartedness, hope—were distorted by the mania of prison: I was stretched between the beauty of the blooming eucalyptus tree in our front yard and the ugly iron legs of a two-man gun tower. There were times when Shannon would cry nightly at my cruel, helpless bouts of silence, disappear to her mother's in Los Angeles for a weekend. And if I must be confessional, there were worse failures on my part than mere silence. I carried around this strange, whirling, uncontrollable force in my head: a chained dog wanted out, and sometimes got out.

When she'd leave, Finn and I would get through Saturday and Sunday without saying a word to one another. The house a sanctum of silence: meals where the fork colliding with the plate was loud as a doorbell; dishwashing where the stream of water sounded like a small river. Of course, I would naturally see Shannon all weekend long in my son's tentative step, his soft blue eyes, feel the infinite weight of guilt as he sat on the porch playing with his Game Boy, lining the raining digital blocks one upon another.

I knew where she stood. She had no respect for my job. We were all crooks, she said, her own husband included. She went into a litany of attack against the system of incarceration. I'd never shared the gore of those stories, the filth and horror birthed of condemnation, of total control; but she knew enough about the looks on my face that hadn't been there before, all the ways in which I'd changed in public (which was basically in having no inclination to be in it), the distance between us in private, in our bed, the absence of the future in our discussions. She accurately recognized that I believed in the future less and less, and that it came from my job. I know now that I felt as if I were stuck on a stretch of time that kept repeating: I couldn't ever untangle a single thread of the knotted past, not my past necessarily, or our past together, but *our* past at large; that is, the past of this jacked-up species. It was way too late to try and untie it.

She went on. She said she hated my stoicism, that it was selfish to internalize half of my life. She hurt me. I said, "So you want me to share that? You want some histrionics and filth? Okay, all right. Stay right here then. Don't fucking move."

I found Finn in his room, standing next to his desk, quietly looking out the window. I said, "Stay in here, son. Keep the window shut. Sit down on your bed."

I patted the top of his head and he sat down as instructed. I locked his door, went back into our room, walked over to the sliding glass, shut it, secured the windows, closed the door and locked it, and looked down on my wife. I carry that image to this very second, Shannon's ticket, at any moment, to up and leave me: my wife huddled like a praying Muslim on the floor, her knees tucked beneath her breasts, crying into the cup of her hands like a helpless child, and me, filled with evil, ready to end her innocence and impart wisdom.

TODAY IN COURT Shannon finally breaks down. The judge allows the district attorney, a red-necked endomorph named Espaniola, a small space to narrate, and he really lets go. Says he can't believe that someone like our son ever walked the streets of our little town, says Finn represents the worst of this generation. We can see only the back of Finn's head. Is he wavering under this tag-team indictment?

She whispers, "How can the judge let him get away with that? It's only pretrial. Son of a bitch doesn't know our son."

I don't dare say the truth, that 95 percent of the judges are former DA's. It's as if providing an answer would somehow make me responsible for the fact, or open me up as a target. That somewhere out there you've a number denoting the low percentage of correctional officers who pose as decent fathers. And anyway, I want Shannon to stay tethered to mystery. The less she knows about this process, the more she will reflexively hope for Finn.

I say, "I don't know," grabbing her hand.

She wipes at her eyes with the sleeve of my coat. I let my arm go limp, be a tool. She whispers, "That crook of an attorney just let it happen without saying a word."

I say, "Don't worry, darling. He'll get in his shots when it's time."

"He better, damnit. They're trying to hang my son."

We are paying Mr. Lupo top dollar to defend Finn. There's a saying in prison amongst the inmates: *The blindfolded lady can't see, so you might as well do it.* Mr. Lupo has that kind of lawlessness. I knew it when I'd asked him to visit our son, and in the client-attorney room he let Finn use his cell phone to call me. It's a violation of the rules, and if caught he could have lost his visiting privileges. But he did it to show me that it's about the fight now, not about truth; it's about that ugly American realm of justice where you load up the arsenal and use whatever weapon necessary to win. And that if I wanted what's best for Finn, I'd dismiss—if I still had it—any notion of nobility.

I remember he'd invited me to his office to sign the deal in person. We ended up discussing the details of his last trial, a case that went the distance and ended in acquittal for his client. Talking again with him made me think of the pen. Mr. Lupo's face took on that controlled fervor I'd become conditioned to seeing in the posture of your average lifer, one which had no difficulty demarcating the evaporating line between survival and evil and putting a face and shape upon—

and the rope around—a single hostile force. The incarcerated lifer lassoed the system, and Mr. Lupo, an integral part of that system, lassoed his litigationally opposed twin, the district attorney. Then, through proxy, he condemned the trial judge, as Mr. Lupo called her, the prosecutor's older, wiser stepsister.

"That judge was a thief," he'd said, shaking his head as the cigarette smoke twirled out his nose, thin wisps of verbally vanquished ghosts. "We'd go back into chambers and I'd catch her whispering to the DA. They probably had after-hours margaritas and hush-hush eros. So you wanna play hardball with me? No problemo. I have more information on her now than the FBI."

For a moment, the notion of justice seemed completely lost to the counselor and the courtroom was merely the beatified alleyway where two rival gangs met to scrap over turf. Then he regained his composure, said, "But I'm in with the judge presiding over your boy's case, Mr. Piedra," and whether he was or not, I thought, *This is the wily, vicious wolf I want in my son's corner.*

And then I paid him. I shook his hand as hard as I could. I wanted him to know that I'd kill him if he scammed me, or at least break his hand. I wouldn't do either, of course, but he bought the bluff. After all, the client he was now hired to defend came from something out there, from someone.

I DON'T KNOW why it didn't end, I really don't. By that I mean that I don't know how Shannon stayed through it all, why. There were days when I'd thought, *There is nothing I can say to remedy this. Nothing I can do.* I began to relate to the heroin addicts in the prison, their defeatist whining: once you've gone into the woods, they claim, you never return. And all it takes is the first hit. When I'd drive home from work, I couldn't afford to think about dinner, or young Finn, or anything related to our house, because I knew each day for several years that she'd be gone.

But she didn't leave. All of those same friends who advised that she not have Finn years earlier now swarmed our phone lines suggesting that she abort the marriage, that my anger was unacceptable. I could hear the echoes of disdain from the other room. Not from them, but from her, from my wife, Shannon. Because she's so genuine, it's easy to see when she's troubled, and yet for that same reason, not everyone has a right to open the book of her life. Her pain was her business, or ours.

I like to think I'm the reader she writes for. One day I said to myself, "You either turn it off here or turn it off at work." I made my decision: I quit cold, seeing the light of my wife's Honda Accord vanishing for good down the road in my head.

So I committed myself to losing the edge at work, letting it dull down into temperance. My life wasn't any easier. It never is, I guess. I just switched onuses, took on a new burden. The lie of the epiphany is that it's the last lesson. It didn't take long for my metamorphosis to bear consequences. I became a pariah at the prison, a loner on the yard, unreliable in the eyes of my peers. I stopped getting invitations to barbecues and waterskiing weekends. But the truest sign of this change was that certain inmates started talking to me, and, for the first time really, I talked back. I became known on the yard as a cool CO, mellow, someone to share stories with. You know how this goes: the muddy tracks run both ways. For longer than half a decade now, I've taken that same fear I had each day driving home to Shannon and twisted it into a new dagger at work, one that hasn't yet hit its target. Each day when my shift ends, I am always a little surprised that nothing catastrophic has happened to me, some crazy situation/setup where no one got my back.

Still, I have no complaints. Shannon and I eat frozen yogurt together on Tuesday nights and drive to the Farmer's Market on Sunday afternoons for asparagus and artichoke. We watch each town production of a little Central Valley theater troupe, the Fabulous Thespian Raisins, and haven't missed a Fresno State football game in four seasons. We have extended family over once every few months and jog together at sunrise or sunset three times a week. We're twelve years from having this house paid off, and we just bought a timeshare in Tahoe for the summers. I have a good retirement package with the state, am part of a strong union. What I'm saying is that we saved our marriage, though survival always has a price, even if you can't see it.

WE MEET with Mr. Lupo and he gives us the story.

He says that just as Finn came out of the Prasad Island Market in downtown Tulare he saw, from afar, two men breaking into his car in the corner of the lot. He didn't run toward them. He didn't shout out for help. He didn't call the police on his cellphone. Finn went back into the store and purchased an eighteen-ounce bottle of El Calderón original tomatillo salsa.

When he came out a couple minutes later, they'd just about finished the job. Both *paisas,* the police report revealed, high on crystal meth. One was carrying the stereo he'd extricated from the panel with a screwdriver as tiny as a golf tee, the other had the front two hubcaps stuffed up into an armpit each. Right there at high noon, walking out the lot without a getaway car or the apparent need for expedience. They crawled through a clipped pocket of fence and commenced down an adjacent alley in a casual stroll.

Finn got into his newly stripped car and started it, drove out of the lot and down the street, around an apartment complex where the alleyway came to an end. He parked in the dark hollow of a carport and waited on the undamaged hood of his car, fingering the glass neck of the salsa bottle.

Finn watched them pass the carport. They were laughing about something, rattling along in Spanish. They reached the public street, the inner bulb of a cul-de-sac, and Finn finally stood. He speed-walked until he was just behind them both. The radio thief turned his head and shoulder and Finn cracked him with the fat end of the bottle. He collapsed to the ground, his face and hair covered in green salsa, blood pooling into a perimeter around his head.

The other thief took flight, tripped over his feet, and dropped both rims. They crashed like cymbals. Kids ran into the house, adults spilled out. Finn walked over and reclaimed his rims. When the police came, he was squatting in the shadows, reattaching a rim to a tire. Marco Antonio Gutierrez lay in a breathless bundle in the gutter, dead of a blow to the temple.

"If only he'd hit him in the store's lot," Mr. Lupo says.

ONE OF THE LOCAL WRITERS for the *Fresno Times* picks up the story. There is an outcry in the community. The NAACP writes an editorial in the opinion section of the paper, hosts a seminar at Grace Cathedral about the dangers of provincial racism. That same night, our house gets egged. I clean the yard of shells, spray the shaving cream off the cars, collect the toilet paper from the eucalyptus, rooftop, and fence line. I think, *Better this than bullets.* Shannon watches me from the window of our room. I wait on the porch in the black cloak of early morning, but they never come back.

Finn's crime makes the leap to state news, and then the unthinkable: debated on a six-minute segment of *The O'Reilly Factor*. Mr. Lupo defends Finn, reveling in the national attention. We take the phone off the hook for days at a time. The prosecutor wilts under the media hype and public pressure and files new charges against Finn as late as the fourth court date. Second-degree murder, now enhanced by a hate crime. The only fortune I can find in the whole deal is that Finn's grandfather, my Papi, is underground. He would not understand how a boy with a quarter Hispanic blood—*his blood*—might be cast as a racist. How our last name could be besmirched by the Irish white skin of Finn's mother.

WHEN I READ the call list posted to the door of Courtroom 36, I think about the new charge and how it will shape the final destination for my son. I see the image of some gossipy skinhead excitedly spreading the details to his homeboys, such that Finn, a teenage hero on arrival to his white brethren, can't pass a single sureño in the sureño-controlled yard without fear of their vengeance.

IN THE LIVING ROOM, Shannon is weeping as she writes. The curtains are drawn, but the room is still blue-gray. The sun has yet to visit our house today. It's 4:54 in the morning.

I say, "Darling."

She doesn't look up, hasn't looked up for weeks now.

"Will you come to bed?"

She keeps writing. It's a card for Finn. He's been eighteen for almost five hours now.

"I'm going to make you tea."

"Albert," she says. "Don't."

This is the easy part. We must prepare for more birthdays—nineteen, twenty, twenty-one. We must prepare for Thanksgiving and Christmas in the white-walled insult of a visiting room, lost amongst the hordes of guests, idly chatting with our son while avoiding virtually every topic of meaning. I've seen it a thousand times: thank God for Monopoly and Scrabble. We must smile through microwaved burgers, ready ourselves for rudeness from the guards and from other visitors.

I know my beautiful wife. She'll wonder why the visitors lack the camaraderie of the disenfranchised. When some angry asshole cuts in front of her at the vending machines, Shannon will shout out, as if a life has been lost, "We're all on the same team here!" There's no way I can explain to Shannon the Machiavellian street ethic pervasive in the joint, and in those very families from whence the convict sprang, while still toeing the line for hope. That whatever side you're on, the goal is to get proximal to your son. Any speech I render, really, will be a reminder to her of days past, when Finn was young and impressionable, our little sponge soaking in all this hatred I used to have of my fellow man.

MR. LUPO has us in the lobby of Courtroom 32 between sessions. He talked to the DA, to the judge, to Finn. Our son wants to take the deal. Shannon says, "Deal? What about the damned trial?"

Mr. Lupo is shaking his head ardently. "We don't want it to go to trial."

"So he wants prison time?" Shannon says. "You're telling me that's what he wants?"

"Oh, no. No, no. That's what he's gonna *get*. One way or another, it's gonna happen. It's just a question of more or less. More time, less time. An acquittal isn't likely. There are four different witnesses who can corroborate the prosecutor's case. More importantly, they have a body. And then there's the media."

Shannon says, "So what did we hire you for?"

Mr. Lupo looks at me and I say, "What's the deal?"

"I got 'em to reduce the plea to manslaughter, drop the hate crime. Five years with good time."

Shannon gasps and I put my hand under her elbow. "We don't want it," she says.

I don't say anything. I know that Mr. Lupo will explain his position soon enough. I'm certain that it's one of pragmatism, rationalization, right up his amoral alley. I can't stand the guy, even when I agree with him, and he's helping my family. My wife is a good mother bound almost blindly to hope, a lawyer's polar opposite, and I can tell that he thinks she's a hindrance to progress, a potential liability at trial.

"No way," she says again.

"Your son is my client, ma'am. I'm obligated by law to do what he asks."

"Is that a threat?" Shannon shouts. "We hired you, we paid you, and we can fire you!"

Stepping back, Mr. Lupo says, "Mr. Piedra."

I stroke Shannon's arm, put my other arm around her waist. I'm thinking of Finn, just as she is, but in a different way.

Mr. Lupo says, "He'll go up for fifteen to twenty years if he's convicted by a jury."

"No," Shannon says. "No."

"Mrs. Piedra," says Mr. Lupo. "The DA has an exceptionally strong case. He's offering us this because he thinks he just might not. That's the work I've been putting in, planting his head with seeds of doubt in chambers. I don't know how much longer we can hold out on this. We don't have one single witness. Finn's youth and slightness of frame are all we've got. It'll get us down to five, no lower. I'd thought going in he'd offer eight, but we got lucky."

"Albert," Shannon whispers, her head in my chest.

Mr. Lupo says, "He can be free in thirty-two months."

Shannon pushes herself away and walks off, a concession. I feel more passion for her now than I had at Finn's birth. I want to bust Mr. Lupo's nose for his unspoken degradation of my wife. But—*see?*—we still need him to get the deal down on paper, and so I shake his hand for Finn, for Shannon, for us.

THERE ARE MILLIONS of moments in the story of a family. Birthdays, vacations, Little League games. Picnics and TV dinners. Sweeping floors and scrubbing walls and summer matinees. Sleeping in on Saturdays. How is it that one obscure and meaningless meal remains at the fore of my mind these days?

It was mid-March, Finn's freshman year in high school. We were at Atari-Ya Tai Kai in Downtown Fresno. I remember that Shannon and I decided to order a plate of nigiri sashimi, really splurge. Finn, usually quiet, was talkative. The fish was fresh that day, pink, tender, a rarity in this valley.

There was a couple next to us, the trucker type, in jeans, a flannel shirt, and a billfold each. Now that I think about it, they were probably *both* truckers. I would not have given them any notice—a common sight in the longest agricultural stretch in the world—had they not been arguing loud enough for us to hear them at our table, detail by adulterous detail. The affair, hers, was unforgiven, though it was years past when they'd first wed. I felt so overwhelmingly uncomfortable that I began to talk about work.

"We had a riot today in two yard."

Finn sat up—I saw it—and gave me his full attention. I didn't even bother looking over at Shannon, who—I could hear—had stopped eating.

"Bulldogs and northerners. Went at it for ten damned minutes."

"Who started it?" Finn asked.

"I don't think anyone ever starts it," I said.

"Someone always starts it," he said.

MY BOY DESCENDS the two-step staircase of the troop transport—the Silver Bullet, we call it—in three tiny, synchronized hops, hooked at the ankle, wrist and waist to a nazi low-rider with a shaved, egg-shaped head who does the same. There is one big mountain block of a shadow from which the men emerge, chests inflated, heads tilted almost delicately on their necks, two by two, fifty-six in full capacity, their breaths rising into the cool cobalt air like prayers. The lavender hills of the Gavilan Range are bruised purple where flecks of sun have already crept through, the promise of a bright blue summer day in our Central Valley, and the beauty of it renders the ultimate silence in the line. No jiving from the youngsters, none of the usual jiving from old pros: this is where the story begins for first-termers like my boy, Finn, and where it ends for the lifer witnessing his last new horizon. So mystery and reverence go hand in hand, forever chained.

This is all slight variation on the same theme, except now, I realize, it is truly and finally personal. My boy walks with such transparently false bravado that even here, through a hazy framed tunnel of archaic binoculars sixty yards away in the two yard gun tower, I can see the shortness of his breath. He's looking to his left at the yard, its eerie emptiness seemingly benign, like the oceanic blue at the proverbial end of the plank. This boy, who legally turned into a man behind bars last month, and who, with luck and courage and flexibility, can hope for nothing better than to become a man behind bars. I don't know what that means, really, except that he'll have to survive something he wasn't ever meant to encounter, in that yard, with those people, officially—as of today—his peers.

I know what his mother does not know about this process: that what is best for our family is not really *good* for our family. That if Finn gets out, it will be because he has acclimated himself successfully to the dark underbelly of our species. He'll walk in through the doors of our modest house with a swagger his mother will not recognize, and he'll head back into his room, where he'll stay for three days. When I finally summon the intrusive nerve to open the door, he'll be squatting in a corner, the adolescent posters discarded in a crumpled heap in the garbage can, the walls thus naked, desktop barren, silent as a morgue. He'll call everyone "homie" and skip birthday parties and go quiet in conversations involving indictment or judgment or the State of California. When people say, "Thank you," he'll pause before saying, "You're welcome," if he says it at all, and he'll issue fake flatteries when his parole officer visits the house, the quiet rage barely detectable on his face. He won't rush to help the elderly, he won't pray with his mother before breakfast, he'll wait until everyone leaves before coming out of locked doors to sit in the solitude of shadows. He will not be a boy, he cannot be. And for the same reason, he will not be the kind of man a mother adores.

And yet I feel something here watching my boy that I've never felt before, not in all these years: he's extraordinary. Not average, as Miss Nurry would have liked to have said a decade ago, not average at all. He's lugging the weight of the world around on his shoulders, carrying the brand of condemnation in his heart, and for the first time in a long time I realize what I have to do with my life. I know it, as sure as the chill wind that blows through this valley now, icing the veins of my son. The line of men inches into Receiving and Release, and Finn is gone.

At 0500, I make my way down the tower, the birdsong of early morning surrounding me. I say, "Howdy" to Eggerson, who is on his way up. He's a simple, predictable kid who hasn't yet been shocked into bearing a grudge. His badge is the symbol of justice, an untarnished image. He's nine months into this story, pink-cheeked with passion. He thinks I'm time-battered, weak, and that he'll keep the faith that I've lost.

When he reaches the tower, I call out, "Good luck, Eggerson!" and he tilts his head like an especially intelligent dog whose just heard the key word: "walk," or "bone," or "steak."

I cross the yard right up the gut of its dead, ice-laced grass. The field is torn by mounds of dirt, gopher holes, fist-sized rocks, the enemies of ankles and knees. I think of the *paisas* and their nightly third-world *fútbol* games—"¡Bola! ¡Bola! ¡Bola!"—and dig in as much as I can, each second precious as a breath of air. I pass Dorm 250 on the right, Dorm 230 on the left, brutally simple blocks of granite and cement, fifty yards from Dorm 210, and the yard transfer. Finches skitter across the rim of the steel goalpost, paying me little attention in their frantic search for space. I tug on the frozen net as I pass, a greeting of sorts.

Greene is posted at transfer, chewing through a bagel and hummus. He's a health nut, a former cross-country star at Fresno State. He loves to watch the convicts run in the deepest heat of afternoon. He'll sit in the stands like a spectator. He's one of the few here who'll share a word with me. Well before I reach him, he shouts, "Albert! Morning!"

I say, nearing, "Morning," knowing he doesn't hear me.

"This damned yard is already packed! Where the hell they gonna house these new arrivals?"

I'm almost there. I say, "I don't know."

"Probably the gym, huh?"

I reach Greene, put my hand out, and shake his. "I don't think it matters, does it?"

He can't answer the question because he's never really thought about it. Once you're in for it, you're in for it. "I'll see ya, Chuck."

I make my way up transfer, a stretch of walk two stories high in barbed wire, strong with the scent of this valley. Along the base of the fence, lilies are lined in simple geometry, clustered rows of ten, a lifer named Flintcraft's lifetime project. Their colors of yellow and pink and white are faint and subtle in the grayness of morn, out of place in this house of simple clarity.

At the callbox, I announce myself, open the door at the click, troop through the sally port. I feel my endorphins kicking in, like a shot of adrenaline. The click comes again, and I lean into the last door and push it outward, this solid steel door light as cardboard.

I'm into the hallway and past the glass-cased photos of the officers, my own portrait young, sure, and misleading. I walk through the empty lunchroom, beeline to the closed door at the end of the building. Knock, wait, hear the coiled squeak of weight being released from a desk chair. Then the steps of authority: orderly, spaced, heel to toe.

The door opens and I say, "L.T."

"Piedra. Come in."

The photos of his children fill his office, across the walls, the plane of the desk, a coffee table. They're all colorful and growing and full of life. "It's all right, L.T."

"Okay," he says, and I know he knows. He's been expecting it from me for a long while, and he doesn't move. The time has come: this story starts. I hand over my badge, nod, and he nods back.

"We have to brave it now," I hear myself say. "We must face it."

what you can do after shutdown

WHO KNOWS WHAT GOES ON IN A MAN'S CELL AFTER shutdown?

You can do lots of things. A whole range of activities. You can make caramel candy with the leftover butter and sugar from chow. Just get your empty Coke can and cut out the bottom, leaving a two-inch ridge around the perimeter. Then put your lighter to it. Make sure you keep stirring the sugar and butter or else it won't come out right. Use a chow hall coffee straw and let it sit for the night.

You can make cheese with your milk, although that takes a few nights. What do you do but let it sit and keep out the light? That's the blessing in disguise here in East Block: there's hardly any light to interfere with the process of making cheese. Put it in the corner of your cell and you've got nothing to worry about. Just let it sit.

You can stay up and read Sidney Sheldon novels if you're the studious type. Just lay your pillow against the bars and catch some of the yellow light on the tier a few cells down. You might have to adjust the angle, crook your head, or stretch your neck out a bit. And if you're out toward the darker end of the block, you'll have to slide your arms through the bars and hold the book outside the cell. It's all about utilizing leftovers. And whoever can't find a Sidney Sheldon novel in the pen ain't ever been there.

If she's still around, you can write your girl.

Or you can make a shank if you haven't already. You don't need anything but a single piece of paper and the socks on your feet. Take that paper and start rolling it airtight from one corner to the other. If it don't take ten minutes, you ain't done it right. Another way of knowing is that your thumb and index finger should be real sore from the rolling. It'll look like a straw. Then fold it in half once and then again. Get your teeth and chew out some of that elastic in your sock. Wind it over and over and over and over again until the insides of your palms are sore and you can no longer see the paper. When you can hold it like a sturdy handle, you got everything you need. Just sharpen it along the floor of your cell, back and forth, like sandpaper: It'll split skin and maybe more. So make a shank if you want.

And you can throw out your line and fish, too. Like a fly fisherman perfecting his stroke on a timer. Just pull in all the refuse on the tier and then shoot it back out again. You can play accuracy games to make it exciting, and compete against your homeboy two cells down. Plus a lot of good stuff shows up in those piles. Uneaten sandwiches, nudie mags, and scandalous love letters. Sometimes folks just get tired of things, no matter how good they are. But try not to make too much noise. The fellas are sleeping and ask only that you respect the program. In fact, you might have to switch the floater on your fishing line from that *Reader's Digest* to an empty milk carton. And if you ain't got a line, rip off the sheet of your bunk and make one.

If you're the artsy type, interior decorate. And if you're a tagger and the bare wall is your canvas, go to work. We got the only cops in the world who could care less about graffiti. The more conventional folk scratch off some of the tar along the roof of the cell and paste it to the back of what needs to go up. It'll hold paper, cardboard, and, in a healthy amount, empty Coke cans. You might want to put it up for a pencil holder or as a fancy kind of toothbrush canister above the sink. It works for disposable razors, too. If they refurbish your cell and the tar's no longer there, bring back some SOS from chow. Breakfast gravy sticks to the wall like it sticks to the insides of your stomach.

Or sweat out some burpees and push ups if you gotta expend some energy. Make a program out of it and track your reps from week one to week four to week twenty. And shadowbox. Better yet: grab the mattress of your bunk, stand it up longways, and roll it up like a big crepe. You got yourself a heavy bag. When it starts looking like an egg carton from all the apple-sized indentations, just flip it over between rounds, and then back over again. You'll be strong and fast and won't need to waste time making a shank. Just sweat it all out.

Afterwards, take a bird bath in the back of the cell. Plug the sink with a ball of toilet paper and then fill it up with bath water. Get naked if you aren't already and double-check the tier with your pocket mirror. You don't wanna go to the hole for bathing. That's like winning a game on forfeit: Everybody knows you never earned it. Then when everything's clear, clean the little squares of skin patch by patch, using a rag in your cell like a bird with its beak in the fountain. Not even the birds sleep sticky, so why should you?

If you gotta take care of business, pull the curtain around your bunk, get your nudie mag, and don't growl or grunt. Nobody likes that type of thing, not even the cops. Show some respect. And please keep all your bodily fluids inside the cell. This is our house, after all, and if we don't take care of it, who will?

Do not throw paper airplanes out of your cell.

Do not bark like a dog.

Do not bark like a seal.

Once you hear this—"East Block! East Block! It is now ten-thirty!"—you must end the conversation with your homeboy and get off the wire. It's all right if you forget because explicit instructions will follow. Like this:

"We ask for your cooperation and participation in shutting tonight's program down! If you do not have matters that are of the utmost importance, we ask that you take care of them in the morning!"

"Front bar! Front bar! Pay your respects to the back bar! Back bar! Back bar! Pay your respects to the front bar! To all my African brothers! *Usiku mwema!*"

That's good night in Swahili. So if you're black, you yell back, "*Usiku mwema!*"

"To my brown brothers! *¡Buenas noches!*"

If you're an *ese*, "*¡Buenas noches!*"

"To the 'woods, Indians, and others! Good night!"

And if you're white, Indian, or Asian, you yell, "Good night!"

If you're the quiet type and all the shouting irritates you, worry not. You needn't say a word 'cause everyone else'll be yelling, anyway. With the chaotic echoing throughout the block, it's impossible to keep track of those who participate in the shutdown and those who don't. So you're covered. And if you're the opposite—the talkative, hustling type—and that's how you do your time, just kick it on the toilet in the back of the cell and talk to yourself all night. Nobody cares. But try not to get too emotional. Make sure the dialogue is monotonous and uninvolved. Don't pick a subject matter that'll make you mad. Avoid talking about your girl, your lawyer, your case, the three-strikes law, or chow. Cut the deal and then walk with the cash. You know how it is: the heated discussions always get us into trouble.

But whatever you do, don't stop and think about it all like that poor bastard last night. I mean it ain't right. Not for you, not for us. Everyone deserves proper burial and you just ain't gonna get it. They'll toss you on a gurney and wheel you and your wrist around like a life-lesson parade. There's not a man alive who wants to see the pruned lips of a cadaver, not even in East Block.

And don't ever forget that: *We are alive.* Chow's up in ten minutes and you can bet we'll back-pocket your picture before the SOS hits the tray.

acknowledgments

I owe a great debt to some good people who lent their spirit to the creation of this book. First, humbly, to the dead, my teachers: Hemingway, Faulkner, Steinbeck, Baldwin, Dickens, Dostoevsky. Thank you for the consummate body of your mastery and for generously appearing in the midnight séances of this upstart who presumed to summon you.

Mille grazie to poet Samuel Maio for the late-night talks on poetics, the planting and nurturing of real literary ambition, the hardback first editions, the healthy knee-slapping over "the ineffable, indecorous, incestuous amongst us," and (to balance things out) what it means to be decent.

A thousand shout-outs to Uncle Jack, Uncle Raymond, and Uncle Tony, three cats who kept it more than real in their letterly words of literary encouragement during my stay at the "Third-Class State Resort."

A royal thanking to a bona fide techno renaissance man, Nikola Stojanovic, for making me comfortable in the photography session.

Tomek Mackoviak and Dalia Sirkin, both nice, agreeable people prior to the shock of meeting the disgruntled poet they have in common, had their sober and clean visions of life forever altered on a dark, lonely downtown San

Jo streetcorner where this same disgruntled poet desperately pushed his barely legal goods into their nervous hands for consumption, and for which he either now thanks them, or apologizes.

Official deference to the early editorial wisdom of Brandon Mise, Howard Junker, Tom Divorsky, Tim Bradford, and Leanne Roripaugh, and orchestral applause for the loads of work our lit mag chiefs do to keep us writers alive.

A head and shoulder nod/kowtow to David Sanders, who bit first on this bait, and with faith. Plus a gang of respect to my punctilious editor, John Morris, who kept me close to the house of proper grammar any time I got too streety and strayed too far.

And, of course, love and gratitude to Master Sergeant Mom, for all the (famous author) stamps and (industrial) staplers and (fancy) Scotch tape and (corporate) manila envelopes left on my desk through the years, the Abr'am Lincolns slid beneath the door, the buying sprees at Barnes and Noble, all of which amount to, really, thanks for the hope.